THE TROJAN BOY

THE
TROJAN BOY

Ken Begg

124971

COLLINS
8 Grafton Street, London WI
1988

William Collins Sons & Co. Ltd
London · Glasgow · Sydney · Auckland
Toronto · Johannesburg

First published in Great Britain by Collins

ISBN 0–00–232098–3

Printed and Bound in Great Britain by
Hartnolls Limited, Bodmin, Cornwall.

Jesus wept; Voltaire smiled.

VICTOR HUGO

ONE

AVEDISSIAN LAY IN BED and looked up at the chink of light that appeared in the vee of the curtains. Another day was dawning, another pointless, mindless day when he would go out and try to persuade people to buy products that they did not want and that he did not believe in anyway. What was the point of it all? he wondered, but he had wondered that every morning for the past two years. His next thought was to consider how many gins he had downed the previous evening, and then to feel depressed when he remembered. He got up and padded to the bathroom.

The milk he poured over his cornflakes was a little sour but he pretended not to notice until his palate threatened action if he were to go on with the charade. He emptied the contents of the plate into the bin and settled for coffee. Why didn't he have a system, he asked himself, a system for buying groceries? It wouldn't take much effort to compose a shopping list; after all, he lived alone and his tastes were simple enough.

Apathy was the problem, he admitted, but how did you escape from that? Didn't you have to care first? And what had he got to care about? His career had gone, his wife had gone, so why should he care about mere details? If the milk went sour he would buy more. If the bread ran out he would buy more. The system was adequate. He donned his overcoat, picked up his brief-case and left for the office.

The woman looked up from her desk as he entered and glanced at her watch before saying, 'Mr Firbush wants to see you.'

'When?'

'Right away,' she replied with some satisfaction.

Avedissian hesitated before knocking on the door but knew that he was only delaying the inevitable. He rapped softly with one knuckle.

'Come.'

'You wanted to see me?'

'I did indeed,' said Firbush. 'Come in. Sit down.'

Avedissian felt rankled at being spoken to like a schoolboy but his face remained impassive. He sat down.

Firbush adjusted his metal-framed, blue-tinted glasses and said, 'I want you to tell me why sales in your area have dropped by fifteen per cent in the past two months.'

Avedissian shrugged his shoulders and admitted to himself that the question was not entirely unexpected, but coming from a little toad like Firbush it was hard to take. He said, 'Maxim Health Products have introduced a new range. They compete directly with ours.'

'So . . . what?'

'Their stuff is better.'

There was a deathly silence in the room before Firbush snapped the pencil that he had been holding.

Avedissian realised that Firbush had broken it deliberately for effect and had probably seen it done in a film once. He wondered if the man practised his interrogation techniques in front of the mirror.

Firbush spoke in a hoarse whisper, 'Avedissian, don't you realise it is your job to convince the medical profession otherwise?' His voice rose as he added, 'It's your sole function in life!'

The thought appealed to Avedissian like horizontal sleet but he controlled himself and said, 'Of course.'

'Then why don't you do it? You *are* a doctor, damn it, at least, you were once, so why can't you do it? You must know how.'

'As a doctor . . .'

'Ex-doctor!'

'As an ex-doctor, as you have so kindly pointed out, I find it impossible to recommend something that I know to be inferior.'

The calmness of Avedissian's reply seemed to annoy Firbush even more than the answer. Firbush lost his temper and his face went deathly pale behind the blue-tinted glasses. He leaned over the desk and clenched his fingers into tight fists. 'Now let me tell you something, Avedissian,' he hissed. 'The real trouble with you is that you think you're too good for this job. You're just a toffee-nosed medic who doesn't want to soil his hands with a bit of honest work!'

'I'd question the honest.'

'You're not a doctor any more, Avedissian!' gloated Firbush. 'They took your name off that magic list and there is no way that you're ever going to get back on. They don't forget about murder after a couple of years!'

'It wasn't murder!' said Avedissian, more forcibly than he had meant to and immediately regretting it, knowing that he had swallowed the bait that Firbush had put out for him.

Firbush smelled blood. 'Oh yes it was,' he said slowly. 'That's what the court called it. That's what it was.'

Avedissian had no defence to offer. He remained silent.

Firbush moved in for the kill. He said, 'You're all washed up as a doctor and you're all washed up with this company! You're sacked!' He waited for some kind of appeal but none was forthcoming.

Avedissian shrugged and got up to go to the door. He was about to open it when he heard Firbush mutter, 'Your wife had the right idea, poor sod.'

The comment pushed him over the edge. He turned and crossed the floor in three strides to grip Firbush by the lapels.

Panic appeared on the smaller man's face as he realised that he had gone too far. This had never been in the plan. Avedissian should have left with his tail between his legs and he, Cyril Firbush, should have gone home to tell his wife how he had been forced to sack a doctor . . . most unfortunate, but someone in the company had to make the tough decisions and, after all, he was the man at the top . . . But now, as he was transported from executive leather, like a missile leaving its silo, to be dragged across his own desk, scattering papers with his trailing Oxfords, something had gone desperately wrong.

Avedissian pinned Firbush to the wall like a butterfly. 'How dare you!' he hissed.

'She killed herself, didn't she?' squealed Firbush in a desperate attempt to salvage dignity but the look on Avedissian's face turned his bowels to water.

'Understand this! I did not murder that child. What I did do was to end his suffering in a world where the law dictated that he be allowed to go through hell for another month or so. I was struck off for it but I do not regret it. As for my wife . . .' Avedissian increased the tightness of his grip. 'Linda took her own life after what the newspapers and the poison pen letters and the myriads of sanctimonious little farts like you did to us in the name of . . . Christian values.'

'Now see here . . .'

'What gives you so much pleasure in other people's pain, Firbush?' demanded Avedissian.

'This is outrageous!'

'For two pins I'd . . .' Avedissian teetered on the brink of violence but kept his balance. He pushed Firbush away from him and sent him tumbling to the floor. Firbush scrambled to his knees and clawed at the buttons on his intercom. 'Miss Carlisle . . . Miss Carlisle!'

Avedissian brushed past Firbush's secretary on the way out. 'Coffee for one,' he said.

It was after eleven in the evening before Avedissian got home to the dreary flat that he had called home since Linda's death. He had had so much to drink that he encountered trouble with the lock and had to make three attempts before the tumblers were satisfied. The door swung back to let the musty cold of the hall engulf him and surround him with loneliness. This was the moment he dreaded most each day, the one when he would come home and know that he was totally alone in the world.

Avedissian snapped into his countermeasure routine. He switched on the lights, lit the electric fires, and turned on the television to provide the distraction of noise. He paused briefly to look at the screen and saw that a woman was jumping up and down in requited greed on a quiz show. The host was flashing his practised smile at the camera and pretending to share in her joy.

'Shit,' muttered Avedissian but he did not switch it off. That would have meant silence, being alone with himself, and that was to be avoided at all costs. After a moment of contrived tension the woman decided to 'go for the big one' and Avedissian decided to go to the kitchen.

A rectangular lump of Spam made a slow, constipated exit from the tin after much coaxing with a table knife; it slid out on to the plate in a trail of slime. The opener slipped from the lid of a tin of beans for the third time and Avedissian abandoned technology at two hundred and seventy degrees for brute strength and a knife. But, as the lid snapped back, it caught his thumb and ripped the skin over the knuckle. Blood began to flow.

Avedissian put his thumb in his mouth and kept it there

as he went to the bathroom to search, one-handedly, through the cabinet above the basin for a plaster. He was rinsing the wound and cursing his luck when the doorbell rang.

Avedissian swathed his thumb temporarily in toilet tissue while he answered it. Two men stood there. One said, 'Mark Avedissian?'

'Yes.'

'May we come in?'

'Who are you?'

The man doing the talking flipped open a wallet and held it up. 'Police, sir.'

Avedissian closed his eyes briefly before opening them again and saying with resignation, 'Come in.'

Nightmares of the past had been rekindled in Avedissian's head by the sight of the warrant card. What could they possibly want this time?

The two men entered and looked about them like tourists in a stately home.

'Sit down.' Avedissian indicated chairs.

'Trouble, sir?' The man was looking at the wad of tissue on Avedissian's hand that was now crimson.

'Just a cut,' murmured Avedissian. 'If you'll excuse me for a moment.' He turned to go back to the bathroom.

'Of course, sir. Anything we can do to help?'

Avedissian declined and left the room. He closed the bathroom door and leaned his back on it muttering, 'Firbush! The little turd.'

He dressed his thumb and composed himself before returning to join the policemen.

Both men had stood up in his absence and were wandering about the room; one was holding the photograph of Linda that he kept on his desk. Avedissian stared at it and the man put it down.

'We have had a complaint from one Cyril Frederick

Firbush, sir. Mr Firbush says that he was the victim of an unprovoked assault at your hands.'

'I wouldn't say that it was unprovoked,' said Avedissian quietly.

'Then you admit the offence, sir?'

'It happened.'

'Would you care to give us your version of the incident?'

'I don't think so,' said Avedissian, feeling drained.

The policemen exchanged glances and shrugged. 'Are you quite sure, sir?' said one of them.

Avedissian smiled wanly at the man's attempt to help him and said, 'Quite.'

'Have you ever been in trouble before, sir?'

'Once.'

Another exchange of glances. 'Really, sir. What?'

'Murder.'

So it had come to this, thought Avedissian as he filled his glass. He was unemployed and due to appear in court on a petty assault charge. The discomfort of shame vied with the numbing effect of the gin and, for the first time in many years, he thought of his parents and was glad that they had not lived to see him in his present state. He lay down on the bed and closed his eyes.

Despite his name, a legacy from an Armenian great-grandfather, Avedissian was English and had been brought up in a village near Canterbury, that most gentle of English towns. His childhood, as the only son of a prosperous business-man, had been a model of middle-class order and pride in achievement.

Having been a bright child Avedissian had had no difficulty in showing the academic success that his parents had valued so highly and, although they had been dead for many years now, they had lived to see him commissioned in the forces and had later supported him in his decision to leave the army and go through medical school.

His mother's pride had been the straightforward pride of a mother in her son and Avedissian smiled as he remembered with fondness the ridiculous floral hat that she had worn at his graduation ceremony. But his father's attitude had been different.

John Avedissian had always been as concerned about his son's development as a person as about his academic achievement, although he too had been proud when Avedissian had graduated as a doctor. To be his 'own man' had always been the goal that John Avedissian had set his son. 'Make up your own mind what is right, then do it,' he had urged. 'Don't run with the herd. It's difficult, make no mistake about it, but resist! Be your own man.'

Difficult! Avedissian snorted at the memory. Just look at what being his own man had done for him! Had his father not realised that people who told the truth, people who did what was right, were an embarrassment to society? What society really wanted was people who played the game; people who knew the rules and played the game . . . or was that self-pity and gin-nurtured cynicism? Avedissian refilled his glass.

The magistrate was lenient. He saw in Avedissian a fellow professional who had fallen on hard times and, in the unspoken way of these things, he back-pedalled when it came to meting out punishment. That Firbush had come across as an ingratiating, slimy little Uriah Heep of a man had also helped Avedissian. The crumpled suit and the rather grubby, un-ironed shirt could not belie the fact that Avedissian belonged where Cyril Frederick Firbush, for all his golf club tie, did not. Justice might be blind but it would take more than a comfortable little homily to destroy Mr Giles Carrington-Smythe's eyesight.

Avedissian paid the fine and walked out into the afternoon, not reflecting too deeply on whether he had got off lightly or not. His immediate thought was to find a nearby pub and order up a large gin. He checked his watch. Ten minutes to closing time.

Two had passed by the time he reached The Earl of Essex and entered the cool, dark interior.

'Just in time, sir. What'll it be?'

Avedissian ordered a large gin and took it to a table after telling the barman to keep the change.

The barman was effusive in his thanks but that only annoyed Avedissian. Whatever happened to dignity? he wondered. Why didn't he tell me to stick my money? Because he was afraid to lose his job? No, that wasn't it. Someone was giving him money, therefore he was happy. A nice simple philosophy.

Avedissian took a large gulp of the gin. Maybe Firbush was right. Maybe he was too grand for the standards of the market-place, but that was hardly a consideration because he was no longer in the market-place. He saw the reality of his situation in the dregs of his empty glass and did not like what he saw. He was lost and alone. One thing Firbush had been right about was the fact that his career as a doctor was over for good. He would never practise again and that thought recurred to gnaw at his insides like an ulcer.

The idea of living without being able to work at what he loved had been bearable, though only just, when Linda had been alive. But with her death the sun had gone out. Not only could he not accept his wife's suicide, he could not understand it and that made it all the worse for they had been so perfectly matched. They had shared an intellectual harmony that had given them such pleasure; it seemed unthinkable that one of them could have had such secret thoughts of death. Did it mean that he had never really known her at all? Had it all been arrogant presumption on his part? Had Linda possessed a secret self, a frightened lonely self who had been unable to confide in him? The thought was unbearable.

'I'm sorry, sir, we're closing now.'

Avedissian did not hear the statement until it was repeated. He glanced at the man in the white jacket and nodded.

'Thank you, sir.'

Avedissian got up and smiled. 'Perhaps you are right and I am wrong,' he said.

'Yes, sir,' said the barman without considering as he picked up the glass and wiped the table.

For Avedissian the days came and went. He was marking time in a meaningless void where the only regulation was that imposed by the liquor licensing laws. One Friday evening as he returned to the flat with his senses suitably numbed he was aware of two neighbours talking in the hallway as he entered the building. 'Disgusting,' said one. 'Absolutely,' said the other.

It was when he was climbing the stairs that he suddenly realised that they had been talking about him and the thought soaked him like icy water. Disgusting? Him? His mind cleared but his feet still displayed unsteadiness as he unlocked the door and made for the bathroom. He switched on the light and stared at the dishevelled spectre in the long mirror, dark circles under his eyes, three days' stubble on his chin, the stain on the front of his shirt. 'God Almighty,' he whispered as he saw himself clearly for the first time in a long while.

Avedissian leaned heavily on one tap while he turned on the other one and began sluicing cold water up into his face. The act of bending over the basin forced some gin-flavoured bile up into his throat where it burned and disgusted him. Angrily he rammed two fingers into the back of his mouth and vomited the contents of his stomach into the basin. The smell made him retch again.

He searched for a disposable razor in the cabinet above

the basin and threw aside everything that got in his way until he found one and started to shave zealously. He ran the bath until it was three-quarters full and immersed himself two or three times before scrubbing his body all over until his skin hurt.

Almost exhausted by the effort, he lay back in the bath and felt anger and frustration leave him, but only to be replaced by an apathy that sucked him down slowly like quicksand. Fighting against it, he got up and dried himself vigorously. At least, it started out with vigorous towelling but quickly degenerated into slow patting as his arms grew sore and tired. He looked at himself in the mirror again and blanched. He was still six feet tall and his hair was still black but these seemed to be the only similarities to the man who had strode the corridors of St Jude's. The man in the mirror had a sunken chest and a ring of flab round his middle. His shoulders drooped and he needed a haircut. The tan from two holidays a year had been replaced in this version by pallid white. The eyes that had been piercing blue were distinctly lack-lustre with whites that were yellow and flecked with veins. Avedissian put out his tongue and put it away again. He would feel better after a drink.

The letter was sandwiched between the electricity bill and an exhortation to provide life insurance for his loved ones. It looked interesting; pristine white and postmarked Cambridge. The paper felt pleasingly expensive as Avedissian unfolded it and saw the embossed coat of arms of Trinity College, Cambridge. He read it with disbelief then re-read it. He was invited to attend for interview on Thursday next at ten o'clock in the morning with a view to employment 'in a professional capacity'. What the hell did that mean? he wondered. He had not applied for any job and he did not know anyone in Cambridge.

Avedissian looked for signs of mistaken identity but

reminded himself of what his father had said: if anyone said 'Avedissian', they meant it. It wasn't a name you mixed up with Smith or Brown. He read on. Expenses would be paid on a scale according to 'Grade 3' and at a rate of £34.15 per night plus second-class travelling costs. Was this some kind of sick joke? Why the hell should he go to Cambridge on the strength of an unsolicited letter? Because he had nothing else to do, that was why.

Chesterton Road was dark but the night was warm and friendly, one of those English summer evenings that optimists like to call 'typical' but which in reality are beautiful exceptions. The scent of blossom filled the air as Avedissian climbed the steps to check in at his hotel.

The hotel was all right but only in the way that many hotels are all right, anonymous decor, anonymous guests. But what it did have in its favour was its location. It stood on the banks of the River Cam.

After a snack taken in the bar, Avedissian walked slowly along the towpath and listened to the sound of talk and laughter coming from the houseboats moored against the sluggish flow. He had to duck his head as he came to a bridge span that was in no hurry to rise, and heard his footsteps echo on the damp stone.

There was a smell of lichen from the underside of the arch. It awakened in him a long-forgotten memory from childhood, a memory of summer days spent fishing beneath weeping willows. There had been a stream running through his village and he and his friends had spent a great deal of time on its banks. The underside of the bridge by the village church had smelled like this one.

Across the water the patrons of a riverside pub had spilled out into the courtyard to laugh and drink beneath the stars. The symbolism of laughter and gaiety being on the other side of the river while he walked alone in darkness did not escape Avedissian but he felt embarrassed at having even considered it. He continued his walk, leaving the towpath and climbing some steps up to the road beside Magdalene College. It had been a long time since he had been in Cambridge. He decided to see if he could still remember where Trinity College was. He could.

Avedissian awoke to the sound of bicycle bells and had the feeling that the sun was itching to fill the room. He checked his watch and relaxed; there was plenty of time. He felt good because he had refrained from drinking on the previous evening and the walk by the river had ensured that he had slept well.

Analysing how he felt about the interview was a different matter and not easy. His overriding feeling was one of curiosity but there was an element of annoyance there too. He was dancing to someone else's tune and that rankled, for by turning up at all, without question, meant that he had conceded the first round.

As Avedissian bathed, in preference to struggling with an ill-fitting shower curtain and makeshift sprinkler that had obviously been added for the benefit of the American summer trade, he wondered what role he should play at the interview. He could not appear as the eager candidate when he did not even know what the appointment was and had not applied for it in the first place. On the other hand he would hardly be negotiating from a position of strength for he was almost on his uppers. He suddenly realised that this had a lot to do with his feeling of annoyance. It stemmed from the fact that his interviewers must know this.

Avedissian walked out into the morning sunshine and crossed the road to look at the river as he walked towards Trinity College. It was good to be able to walk somewhere with purpose again. He opened the tall iron gate and entered the college grounds, pausing to admire the rolling greenery that swept back from the river, before looking for the entrance that the letter had decreed. He paused again on one of the bridges and watched the water slide slowly underneath. A solitary punt was moored nearby.

The courtyard was quiet as he crossed it, looking up to see the minute hand on the clock tower move on to three minutes to the hour. As he entered the building a uniformed porter stepped forward to meet him and before he could say anything, the man said, 'Dr Avedissian? This way, sir.'

The slowness of the lift's ascent obliged Avedissian to say something. 'It's very quiet.'

'The vacation, sir,' replied the porter, without taking his eyes off the floor indicator.

'Of course,' said Avedissian, ending the conversation.

The corridor smelt of dust, leather and floor polish. Avedissian liked it. It had the timelessness of a library.

'In here, sir,' said the porter, opening a door and flattening himself against it to allow Avedissian to pass.

Inside the room Avedissian was met by a smiling woman in her early thirties. She held out her hand and said, 'How nice to meet you, Doctor. I'm Sarah Milek, Sir Michael's assistant.' Avedissian found the smile reassuring and was pleased to hear a name at last, for his letter had been unsigned.

'Sir Michael who?' he asked.

'Just Sir Michael,' replied the woman. 'Follow me, please.'

Avedissian followed the woman into a pleasant, sun-filled room where four men sat waiting at a table. They had their backs to the window. He would be facing it.

'Dr Avedissian,' announced Sarah Milek before turning to leave.

A silver-haired man got to his feet and gestured to Avedissian that he should sit. 'How nice of you to come,' said the smooth, cultured voice.

Avedissian managed a smile but felt patronised.

'May I introduce Mr Bryant, Mr Stapleton, Mr Carlisle.'

Avedissian nodded to each of the three men in turn. Stapleton and Carlisle said 'Good morning' but Bryant looked through him.

The silver-haired man, whom Avedissian took to be 'Sir Michael', opened a file in front of him and moved his glasses to the tip of his nose before shuffling his way through a pile of papers and apparently back again. 'Let me see now . . .' he muttered, beginning the process all over again.

Avedissian noticed Bryant move impatiently in his seat and saw him raise his eyes briefly to the ceiling. The other two remained impassive but Avedissian was aware that they were watching him. The knowledge made him determined to maintain a sphinx-like expression.

'Ah, here we are,' said Sir Michael. 'Mark Avedissian, age thirty-seven, married with no children. Wife deceased. Three years with Her Majesty's Forces, commissioned, served with the Parachute Regiment, resigned commission to enter medical school, graduated third in class in 1973, specialised in paediatrics, last position, consultant paediatrician, St Jude's Hospital, Southampton. Bit of a change, army to medicine, what?'

Avedissian remained silent.

'Care to tell us why?'

'No,' replied Avedissian.

'Too tough for you, Avedissian?' asked Bryant, attracting a sidelong glance from Sir Michael who cleared his throat in disapproval and continued before Avedissian felt obliged to reply.

'Convicted of administering a lethal dose of barbiturates to one Michael Fielding, a patient in your care . . . Parents and judge sympathetic to your motives but law has to be upheld . . . Short prison sentence and removal from the Medical Register . . . Subsequent employment as a medical representative with . . . several companies in fact. Would you agree that that is an accurate, if superficial, account of your curriculum vitae, Doctor?'

Avedissian agreed that it was.

Bryant said abrasively, 'You have been sacked from five companies in the last two years, Avedissian.'

'Yes.'

'Is that all?' demanded Bryant. 'Just "yes"?'

'Why am I here?' asked Avedissian, seething inwardly but outwardly remaining calm.

Sir Michael looked as if he were about to reply but Bryant got there first. 'Good question,' he snorted and sat back in his seat. He stared down at the desk pad in front of him.

Sir Michael looked briefly at Bryant before turning to Avedissian and saying, 'We think that you may be able to help us.'

'How?'

'First we have to ask you some questions.'

Avedissian sighed slightly but then nodded.

'Why did you leave the army?'

'It wasn't for me.'

'You were a first-class officer with a promising career.'

Bryant showed signs of impatience again and interrupted Sir Michael's leisurely approach. 'You decided it wasn't for you after you were sent to Northern Ireland. Isn't that right?'

'I did serve in Northern Ireland,' agreed Avedissian.

'And you lost your nerve.'

'No.'

'Oh, became a pacifist did we? Got all moist-eyed over the bleeding hearts in the Emerald Isle did we?' sneered Bryant.

'I did not become a pacifist,' said Avedissian with a levelness of tone that seemed to annoy Bryant even more.

'Perhaps killing babies is more your style, Avedissian?'

'Why you son of a bitch I'll . . .'

Bryant leaned back in his seat and grinned with self-satisfaction. 'So you're not a complete wimp after all, Avedissian. Good to know.'

Sir Michael seemed embarrassed at Bryant's psychological game. Stapleton and Carlisle remained impassive.

'Your wife committed suicide?' asked Carlisle.

'Yes.'

'How do you feel about that?'

'That's a bloody stupid question.'

Carlisle ignored the comment and asked, 'Any dependent relations?'

'None.'

'How would you like to practise medicine again, Doctor?' asked Sir Michael.

Avedissian was angry. 'Just what is this bloody farce?' he demanded. 'You know damned well that I can never practise again. It's against the law.'

Sir Michael took off his glasses and sat back in his chair. He looked into the distance over Avedissian's shoulder and said, 'In any society, Doctor, it is essential that people be subject to the law. However, there will always be a criminal element who ignore it and, at the other extreme, there will always be the necessity for a small group of people who are not entirely subject to every nuance and letter of it.'

There was a long silence in the room while words kept sticking in Avedissian's throat. When he did finally manage to interpret what he had been told he cleared his throat and said, in acute embarrassment, 'Am I being recruited into the Intelligence Services?' He thought it sounded like a bad line from a village hall play and was relieved when no one laughed.

'In a manner of speaking,' said Sir Michael.

Avedissian felt as if he were alone on a tightrope, the butt of some tasteless joke. In an effort to defend himself he said, 'I am, or rather was, a paediatrician. I am thirty-seven years old, heterosexual and I am not a graduate of this university. That, I would have thought disqualified me on all counts.'

The four men at the table remained impassive. Sir Michael said, 'We have need of a doctor, you are a doctor and you are available. The fact that you have served with the armed forces has some bearing on our choice.'

'Why do you need a doctor?'

'I can't tell you.'

'If you are looking for someone to feed scopolamine to Russian spies then it isn't me.'

'No Russian spies.'

'And if I say no?'

'Then you can go back to becoming an aimless drunk,' rasped Bryant.

A spark of anger flared in Avedissian but he controlled it, for whatever way he looked at it, the comment was not without foundation. 'Very well, I agree,' he said.

'You will now sign this,' said Stapleton, bringing out a document from his briefcase. 'It's the Official Secrets Act.'

Avedissian signed and said, 'Now can you tell me what this is all about?'

'Not yet,' answered Sir Michael, collecting his papers and getting up to leave. 'Mr Bryant will tell you all you need to know for the moment,' and with that, he, Stapleton and Carlisle were gone.

Avedissian was left alone in the room with Bryant who said, 'You will not be returning to your home. Your things will be collected and brought to you. Miss Milek will give you your instructions.'

As the door closed behind Bryant, Avedissian felt hopelessly alone and filled with foreboding about what he had let himself in for. He crossed to the window and looked down at the courtyard to see a black saloon disappear through an arch. The sun shone on the cobbles and it was quiet, deathly quiet.

Sarah Milek came into the room and joined him at the window. 'Welcome aboard,' she said softly.

'Do people really say that?' asked Avedissian, still looking out of the window.

'When they can't think of anything else.'

Avedissian turned to face her and said, 'I'm sorry, that was rude.'

'Don't mention it. I understand life has not been treating you too kindly, and now this . . .' said Sarah Milek.

'What exactly is "this"?' asked Avedissian.

'I'm sorry. I can't tell you any more than I've been instructed to.'

'Which is?'

'Nothing really. I'm to give you this.' Sarah Milek handed over a sealed envelope which Avedissian accepted in silence. 'Open it here,' she said. 'It contains all you need.'

Avedissian sat down at the long table that had been used by Sir Michael and the others. He opened the envelope as Sarah Milek turned to leave. When she reached the door she turned and said, 'Take your time. When you're ready the porter will let you out.'

Avedissian examined the contents. One hundred pounds in cash, a railway timetable and a travel warrant. A brief typed and unsigned letter instructed him to present himself in the lobby of the Brecon Inn in Ebbw Vale on Saturday at ten in the morning. There was a suggestion that it might be sensible to spend the previous night at the inn.

The porter opened the front door as Avedissian emerged from the lift and walked towards him. Almost on impulse Avedissian pointed to a building across the square and asked, 'What building is that?'

The porter seemed embarrassed and looked briefly at his feet before saying, 'I'm afraid I have no idea. I've not been here very long.'

'No, I didn't think you had,' said Avedissian. The "porter" was no more part of Trinity College than he was.

Avedissian bought himself a large gin at a riverside pub

and ordered something from the bar menu. The verandah doors were open so he took his drink outside and leaned on the railing to enjoy the green pleasantness of a perfect summer day.

'Would you like to eat out here?' asked a girl whose accent proclaimed her as a student doing vacation work.

'Please,' he replied.

After lunch Avedissian walked by the river and thought about the morning. On the positive side he felt that he was employed again and that must be good . . . or was it? He could not make up his mind. He had no idea what his job was but the one good thing seemed to be that it did not involve selling and that was a big plus.

Avedissian was temperamentally unsuited to selling as a career for, apart from the occasional person whom he liked instinctively, he tended to regard people in general with reserved suspicion. They were idiots until they proved different and, if they didn't, then he had no further time for them.

Unfortunately, his career as a representative with several companies, as Sir Michael had so euphemistically put it, had brought him into contact with a succession of people who had failed the Avedissian Test when he had been in no position to flunk them. Clients had felt that he had not treated them with due deference and company superiors had felt that he had not acknowledged their true importance. In the end both had conspired to make his life a misery.

All that was behind him now. The question was, what lay in front? He paused to watch two little boys play with model boats in the water before leaving the towpath to rejoin the road by crossing the footbridge. He had a hundred pounds and a travel warrant in his pocket and he had to be in Wales on Saturday.

TWO

KEVIN O'DONNELL WAS DYING and, like so many at such times, he was unprepared for death and struggled to say so much before it was too late. Martin O'Neill cradled the dying man's head in his arms and tried to comfort him but he was too badly hurt himself to be of much use and blood flowed freely from a shattered left arm. It started to rain, turning the pools of red a muddy brown and plastering the men's hair to their heads as they huddled in their backstreet doorway.

'I'm thirsty,' croaked O'Donnell, but there was only the summer rain to moisten his parched lips.

O'Neill looked up sharply as he heard the shrill sound of a whistle in the distance. Next would come the clatter of army boots and the revving of laboured engines as the British combed the area. O'Donnell had heard the sound too and reacted with new urgency.

'Listen . . . Listen to me. There's an envelope in the safe at the Long House. Get it, hide it, let no one else see it. Promise me?'

'I promise.'

There was a trickle of blood at the corner of O'Donnell's mouth and a gurgling sound from his throat that said his lungs were filling up. He gripped O'Neill's lapel and pulled him closer. 'One . . . last order.'

O'Neill brought his ear close to hear it then sat upright and repeated, as if in a daze, the words he had just heard.

27

'That's right,' O'Donnell gasped. 'Obey it . . .'

O'Neill nodded dumbly as O'Donnell's head fell back and he was dead.

O'Neill clutched his wounded arm to his side as he struggled to his feet. The shouting was coming closer but the pain in his arm was becoming unbearable. He set off down the lane but had to stop as lightheadedness blurred his vision, for he had lost too much blood. Knowing that he was in imminent danger of passing out he knelt down in another doorway and put his head on the ground to restore the blood supply to his brain. He had to make a decision.

The British had already achieved a major victory. They had killed Kevin O'Donnell, the IRA's senior commander in Belfast and, whether they knew it or not, the most listened-to voice on the war council. They must not take him alive as well, for he knew too much and the British would make him talk, of that he was sure. There was no level of bravery that could stand up to modern interrogation techniques and only a fool would believe differently. By the time that sound machine had scrambled his brain he would be ready to kiss the Queen's arse and recite nursery rhymes for the Duke. There was no real decision to make. He would have to take his own life.

The ultimate test of loyalty had come and here, in a dark street in Belfast with the rain pouring down, his life would come to an end. Had it been worthwhile? Would anyone miss him? And what of O'Donnell's last order? Had the dying man taken leave of his senses? Surely he could not have meant it? But he had, O'Neill was sure of that. He had seen O'Donnell's eyes when he had said it and the man had been perfectly lucid. But now it seemed to be academic anyway for circumstances were dictating that he would be in no position to carry it out. He reached inside his jacket and pulled out his pistol.

The pain from his arm was becoming unbearable and

O'Neill knew that he could not remain conscious for much longer. Just as long as he could pull the trigger. His vision blurred again as he tried to focus on the meagre output from a faulty streetlight on the other side of the lane. The filament dissolved in the rain to form a misty halo that grew and grew until it swallowed him up and all was quiet.

There was a smell of fried onions when O'Neill awoke and he could hear the yells of children playing. His first black thought that he might be inside a British prison was allayed for the moment, for prisons did not smell of fried onions. They smelt of cabbage and urine. And they did not sound of children, they clanged and echoed. A stab of pain from his arm made him consider a hospital but that idea did not gel either. It did not feel like a hospital because it was cold. Hospitals were not cold. They had the heated dryness of a hairdresser's and the smell of a school sick room.

O'Neill started to shiver then found that he could not stop. The involuntary convulsions stirred his arm to new extremes of pain and made him cry out as he clutched at it to minimise the effects of the tremor.

A woman came into the room and hurried over to him, alarmed at what she saw. 'Easy,' she soothed, pushing him back gently on to the pillow. 'You're all right. You're safe now. Try to relax.'

O'Neill searched the woman's face and found reassurance. The convulsions became more intermittent, each one being met by the woman's renewed insistence that all was well. O'Neill thought that she looked about forty-five but had to admit that the truth could have lain anywhere from twenty-five upwards. The lines around her eyes and the thickness of her waistline said that she led the kind of life that brought age early to a woman. Her fingers smelled of nicotine as she brought the blanket up to his chin.

29

'Where am I?' O'Neill asked.

'The Flats.'

O'Neill's eyes asked the question.

'The Doonan Flats. My husband and his brother brought you here.'

'But the Doonan . . .'

'I know, they're a good bit away from where they found you but that's probably all to the good.'

'How did they find me?'

'They were out drinking. What else! They were over in Clancy's when they heard that the Brits were on the warpath. Someone had seen two of ours in Tannahill Road, so Con, that's my man, said that he knew where they would be making for. He was brought up round there, see. He would go lend a hand. He and his brother drove through the backstreets in Michael's car and, unfortunately, they found you.'

'That was brave of them.'

'Brave!' scoffed the woman. 'It was bloody stupid. It was Guinness not bravery!'

'You're not for a free Ireland then?'

'Free Ireland! Now what would I be doing with high-sounding phrases like that? I want a decent house, I want a job for Con, I want a future for my kids. These are the things I'm interested in.'

'And don't you think that you'd get these things in a free Ireland?' asked O'Neill.

'Governments are governments. They are politicians and they don't give a stuff for the likes of me, whoever they are.'

'If you feel that way why didn't you turn me in?'

The woman threw back her head and laughed bitterly. 'Turn you in?' she exclaimed. 'Me, a Catholic woman living in the Doonan, turn in a Provo? Do you think I'm mental or something?'

O'Neill conceded the point silently and tried to raise

himself on to his good elbow. He said, 'If you will just give me a hand, I'll be getting out your road.'

Political considerations became personal ones. The woman said, 'You will do no such thing. Besides, Con and Michael have gone to get medical help for you.' She saw the look of alarm appear in O'Neill's eyes and added, 'Don't worry. They are daft but not that daft. There's a woman, used to be a district nurse, her brother's in the Maze, she's quite safe.'

'Thanks,' said O'Neill.

The woman sat down on the edge of the bed, her face showing the signs of strain that the last few hours had brought. 'Would you like a cup of tea?' she asked quietly.

'I'd love one.'

The woman's husband returned, accompanied by his brother and a small woman in her fifties. In her hand she carried a battered leather case.

'Connor McShane,' announced the man holding out his hand but taking it back in embarrassment as he realised that O'Neill was in no position to accept it. O'Neill nodded.

'And this is my brother Pat.' The smaller of the two men grinned and O'Neill nodded again.

'And this here is Mrs O'Hara. She's going to have a look at your arm.'

'I'm obliged to you,' said O'Neill.

The woman did not smile but put down her case and took off her coat while the rest retreated to a respectful distance. She gingerly started to cut away the blood-caked sleeve of O'Neill's shirt with scissors that seemed none too sharp judging by the difficulty she was having. O'Neill watched what she was doing impassively but was afraid inside for he feared that the bullet had shattered the bone.

'I'll need some water,' said the woman. 'His shirt is stuck to the wound. I'll have to bathe it free.' McShane's wife left the room and returned a few minutes later with some warm water in a bowl.

'This will hurt,' said the nurse as she began teasing the cloth away from O'Neill's arm. A sharp intake of breath from O'Neill verified it. He was watching the faces of the onlookers when his shirt was finally freed from the wound and saw them wince. He looked down to see the smashed pulp of tissue and bone that had been his left elbow and felt despair threaten.

The nurse's shoulders sagged. 'You need a hospital,' she said.

'No hospital,' replied O'Neill.

'There's nothing I can do for you.'

'That's what they always say in the pictures before they go and patch it up anyway,' said O'Neill with a desperate attempt at humour.

The nurse's face showed both cynicism and pity. 'Not in your case,' she said. 'Your arm will have to come off.'

The fact that O'Neill, only a few short hours before, had been preparing to take his own life did not seem to matter now as he was stricken by the thought of mutilation. In his mind he could see the empty sleeve, turned up and secured with a safety pin which would rust with the passing of time. He could see the little stump at bedtime, flapping like the useless wing of a penguin.

The hell was all inside O'Neill's head. Outwardly he was calm but he saw that McShane was construing this as bravery. The man's face was bursting with emotion as he turned to his brother and said, 'See! What did I tell you? With one arm they are still more than a match for these Brit bastards.'

McShane came over to O'Neill's bedside and knelt like an adoring shepherd. 'I tell you, mister,' he said to O'Neill. 'When I saw you in that doorway preparing to take on the Brits single-handed, I've never felt so proud in my life.'

O'Neill looked at the man. Should he tell him the truth? Tell him that he had never had any intention of taking anyone on single-handed? Tell him that he had, in fact, been preparing to blow his own brains out because this was the real world and the real world was a long way from a John Wayne film? Tell him that the real struggle was for professionals not romantics, it was for men who calculated the odds with their brains not their hearts, men who figured out risk against return? O'Neill decided that there was no point in telling him anything. Let the myths flourish with the folk songs. After all, the British had television.

'Can you fix me up so I can move out of here?' O'Neill asked the nurse.

'I'll do what I can but it will just be a case of covering the whole mess up and strapping your arm to your body. We'll keep the tourniquet on but you'll have to remember to release it at intervals or gangrene will set in.'

The nurse cleaned up the wound before smothering it in white dressing. O'Neill was exhausted for it had been an agonising fifteen minutes, during which the woman seemed to have consistently sought out the most sensitive areas to linger over and probe and prod for bone fragments. Suppressed anger and frustration had welled up inside him like the rolling waves of a rising tide, till now he felt too weak to move.

'He will have to rest for a bit,' said the nurse as she packed her case.

'We can take him where he wants to go later tonight,' said McShane.

'No,' said O'Neill weakly. 'You've done enough. Phone this number.' He recited a series of digits. 'Tell them that you have a parcel ready for collection, then tell them what they want to know.'

'You can rely on us,' said McShane.

*

Two men came for O'Neill at nine in the evening. Any later and the risk of a spot check would have been greater, but at that time the traffic was just right. McShane and his brother stood on either side of the doorway like football fans seeing their team out of the tunnel. O'Neill stopped and thanked them both.

'Anything for a free Ireland,' said McShane self-consciously.

'Don't go selling your story to a newspaper now, will you?' said one of the men who had come for O'Neill.

McShane laughed nervously for he had seen the veiled threat. O'Neill looked at McShane's wife and saw that she had not bothered to laugh. 'Thank you as well, missus,' he said.

'You're welcome,' said the woman as she turned away.

The dark blue Bedford van took off from the kerb and the driver said to O'Neill, 'We can't take you home. The Brits know you're missing. They turned your place over last night.'

'What about Kathleen?'

'Your sister told them that you were away for a few days but they turned it over anyway.'

'So where are we going?'

'The Long House. They've got a doctor for you.'

'I want to see Kathleen.'

'It's difficult. The Brits are watching your house all the time.'

'The army?'

'The woman at number seventeen has a new lodger, works the boats . . . you know the game.'

'At least it's predictable,' said O'Neill.

'We'll try to set up some kind of decoy so that your sister can slip away.'

'Thanks.'

*

The Long House was a warehouse. It was owned by a wholesale newsagency that distributed stationery, magazines and periodicals throughout the north and as such, with the ephemeral nature of news, it was ideal cover for the IRA, with delivery vans coming and going at all hours. They had been using the building successfully for two years without problem, utilising its extensive cellarage for administration, meetings at top level and, when the circumstances dictated it, for living quarters. Circumstances dictated that O'Neill stay there for the present.

The doctor was already in the room when O'Neill was helped in by the two men who had brought him. They laid him gently on the table as the doctor continued to scrub his hands and forearms in the sink.

The thought of someone else poking and prodding at his wound prompted O'Neill to ask, 'Can you give me something? The pain's bad.'

'You'll feel better in a moment,' said the doctor, drying his hands and picking up a syringe.

The tiny prick of the needle was followed by a warm feeling of well-being and peace which spread inexorably through O'Neill's body, bringing a tranquillity that he had seldom experienced. He did not feel drowsy, more weightless, as if he were floating in a world free from pain and care.

'How's that?' asked the doctor.

'What did you give me?' asked O'Neill.

The doctor told him.

'I can see the attraction,' replied O'Neill.

'You do know that your arm will have to come off?' asked the doctor.

'The nurse told me.'

'The Bairn says I have to do it here. We can't risk a hospital with what you know.'

'I'd like to see my sister.'

35

'The Bairn says no, not until after.'

'There might not be an after. That's why I want to see her.'

'The Bairn says no.'

'Bastard,' said O'Neill softly.

'He's taken over from O'Donnell,' said the doctor. 'He's the new commander.'

Finbarr Kell, known as 'The Bairn' to everyone within the organisation, but never to his face, scared O'Neill. For years he had been convinced that Kell was a hopeless psychopath but, within the organisation, his credentials were impeccable and he had risen relentlessly till now he was their new commander. O'Neill had never known anyone so lacking in compassion of any kind.

Kell seemed to O'Neill to have been born to violence and baptised in hatred. When this was combined with a street cunning that would have made him the envy of a New York street gang and a brain that was devious to the point of genius, Kell inspired fear in all who came to know him.

Hatred, cunning and the bravery of a lion had made The Bairn a living legend. His exploits were the stuff of folklore, or at least they had been until a bomb that he had been setting had gone off prematurely. The blast had fractured his spine and blown off both legs but he had survived, and survived to rise within the organisation.

Since the loss of his legs Kell had been transported around in a contraption that resembled a pram, hence the nickname The Bairn. If Kell had ever possessed the tiniest spark of decency it had been totally extinguished by the accident. He was a cold, cruel man, feared, loathed, but always obeyed. The thought that now he would no longer be subject to the moderating influence of Kevin O'Donnell was not one that O'Neill could take any pleasure in. As the anaesthetic took effect he thought of O'Donnell's last order.

*

Through a sea of pain O'Neill could hear voices. They were far away, as if he were at the bottom of a well and the voices were at the top, but he could hear what they were saying.

'Probably won't make it through the night . . .'

'Surgical shock too much in his condition . . .'

'Desperately weak . . .'

'No blood to give him . . .'

'The Bairn's coming down just in case he comes round.'

'What about his sister?'

'The Bairn says no.'

O'Neill tried to open his eyes but found that he could not. He concentrated hard but still to no effect. It was ridiculous. He was conscious but trapped inside a body that refused to respond to any instruction he issued. He could feel nothing except a burning pain coming from his left arm, but that was the thing that was not there any more. Perhaps he was dead? It was a big disappointment if he was for he was still there, damn it! Locked inside a useless hulk of flesh. Good God, he would be able to hear everything at his own funeral, the volley of shots, the patter of earth on the lid of the coffin and then nothing, endless, eternal, black nothing. But he would still be there!

O'Neill's brain rebelled violently at the thought and sent a tremor down his right side. The tremor shook him free like an air bubble that had been trapped at the foot of a pond and he surfaced to open his eyes.

'Doctor!' said a voice. 'He's coming round.'

A shadow moved over the light and the voice of the doctor said, 'How are you feeling?'

Another voice said in rasping tones, 'Move! I have to speak to him.'

O'Neill recognised the voice as Finbarr Kell's. He struggled against the intransigence of his lips but to no avail.

He was falling into blackness again. Down, down, down. Perhaps there would be sunshine when he stopped falling. That would be nice, sunshine . . . grass . . . flowers.

O'Neill was unconscious for the better part of two days while his body struggled to scrape by on the borderline oxygen supply that his vastly depleted blood volume could transport. On the third day he was through the crisis and started to get better and Kell came back to the Long House in the evening. O'Neill heard the squeak of the pram wheels as Nelligan, Kell's constant minder, manoeuvred him through the door to park him at the foot of the bed.

There was a long moment when neither man spoke but just looked at each other. Kell's head had always struck O'Neill as being too big for his body but he supposed that this was an illusion created by his legless torso. Nevertheless it seemed as if all the pores on Kell's face were quite discernible as the cold eyes, magnified by strong, rimless glasses, surveyed him under a hairless head.

'Well, Martin, it seems that even an intellectual has given up something for the cause at last, eh?' said Kell eyeing O'Neill's bandaged stump. He seemed pleased with his joke.

'I'm no intellectual, Finbarr.'

Kell smiled but there was no humour in it. 'Of course you are,' he said softly. 'All that book learning . . . of course you are.'

O'Neill stayed silent.

'What went wrong?' asked Kell.

'The Brits knew we were coming. They were waiting for us.'

'Bastards!' spat Kell. 'Then they were tipped off?'

'Must have been,' said O'Neill.

'Any ideas?'

'No.'

'I'll find the bastard if it's the last thing I do,' said Kell in a way that utterly convinced O'Neill that he would.

'Meanwhile I need the keys to the safe. Do you know where they are?'

'No,' lied O'Neill. He had a promise to keep before he handed them over. 'Have you checked O'Donnell's room?'

Kell looked at him as if he were mentally defective. 'Of course I've checked O'Donnell's room,' he rasped.

'They'll turn up', said O'Neill.

'No doubt,' said Kell with a look that sent shivers down O'Neill's spine.

'I'd like to see my sister,' said O'Neill.

'Ah yes, the schoolteacher sister.' Kell smiled and O'Neill thought that he looked even more evil when he did that. 'I don't want her coming here. It's too risky.'

'I heard that there's a Brit plant in the street?'

'There *was*. Arm got caught in a hawser winch at the docks. Tore him in half.' Kell smiled again.

'What's to happen to me?' asked O'Neill.

'The cottage at Cladeen. It will be safe there and your sister can look after you.'

'Thanks.'

'Anything for my men . . . Martin.'

The doctor changed the dressing on O'Neill's stump in the morning and seemed optimistic that the risk of infection had passed. He advised waiting another day at the Long House but O'Neill was adamant that he be taken to Cladeen and in the end the doctor agreed. O'Neill travelled in one of the news vans, an uncomfortable journey that lasted three hours, but the thought of fresh air and quiet countryside sustained him.

There was a chill in the evening air when they arrived at the loughside cottage and O'Neill saw smoke rise from the chimney as they turned off the road to negotiate the narrow track leading to the water's edge. The van started to lurch on the rough surface and O'Neill stopped it, saying that he would rather walk, it would be easier on his arm. He watched while the driver reversed the van up the track, and nodded goodbye before continuing on down to the cottage where Kathleen was waiting. She came to meet him.

'So you came back then?'

'Most of me,' said O'Neill, nodding to his left shoulder.

Tears started to run down Kathleen O'Neill's face as she looked at O'Neill's bandaged stump.

'Don't,' said O'Neill softly.

Kathleen came towards him and put her head on his chest. 'I knew it would come to this,' she said. 'I always knew.'

They went inside the house and O'Neill sat down while Kathleen made tea. 'Or would you like something stronger?' she asked.

'Tea will be fine.'

As O'Neill sipped his tea Kathleen looked at him and said, 'It's going to be over now, isn't it?'

O'Neill shrugged and said, 'You don't retire from the organisation, you know that. They don't give you an electric toaster and a Teasmade and wish you well with the roses. It's a commitment for life, or until we win freedom.'

'A political commitment! I'm just saying that it's time you left the field, especially now that Kell is in charge.'

'You know then?'

'All Belfast knows.'

'I'm tired,' said O'Neill.

'Rest then. We'll talk later.'

The subject of O'Neill's 'retirement' came up again as he and Kathleen walked by the lough on the following evening.

'Have you thought about what I said?' asked Kathleen.

O'Neill said that he had.

'Well then?'

'There's something I have to do.'

'Oh there's always going to be something you have to do!' said Kathleen angrily. 'What kind of a life do you think this is? Do you think I enjoy being Martin O'Neill's sister? Do you think I enjoy having soldiers storm into my house whenever they feel like it? Do you think I enjoyed losing every boyfriend I ever had because of who I was? Do you? Do you think I enjoy having parents whisper behind my back and wonder just what kind of woman is teaching their children?'

O'Neill was taken aback at the outburst. 'I thought you understood,' he said weakly.

Kathleen looked at O'Neill holding the stump of his arm and relented. 'Oh I do,' she conceded. 'But enough is enough. You can't go on like this. I can't go on like this. You're crip . . .'

'Crippled,' said O'Neill, completing the word.

'Yes, crippled,' said Kathleen quietly. 'You've done your bit. Call it a day.'

'Perhaps you're right,' said O'Neill.

'Do you mean that?'

'I really do have one more thing to do. It was O'Donnell's last order to me. I promised him just as I am promising you.'

'What was it?'

'You know better than that.'

O'Neill withdrew his arm from the bedclothes and looked at his watch, now painfully aware that it was on his right wrist. He angled it so that it caught the moonlight coming in through the bedroom window. It was three in the morning and he could not sleep for there was too much on his mind. Uppermost was the problem of the safe in the Long House and how he was going to be able to get the envelope from it. He got up quietly and crossed to the window to look out at the waters of the lough.

Would the contents of the envelope help him to understand

the nature of the order? he wondered. Please God that they would for he was by no means confident that he could carry out such an order without understanding the reason behind it.

There would have to be a reason, a good reason, for O'Neill had never been very good at assuming the good intentions of his superiors. In fact, he had discovered some years before that he possessed entirely the wrong mentality for military life of any sort. He had discovered within himself an inherent weakness that had made him uneasy in the field ever since. As he stood in the pale grey moonlight he thought back to that day, the day of the ambush.

O'Neill and six others had been returning to their farmhouse hideout after an operation near the border and, as always when they returned, they were approaching with caution in case an ambush had been laid for them.

O'Neill had ordered the others to wait while he himself had gone on alone to investigate. As he had lain in the grass watching the huddle of cottages a child had run out into the yard. It had waddled across the dirt with its nose running and a full nappy impeding its knock-kneed gait. O'Neill had waited for its mother to come out and get it but she had not. Instead she had called to it from inside the house and there had been fear in her voice. Fear that had warned O'Neill that she was not alone.

Quite suddenly a British Paratroop officer had come out from the cottage and sprinted over to the child to sweep it up into his arms. He was turning to take it back to its mother when he saw O'Neill pointing the gun at him and froze in his tracks. Their eyes met as O'Neill prepared to fire but did not.

Thinking that O'Neill's reluctance had to do with the child he was holding and, rather than use it as a shield, the officer had put it down gently and shooed it away from him. He had then stood up to face death. The simple gesture of humanity had not been lost on O'Neill. He had lowered the weapon and indicated with the muzzle that the officer should finish what he had started. He had seen the look of puzzlement in the man's eyes and then the slight nod as he picked up the child again and disappeared into the house. O'Neill had returned to tell his group that the hideout had been blown. They could not use it any longer. Humanity or weakness? The question had remained unanswered within O'Neill all these years.

THREE

On Saturday morning Avedissian sat in the lobby of the Brecon Inn feeling distinctly ill-at-ease. The feeling was born of not really knowing why he was there or, indeed, who or what he was waiting for. He had just had to say, 'Someone will be coming to meet me,' for the third time to a solicitous member of the staff. But who would it be? Sarah Milek? Sir Michael? Someone new?

At five minutes past ten a taxi pulled up outside and the driver came in. He said something to the desk clerk and Avedissian knew from the way that they looked in his direction that he must be the subject of their conversation. The driver came towards him and said, 'Mr Avedissian?' Avedissian nodded and they left.

The journey took about half an hour but Avedissian was surprised when the driver said, 'Here we are. Llangern Farm road-end,' for the place where they had stopped appeared to be in the middle of nowhere. Avedissian got out his wallet but the driver said, 'All taken care of.' Avedissian gave him a pound anyway and watched as the taxi did a three-point turn and disappeared back down the road to town.

It was still and hot and the hedgerows buzzed with business of summer. Avedissian wanted to sit down but somehow felt that he should remain conspicuous. He loosened his collar and began to pace up and down. At first it was ten paces in both directions but then further as boredom dictated.

After ten minutes he heard the sound of an approaching engine and looked along the road in both directions, unable to decide where the noise was coming from. As it grew louder Avedissian realised that it was not coming from the road at all. A small military vehicle was coming towards him across the fields. It drew to a halt and a shirt-sleeved sergeant beckoned to him. 'In you get, sir.'

There was no opportunity for conversation above the sound of the Land-Rover's engine so Avedissian contented himself with the view and concentrated on keeping his backside in contact with the seat as the vehicle bounced over the Brecon moorland.

Distance was difficult to judge but Avedissian reckoned that they had travelled about three miles from the road when they reached a track leading up to some gates which were almost obscured by a copse of conifers. The vehicle slowed and Avedissian said, 'I take it we have arrived.'

'Llangern House,' replied the sergeant.

The house was impressively large and Avedissian was moved to wonder who had built it where it stood and why. The answers obviously lay in the last century but he did not bother to ask for there were more important things to consider as the sergeant took his bag from the back and led the way inside.

A young man bearing the insignia of a captain in the army, but like the sergeant bearing no regimental badges, stood up to meet them.

'You must be wondering what this is all about,' he said to Avedissian.

'A bit,' agreed Avedissian as they shook hands and the officer indicated that he should sit down.

'Quite simply, you are here for a bit of a tone up.'

The captain smiled as Avedissian repeated the phrase slowly. 'Yes,' he said, 'You know the sort of thing – a spot of running, bit of hill walking, some PT. General improvement in fitness. That sort of thing.'

'But I'm a doctor, not a football player,' Avedissian protested.

'Oh really?' said the captain, 'I didn't know that. Says here you're an ex-Para.'

'That was years ago.'

'Well, never mind. It's a bit like riding a bike really. You never really forget.'

Avedissian did not agree but said nothing.

'We get all sorts here,' said the captain. 'Bit like a health farm I suppose. Wouldn't you say so, Sergeant?'

'Yes, sir. Quite so, sir.'

Avedissian felt even more uneasy.

'Now, Sergeant, perhaps you would show Mr, sorry, Dr Avedissian here to his quarters.' The captain turned to Avedissian and said, 'When you have settled in we would like you to see the MO. Come to think of it, you two should have lots in common, both being doctors and all.'

Avedissian emptied out what little there was in his travel bag and stowed it away in a bedside locker. He put the bottle of gin at the back and concealed it as best he could. He was already depressed for he had felt sure that he would learn something about his job today but now that seemed unlikely. He had been sent to summer camp.

The sergeant was waiting for Avedissian when he returned downstairs and said, 'If you will just follow me, sir.'

Avedissian dutifully trotted along behind him until they came to a glass door marked Unit Medical Officer. The sergeant knocked and stood back to let Avedissian enter first.

'Mr . . . er . . . Dr Avedissian,' announced the sergeant.

The sergeant left and Avedissian and the Medical Officer sized each other up. 'I didn't know you were a doctor,' said the MO.

'I'm not but I was,' said Avedissian.

'Oh I see. One of those,' said the MO.

'Not exactly,' said Avedissian coldly.

'Well, no matter. Take your clothes off.'

Avedissian stripped and answered questions as the MO filled in a large pink form. The questionnaire, Avedissian deduced, had been designed to ascertain his present level of fitness.

'Play any games?'

'No.'

'Jog?'

'No'.

'Take any exercise at all?'

'No.'

The MO completed a list of negatives and said, 'Right then. Let's take a look at you.'

Avedissian marked mental time as he underwent the examination and the MO filled in the blanks on a yellow sheet. Height, weight, blood pressure, pulse, lung function, chest expansion.

'Do you wear glasses?'

'For reading.'

'Ah yes, Anno Domini.'

'Quite,' said Avedissian flatly.

The MO completed his examination and put down his forms. He folded his arms and said, 'Quite frankly, Avedissian, you're a wreck. What the hell have you been doing to yourself?'

Avedissian shrugged his shoulders but did not reply.

'Booze,' said the MO, answering his own question. 'Still, the damage is nothing that a bit of exercise and some decent meals won't cure. You can go now.'

As Avedissian finished dressing and turned to leave the MO asked, 'Did you bring any with you?'

'No,' Avedissian lied. He closed the door and rejoined the sergeant who had been waiting for him in the corridor. He was taken to the quartermaster where the kit that was issued did little to restore his morale, for it comprised three sets of military fatigues, waterproof clothing, two pairs of boots, a knife, a compass, a map-case and mess tins.

'Anything else you will require will be issued to you as you need it,' said the sergeant.

Avedissian was acutely aware of a strong physical element in what had been implied or said since his arrival. It made him uneasy. He was not at all reassured by references to 'a bit of exercise' or 'a spot of this or that' for, to him, it smacked of practised military understatement, the sort of mentality that dismissed World War Two as a 'bit of bother'. His line of thought became defensive.

The sergeant took Avedissian back to his room and left him to consider his options. His first thought was to wonder whether or not he actually had any. He was not in the army, he reasoned. They could not make him do anything he did not want to do. He could leave at any time. That was the theory but when he thought about what would actually happen in practice things were not so clearly defined. If he walked out through the door he would be a figure on the landscape. He would have no job, no prospects and no future. Did that seem attractive? Avedissian introduced a working hypothesis of hoping for the best.

Avedissian came down to dinner at seven as instructed and joined his fellow guests. Like him they were all wearing dark green fatigues with name tags above the left breast pocket. A tall man with short cropped hair came towards him and said, 'I'm Paul Jarvis, we will be working together.'

Avedissian shook hands and feared the worst, for Jarvis was in his mid-twenties and struck him as being as hard as a rock. He prayed that 'working together' did not hold an element of competition.

A tall, spare man with the rank of major rose to his feet and welcomed them to Llangern. It was day one for all of them, he said, and introduced the staff, six in all, who were to be addressed by rank alone. Military discipline would be observed at all times but bull would be kept to a minimum and allowances would be made for the fact that some members of the course were unfamiliar with what that entailed. Avedissian hoped that that would include him and glanced round at the others. There were about twenty of them including five women. All of them looked younger than himself.

'I understand you were a Para,' said Jarvis as he and Avedissian sat down to eat together.

'A long time ago and only for a while,' replied Avedissian, wishing that people would stop referring to his military service.

'And then you became a doctor?'

'Yes,' replied Avedissian. So Jarvis knew about him, he thought. Perhaps he knew the reasons for his being there. 'You seem to know a lot about me,' he said. 'But I know nothing about you.'

'There's not much to say really. I'm twenty-six, I have a BA in history from the University of Leeds and I'm a serving officer in the Royal Marines.'

'You're a commando?'

'Yes.'

'Then what on earth are you doing here? You can hardly need a "bit of exercise", as they keep calling it.'

Jarvis smiled and said, 'I don't, but you do. That's why I'm here.' His smile became even broader when he saw the look that appeared on Avedissian's face.

Avedissian felt that his worst fears were being realised. He now had his own personal Marine Commando to put him

49

through hell. 'This is all a bit ridiculous,' he protested. 'I'm a doctor! I am thirty-seven years old!'

'So was James Bond,' said Jarvis.

'Pardon?'

'The Bond books. James Bond was thirty-seven.'

Avedissian could see that his chances of attracting any sympathy were remote. He changed the subject and asked, 'What's the purpose of all this?'

Jarvis replied, 'I'm as much in the dark as you are. All I know is that I have been seconded to a special mission. I was told that I would be working with a doctor, an ex-Para who might be a bit rusty, and I was to see that he should get back into reasonable shape.'

'Just what does reasonable shape mean?' asked Avedissian bringing his fears into the open.

'Don't worry too much,' Jarvis smiled. 'No one is going to try to turn you into a cold-eyed assassin who can kill a man with one flick of his big toe. My instructions are to see that you can suffer the slings and arrows of outrageous fortune and occasionally hit back if necessary.'

When they had finished eating the major got to his feet again and said that they should all have an early night. He added that, before retiring, they should lay out their clothes in such a manner as to permit dressing in complete darkness. If an alarm should sound they should be 'on parade' in the hall within two and a half minutes. 'Any questions?' he asked.

Someone asked what time reveille would be at.

'Any time,' came the reply.

The laughter had the thinness of new ice.

Avedissian said good-night to Jarvis, who had the room next to his, and closed the door. He went immediately to the bedside locker and reached inside for the gin bottle. It had gone. A momentary flare of anger subsided and he resigned himself with a wry smile. That, he supposed, was one problem taken care of.

He lay in bed and looked out of the window at the full moon, his hands behind his head. Sleep was going to be a long time coming but it did not matter for the sheets were clean and cool, the bed was firm and comfortable and, in the moonlight, he could see his clothes spread out in pre-determined order. He closed his eyes and rehearsed where everything was. He opened them again and confirmed it.

As the moon dipped behind the window-frame Avedissian felt sleep creep up on him. The stars twinkled in the clear night sky over the dark shapes of the Welsh mountains and all was peaceful, save for the alarm that had just gone off.

'Boy Scouts!' muttered Avedissian as he got into his clothes in the darkness. The advantage of not having been asleep when the alarm had sounded and the fact that there was still some moonlight in the room made the exercise a smooth one. He clattered downstairs and joined the throng of people assembling in the hall. Jarvis was already there. He acknowledged Avedissian with a nod.

Several of the course members were standing stiffly to attention, eyes staring straight ahead as if fixed on some invisible Star of Bethlehem. Avedissian adopted a more leisurely stance and Jarvis hid a smile.

'Good morning,' said the captain and checked his watch as the last of the stragglers came through the door, including one of the girls carrying her right boot. 'I couldn't get the knot out,' she said sheepishly. It got a laugh.

'You'll find sweaters and anoraks by the door,' said the captain. 'We're going for a walk.'

At first the walk was brisk but not unpleasant. Avedissian found himself enjoying it and was pleased to note that his circulation had improved to match the cold night air.

Another two miles and the Captain said, 'Right, we'll run for a bit.'

Pleasure gave way to pain as Avedissian's lungs demanded more and more air and the fact that Jarvis beside him appeared to be breathing quite normally did not give him a psychological boost.

'Keep up!' yelled the sergeant as the party started to string out with Avedissian competing successfully for last place. The shouts of the NCOs and Jarvis egging him on spurred Avedissian to greater effort and he increased his pace to gain a little on the pack. He was almost back in touch when they were ordered to return to walking pace. Jarvis asked Avedissian how he was feeling but Avedissian was unable to reply. Oxygen was too precious to waste on mere words.

The outward leg of the 'walk' ended with a climb. The party followed a mountain track to reach the summit of a Brecon peak of sixteen hundred feet. By the time he reached the top Avedissian was feeling ill. He detached himself from the group and fell down on his hands and knees behind a rock to be sick. He stayed on his hands and knees till his stomach was empty and his breathing had returned to normal.

The sun came up. Avedissian had always found the dawn an intensely personal experience and, like most people, had not watched the sun come up that often in his life, so that he could recall clearly the occasions in his past when he had. He was glad that no one spoke for there was no need for anyone to say how beautiful it was. He stood alone on an outcrop of rock and let the red light bathe him in mellow sadness.

It was six-thirty when they got back to Llangern House to a hot shower and then breakfast. This was followed by a morning of lectures on navigation and map reading. Avedissian could not help but wonder about his fellow students. They all seemed to be familiar with the basics but varied a great deal in ability above that level. Were they civilians? Service personnel? What was more important, were they all there for the same reason? The fact that the members of the course split up in the afternoon to do different things seemed to suggest that they were not.

Avedissian and Jarvis were part of an eight-strong contingent, all male, who spent the afternoon in the gymnasium. There they were hounded by two NCOs in something called circuit training, in which they were required to complete a series of exercises in succession and then start all over again. After three circuits Avedissian had to void his lunch. His attempt to linger too long in the lavatory was headed off by one of the NCOs who had seen it all before. Avedissian was permitted to rest . . . after two more circuits.

The official day finished at seven and Avedissian was in bed by eight. He had not felt so tired since his basic training with the Parachute Regiment. Come to think of it, that had been in Wales too, he recalled.

A new day began at five a.m. and followed much the same pattern as the one before. Early morning exercise was followed by breakfast and lectures. Lunch was followed by afternoon exercise. This time the afternoon exercise for Avedissian and four others, including Jarvis, was in unarmed combat. Jarvis did not need it, as the instructors quickly recognised, but Avedissian did. He spent so much time in the air that he considered joining the Air Force. At least they would teach him to land properly.

'A bit rusty are we, Mr Avedissian?' inquired one of the NCOs, sending Avedissian into yet another ungainly heap. 'Never had much time for the Paras myself.'

Tumble crash.

'Bit overrated I always thought . . .'

Tumble crash.

'Crowd of nancy boys, some people reckon . . .'

Tumble crash.

Avedissian was growing tired of his love affair with the mat and the NCO was beginning to get on his nerves. He was just too confident and arrogant, although with good reason he had to admit, but perhaps it could be used against him? He staggered to his feet and pretended to be more disorientated than he really was as the man came into him yet again. At the last moment he side-stepped and brought his foot up into the NCO's solar plexus. The man went down and Avedissian was on him, forearm in his throat, fist raised above his face.

'That's more like it, sir,' said the man with a smile. 'Coming back, is it?'

Jarvis applauded and said, 'About time too. I thought you were auditioning for a part as a bowling ball.'

On Thursday it was announced that the course would be guaranteed an uninterrupted night's sleep before moving on to 'phase two' of their training. On the strength of that promise Avedissian stayed up past his eight o'clock bedtime and joined Jarvis downstairs in the reading room.

Jarvis put down his book and asked how Avedissian was feeling after five days. Avedissian had to admit that, after the hell of the first two days, things had been improving and he was forced to concede that he felt a lot better than he had done for a long time. 'But you must be bored?' he said.

'Not at all,' replied Jarvis. 'The run-up to an operation is never boring. What is it they say about anticipation being more exciting than realisation?'

'Then you've been on a mission before?'

'One.'

'Can you tell me?'

'No.'

'Silly question,' conceded Avedissian and Jarvis smiled. 'What *can* you tell me?' Avedissian asked.

'Just about everything else, I should think. My mother and father split up when I was fourteen and I went to live with an aunt in Cumbria where I suppose I had a pretty uneventful adolescence. I don't think my aunt was ever that fond of me, or I of her if the truth be told, but she did look after me through my school years, and for that I am grateful. Money was tight when I left school so I applied for, and got, a University place under military sponsorship. The Royal Marines paid me a salary while I was a student on condition that I served with them after graduation. It suited both of us.'

'Your aunt must be proud of you.'

'She's dead.'

'Parents?'

'They're dead too.'

'Wife?' tried Avedissian.

'I'm engaged to a girl I met at university. Annie, she's a biologist, doing a PhD at Edinburgh.'

'You can't see much of each other?'

'It hasn't been too bad. I'm normally stationed at HMS *Condor* in Arbroath. It's not that far from Edinburgh.'

'Except when you're on holiday in Wales.'

'Quite,' replied Jarvis with a smile.

The major gave a brief introductory talk to the second phase of the course in the library on Friday morning. The key word that kept cropping up, to Avedissian's dismay, was 'survival'. They would be trained to exact a living from the most unforgiving of terrains, he said. Not that many of them would be likely to need such skills, but it was felt by their sponsors that such training would do them good in an all-round sense.

'Does that mean that we are all here for different reasons?' asked Avedissian.

'Why do you ask?'

'Because personally I have no idea what I will be doing when I leave here. Is that the same for everyone?'

The major said, 'It is certainly true that the members of the staff here, myself included, have no notion why any of you are here. If there is any course member who would like to say anything? . . .' The major looked round the room.

One man said, 'I know why I'm here. I've been appointed assistant and general minder to Admiral Sir John Sharpe at NATO Headquarters in Brussels. There's no great secret about it.'

Another, one of the women, said, 'I'm an army nurse. I hope to go on the combined services expedition to Borneo.'

Two RAF instructors admitted to being there on a re-fresher course.

'I think that answers your question,' said the major.

It did, but it did not help.

Avedissian was convinced that the Welsh mountains had taken a dislike to him, or so it seemed in moments of damp paranoia when he thought that it might never stop raining again. People who lived in houses and ate real food had quickly become a distant sub-species who never in their wildest dreams considered the kind of existence that he and the others were experiencing. A life where hunger and discomfort were the norm, clothes were never properly dry, and feet were never warm. The sole object of each day was to get through it.

Avedissian frequently lost track of time as they roamed the peaks and valleys of the Brecons, like aimless sheep scratching a meagre living from the hillside. Relationships within the group were appraised in terms of new qualities, ability to light fires quickly, success in wood gathering, prowess in rabbit snaring. Avedissian had the personal advantage of having Jarvis at his elbow and took full advantage of this to learn quickly. He had grown to like the

Cumbrian for Jarvis always understated his ability and that was the mark of a true professional.

As Avedissian lay in his dug-out trench with its bracken roof canopy he was enjoying the fact that it had actually stopped raining. The ground still smelled wet but the sky was clear and he could see the stars in an unclouded heaven. His cheek noted that the wind had dropped to a gentle breeze. He took off his boots and rubbed his feet. Sheer luxury . . . and tonight it wasn't even that cold.

It was a night for contemplation, a night for astronomers to work and philosophers to consider. Avedissian was neither but he did consider the course of his life and where it had led him, for one thing the time at Llangern had done was to relax him mentally. He felt able to see things more clearly.

In society's eyes he had failed at two professions and it seemed unlikely that he would be given a chance at a third. His army career had ended in an Irish farmyard when some snot-nosed kid had made himself more important to him than the ambush that he and his platoon had been planning for weeks. Avedissian knew that he should have died that day, but the Irishman had let him live and in the space of a few short seconds had changed his whole way of thinking. He had subsequently resigned his commission and gone to medical school.

Avedissian had enjoyed medical school. The fact that he had been three years older than most of his fellow students had been a help rather than a hindrance in that, with more experience of life, he had been better able to avoid the traditional distractions that face students on their first time away from home. He had worked hard and done well.

His hard work and dedication to the profession he loved had rewarded him with a consultancy at an early age, and with his marriage to Linda contentment had appeared to have been within his grasp. But then came the day when Michael Fielding had been admitted to St Jude's.

57

It had not been a difficult case to diagnose for the brain tumour had been very clear and the fact that it had been sited in an inoperable position had also been beyond doubt. A sad but straightforward case. Avedissian remembered how he had taken the parents into a ward side-room to tell them.

Michael had been their only son and their obvious distress had made it all the more difficult. Somewhere outside a contractor's steam hammer had been busy on the foundations of a new wing for the hospital and on that morning it had seemed like an obscenity. The callous indifference of its thump had punctuated what Avedissian had had to say in all the wrong places.

'He is going to die isn't he?' the woman had asked with brim-full eyes.

'Yes, I'm afraid so.'

'How long?' Her voice had dropped to a whisper as if she were afraid of the words.

'Two months at most.'

'Will he suffer much pain?'

Avedissian had been unprepared for the question and he had dithered long enough for the woman to see the true answer to her question. He had tried to assure the parents that pain-killing medication would be given.

'But will it work?' the woman had asked.

In his heart Avedissian had known that, from the type and position of the tumour, standard pain medication would not have been much use but he had been reluctant to say so to the couple. Once again the woman had read the truth in his eyes and had said, 'I really don't want my son to suffer.'

Avedissian had remained silent.

The woman had taken her husband's hand in her lap and said with plain meaning, 'Anything you could do . . . would be appreciated.'

Michael Fielding had died peacefully in his sleep two days later. His parents were at his bedside at the end and Avedissian had been on hand to comfort them. It seemed to all present that God's will had been done, but Sister Veronica Ashwood had disagreed. In her book, and her book was the Bible, God's will had certainly not been done. Murder had been done and she had noticed the dose that Avedissian had administered.

The trial had been a strange affair of medical fact and religious cant. Never had Avedissian been more convinced of Marshall McLuhan's assertion that moral indignation was a strategy for endowing the idiot with dignity. Any questioning of the rightness of letting a child suffer prolonged agony before certain death had been countered by a barrage of mysteries and miracles and the ways of the Lord being strange. The outcome had been inevitable but Avedissian had known that all along. The Lilliputians won the day and, having smitten Avedissian the Arrogant, they had gone on to set about the child's parents.

Two people who had loved their child so much that they had been unable to see him suffer unnecessary agony had been pilloried in the newspapers. Teams of ferrets on expense accounts had been let loose to dig up tales of miraculous recoveries after medical opinion had pronounced matters hopeless. They had been mainly instances of remission from carcinoma, a well-known feature of certain cancers, but this had not been mentioned. Did these callous parents now regret their action? was what the *Daily Rag* had wanted to know. Perhaps they had been led astray by an evil doctor?

To their eternal credit the couple had not gone for the easy way out. They had refused to blame Avedissian and had maintained a dignified silence throughout. They had been put through hell, but what had that mattered when compared to the *Daily Rag*'s circulation figures and the right of the *Rag*'s reader to feel superior over cheese sandwiches in his tea-break?

A calm night gave way to a misty summer morning, with the air so still that Avedissian was conscious of the sound of his own breathing as he prepared to move off with the group. The sun rose to burn off the mist by eleven o'clock and baked the barren Welsh landscape as they made their way up the unshaded side of a valley to pause for breath at the top.

As they lay in the rough bracken Avedissian became aware of a distant beating sound. He recognised it as the sound of a helicopter's rotor-blade and searched the sky with his hand to his forehead against the glare. He spotted the yellow rescue craft down at the other end of the valley and watched it traverse from side to side in a search pattern.

'Lost climbers?' suggested someone.

'They would have to be really lost to end up in this valley,' observed Jarvis.

Avedissian took his point for there was no reason for climbers to be anywhere near this spot. There was nothing worth climbing in the area. It was just an endless, rolling wasteland.

As they all watched it the helicopter released three flares, two green and a red. The captain got to his feet and said, 'They're looking for us.' He said something to the sergeant who responded by rummaging in his pack and bringing out a Verey pistol. A single red flare was loosed into the sky and the helicopter stopped its meandering, leaned heavily over to starboard and came towards them.

It descended to twenty feet above them but did not land for fear of ditches and boulders. Instead a crewman was lowered on a line and the captain approached him in a crouching run. A brief conversation was conducted through cupped hands and ended with the captain coming towards Avedissian. 'They want you back at Llangern,' he said.

Avedissian pointed to Jarvis and asked above the noise, 'Him too?'

'Just you,' replied the captain.

There was very little time for goodbyes. Avedissian shook hands with Paul Jarvis and Jarvis said that he was sure that they would be meeting again soon. The whirring blades insisted that Avedissian run towards the crewman and accept the sling that was offered to him. The crewman checked that it was properly positioned then signalled to the winchman above them.

Avedissian and the crewman revolved slowly like a dance-hall globe as they left the ground. Avedissian tried to look down but his clothing had bunched up, obscuring his view, and it was not until he was inside the winch bay that he could turn round and look back to the ground. He raised his arm in farewell and saw the gesture returned from the ground as they gained height and altered course.

As the helicopter skimmed over the hills and valleys Avedissian warmed to the idea that his time in the wilderness was apparently over. Thoughts of a hot bath and a good meal took precedence over why he was wanted back at Llangern. He relaxed and watched the countryside roll past the open bay then, as he put his hand to his face, he felt the rough beard that he had acquired and smiled as a distant voice from his past said, Disgusting.

The tarmac at the front of Llangern House felt ridiculously civilised to Avedissian as he walked towards the house. It was so incredibly easy to walk on after the stamina-sapping rough ground of the past week. He was met by the major who was waiting at the door. 'You are leaving us, Avedissian,' he said.

Avedissian's questions were met with a raise of the hand and the reply, 'No idea, old chap. All I know is that you're to be picked up at seven this evening. Time for a bit of a wash and some food, eh?'

Avedissian resigned himself to another wait and had started to climb the stairs to his room when the major called after him. 'Oh, and by the way, old chap. Keep the moustache. Lose the beard.'

That the day was warm did not detract from the pleasure Avedissian took in having a hot bath. He soaped himself repeatedly then made waves in the tub with his knees to clear the suds from his chest. He removed his beard with a fresh razor and brushed his hair into order.

As he looked at himself in the mirror and smoothed down his unaccustomed moustache between thumb and forefinger Avedissian had to admit that he looked an awful lot better for his time at Llangern. The flab had gone from his middle and the muscles on his shoulders and chest looked firm and hard. His hair was a bit on the long side but it only served to make him look younger. He felt better inside too. Total abstinence from alcohol and freedom from the cares of civilisation had cleared his head. He felt alert and capable and ready to serve Queen and Country in whatever role they required. He just wished that they would tell him soon.

After a meal that was overindulgent in terms of quantity if not quality Avedissian was handed a pile of newspapers to read as he relaxed. It was his first contact with the outside world since he had come to Llangern.

The lead story in many concerned the success of the British Forces in Northern Ireland in an action which had resulted in the death of Kevin O'Donnell, a leading IRA figure. Another high-ranking terrorist was believed to have been seriously wounded in the same action. There was speculation as to whether or not the death of O'Donnell might lead to a new wave of violence as O'Donnell was widely believed to have been the moderating influence on the IRA's war council.

There was speculation that interest rates might have to rise after a new run on the pound, which had sunk to an all-time low against a basket of European currencies. Entry to the European Monetary System was advocated as a possible measure for the future.

The failure of one of the royals to turn up for a charity function was commented on in one of the tabloids and speculation about health or pregnancy was raised.

A dismal performance by the England cricket team had the sports pages demanding a change in the captaincy.

Avedissian yawned and put the papers down. He checked his watch and saw that there was still two hours to go. The major came to tell him that his 'things' were now in his room so he went to investigate. Sure enough his clothes from home had been brought to Llangern and, what was more, they had all been laundered and pressed. Avedissian dressed in a plain blue shirt, dark red tie and dark grey suit and was ready to face the world.

At a quarter to seven Avedissian was taken down to the road by Land-Rover and sat chatting to the driver until, at precisely seven o'clock, a black Ford Granada arrived and stopped at the road-end. Avedissian got in and did not look back as the car headed smoothly away from the mountains. The driver was in uniform but not military. Avedissian guessed at some kind of Civil Service rig. He asked the obvious question and was told, 'London, sir.' The man did not elaborate.

It was late when Avedissian followed the driver up the steps of an old Victorian building in South London. Once inside he was faced with more steps to climb until, on the third floor, he was shown into a small room and asked to wait. Sarah Milek, the woman he had first met in Cambridge, came in and smiled. 'Nice to see you again. How was Wales?' she asked.

'Wet.'

'But not today, surely?'

'Not today,' agreed Avedissian. The sun had come out now it was all over.

'Mr Bryant will be with you in a moment.'

Avedissian felt less than enthusiastic on hearing that it was Bryant he would be seeing but he remained impassive. Sarah Milek left the room leaving him with only a tall potted plant for company. Avedissian got up and looked out of the grimy window but there was nothing to see. The window faced the back of the building and all was in darkness save for a single neon sign on the ground floor of the building across the lane. It said, 'Staplex Bindings trade entrance'.

Bryant came into the room and stared at Avedissian long and hard. He said, 'You look less of a dosser than the last time I saw you.'

'You're too kind,' said Avedissian acidly.

'And we've got a deal more spirit, have we?' murmured Bryant. 'Sit down.'

Avedissian sat and waited while Bryant took out a large handkerchief and blew hard into it.

'You're off to Belfast in the morning,' said Bryant.

The colour drained from Avedissian's face. 'You never said anything about my job being in Ireland,' he accused.

'I never said anything about your job being anywhere, as far as I remember,' said Bryant quietly. But he was interested in Avedissian's reaction. 'So the prospect of the Emerald Isle does not appeal?'

'I don't want to go back there,' Avedissian agreed.

Bryant leaned towards him and said, 'Why not, Avedissian? What happened to you in that snake pit?'

'I just don't want to go back there. I'm an ex-Para. It would be stupid to go back.'

Bryant smiled and said, 'Avedissian, if I had my way they would tow the bloody place out into the Atlantic and sink it without trace, but we're stuck with it. You're going. If it's any consolation your 'job' as you call it isn't there. You're going to a Belfast Hospital for training.'

'Why?'

'It's two years since you practised last. You need it. From tomorrow you have been appointed registrar in the hospital's casualty department. It's a busy place and we expect it to get busier now that that little mutant bastard Kell has control of the IRA.'

Avedissian looked puzzled and Bryant told him about The Bairn having taken over from Kevin O'Donnell.

'It's a long time since I worked in an Accident and Emergency Unit,' said Avedissian.

'That's why you're going to Belfast. You'll see more medicine in a week in Belfast than you would in a year anywhere else.'

'What about the register problem?'

Bryant handed Avedissian a sheaf of papers. 'Your new identity.'

Avedissian looked through them and saw that he had become Dr Roger Gillibrand.

FOUR

A CAR CAME TO CLADEEN IN THE MORNING. O'Neill had not
expected anyone to come that soon but Liam Drummond,
the driver, said that The Bairn wanted to see him at the
Long House. Kathleen reminded him of his promise and
waved as the car pitched and rolled up the track from the
cottage to join the main road to Belfast. O'Neill heard the
exhaust pipe hit the ground and was aware of stones flying
from the rear wheels as Drummond's impatience to be away
made him put his foot down too soon. O'Neill looked
sideways at the man and saw that he seemed agitated.
'What's the matter?' he asked.

Drummond licked his lips nervously and pretended to
concentrate on the road.

'Out with it, man,' O'Neill insisted.

'The Bairn has been finding out who shopped you and
O'Donnell to the British.'

'So?'

'It's the way he's been going about it.'

'Well, go on,' prompted O'Neill beginning to lose
patience.

'He has been taking the knees from anyone he suspects
and who can't prove they're innocent!'

O'Neill's insides turned over. Were his worst fears being
realised? 'I can't believe that Finbarr . . .' he started to say
but Drummond interrupted him.

66

'It's true, I'm telling you. He's guessing blindly and capping anyone he thinks is a possible. By the time he's finished there'll be no one over four feet tall in Belfast!'

'You've said enough!' said O'Neill harshly but only because rank obliged him to. Drummond was a good man. There had to be a deal of truth in what he said. They changed cars twice, the last time to a news van which took them to the Long House.

Kell seemed triumphant when they got there and was smiling when O'Neill announced his arrival.

'I've found him!' said Kell.

'Found who, Finbarr?'

'The bastard who betrayed you and O'Donnell.'

O'Neill congratulated him and asked who it was. He did not recognise the name.

'Mary Tynan's boy,' said Kell. 'He overheard O'Donnell and his mother talking about the meeting and what safe house you were going to use. He decided to sell you.'

'Bastard,' said O'Neill. 'How did you find out?'

'A process of elimination,' said Kell smugly. 'There were a limited number of people who knew about the meeting. We questioned all of them.'

'Why did he do it?'

'You can ask him. He's downstairs. In fact, you can carry out the sentence.'

O'Neill descended to the sub-basement of the building accompanied by two others. 'He's in here,' said one of them opening up a heavy wooden door. The room was lit by a single bulkhead lamp encased in a wire screen that dripped with cobwebs.

Lying in the corner, on a dirty camp bed and clad only in his underpants, was a boy of about twenty. His right knee-cap had been shot off leaving a bloody mess of bone and gristle. The room stank of fear and excrement.

O'Neill approached the bed and looked down at the whimpering figure. The boy's head was turning rapidly from side to side and his lips were moving incessantly. 'Oh Mammy . . . Oh Daddy . . .' he repeated without pausing.

O'Neill felt sick at the sight. 'Shut up!' he commanded but the boy appeared not to notice and continued with his chant, 'Oh Mammy . . . Oh Daddy . . .'

'I said shut up!' snapped O'Neill and the noise stopped. 'Why did you betray us?' he asked.

The noise from the boy's stomach said that he had lost control of his bowels again.

'Answer me!' O'Neill insisted.

'Money . . . money. It was for money,' blubbered the boy, trying desperately to avert O'Neill's anger.

'How much?'

Silence.

'How much?' O'Neill brought his face close to the boy's.

'Two hundred pounds.'

O'Neill repeated the figure while he considered O'Donnell's death and the loss of his own arm. 'What were you going to do with . . . two hundred pounds?' he asked.

'A motorbike . . . I was going to buy a motorbike.'

Words failed O'Neill. He turned on his heel and went over to the two men by the door. One of them handed him a pistol and he accepted it without saying a word. Almost without a pause he went back to the boy and shot him once through the head.

O'Neill left the room and went to the lavatory at the end of the passage where he retched up the contents of his stomach. He had difficulty supporting himself against the brick wall with only one hand and, as he looked down into the bowl, the empty sleeve of his jacket that Kathleen had tucked into his pocket swung free. It had a safety pin in the cuff.

*

One of the two men had waited for O'Neill before returning upstairs and asked him if he was all right. O'Neill, avoiding his eyes, said that he was. As they got to the end of the basement corridor O'Neill heard a moaning sound come from one of the rooms. He asked about it.

'Have a look,' said the man with what O'Neill thought was suppressed anger in his voice.

There were three men inside the room. All had been knee-capped. The doctor who had performed the operation on his arm was tending one of them. He looked up at O'Neill as he came in then looked away again without saying anything. O'Neill backed out and closed the door.

'They were the other suspects,' said the man with as much sarcasm as he dared.

The phrase 'process of elimination' repeated itself inside O'Neill's head.

O'Neill was aware that Kell was searching his face for signs of weakness when he returned upstairs. The fact that Nelligan, Kell's minder, was grinning suggested that they had been sharing a joke. That the grin stayed on Nelligan's face when he entered suggested that it might have been about him personally.

'Did you do it?' asked Kell.

'He's dead,' replied O'Neill.

'A lesson for the learning,' said Kell.

'What lesson did the other three down there learn?' asked O'Neill, unable to hide his anger. For a moment it seemed as though he had lit Kell's fuse but the cloud of anger that hovered on Kell's face disappeared to be replaced by a slight grin. 'We sometimes have to do unpleasant things in war, Martin,' he said in a voice that was ten below zero.

Feeling that it would be pointless to provoke Kell further O'Neill changed the subject. 'Did you find the key to the safe?' he asked with his heart in his mouth.

'No, we'll have to blow it.'

'I'll have a look before I go,' said O'Neill hoping that he sounded calm for his pulse was racing. This might be his only chance to get his hands on the envelope.

Kell fixed him with a smile and eyes that seemed to see right through him. 'Why not?' he said.

O'Neill felt as if he were standing on broken glass.

O'Neill left the room and paused for a moment in the quiet of the corridor. He could hear his heart beating. He could never serve under Kell. The man hated him, not just disliked, as he had always known, but hated. He could feel it in the air whenever he was near him, enveloping him like a malignant vapour.

O'Neill walked quickly and quietly along the corridor to the little room that had been O'Donnell's. It was unchanged because The Bairn could not use it. A brick support pillar prevented the manoeuvring of his pram through the doorway. O'Neill was glad. It would not have been right to have the little psychopath in O'Donnell's room.

He knew exactly where the safe key was because O'Donnell had told him before he died. He pulled one of the drawers right out of the desk and turned it around. There, taped to the back with red masking tape, was a small plastic card, the electronic key to the safe. He removed it and put the drawer back on its runners. Now for the safe itself.

The safe was built into the end wall of a long narrow room known as the Council Room, which served as the place where sector commanders met to discuss strategy. It had an oval table and eight chairs in it but very little else. O'Neill tried the door. It was locked. He drew his lips back over his teeth in exasperation and released his grip on the handle slowly so as to avoid noise. What now, damn it? He would have to find the key.

As O'Neill considered where it might be, he heard

Nelligan's voice raised in laughter. Nelligan could always be relied upon to appreciate Kell's humourless wit. Big, dumb, faithful Nelligan. Kell's friends were his friends; Kell's enemies were his enemies. The body of an ox and the brain of a rabbit, and he had no love for O'Neill.

As Nelligan's voice grew louder O'Neill realised that Kell's door was about to be opened and he had no wish to be discovered lurking near the Council Room. He moved swiftly away from the door and returned to O'Donnell's room to wait there with the light off and the door slightly ajar. He heard the squeak of the pram wheels going in the other direction and breathed a sigh of relief. In the darkness he wondered why Kell never had his wheels oiled but, in his heart, he thought that he already knew the answer. The Bairn wanted people to know when he was coming, wanted them to know . . . and be afraid.

The voices faded and O'Neill knew that he would have to act quickly. The key to the Council Room must be somewhere in the room that Kell had just left. He glided silently along the corridor and slipped into it, closing the door behind him and clicking on the light. He looked around for inspiration.

There, on the wall, was a wooden board with keys hanging on it. O'Neill gave silent thanks and went over to read the Dymo Tape labels. 'c ROOM' said one on the third row. O'Neill removed the key and the door opened behind him.

'Oh . . . excuse me. Oh, it's you, Mr O'Neill . . .'

O'Neill did his best to recover his balance. 'I was looking for the key to Mr O'Donnell's room,' he lied.

'It's not locked.'

'In that case . . .' O'Neill smiled and walked towards the door.

'Where's Mr Kell?' asked the man.

Was that suspicion in his voice? wondered O'Neill or was

71

it guilt playing tricks on him? 'I don't know,' he said calmly, 'I was looking for him myself.'

O'Neill did not know the man but guessed that he must be one of Kell's protégés. 'I'll come back later,' he said as he squeezed past him and started walking towards O'Donnell's room. He felt the man's eyes on his back all the way but when he turned round there was no one there. It had been his imagination.

O'Neill let himself into the Council Room and approached the safe. He pressed the electronic key into the slot and heard the mechanism respond. There was a large sum of money in the main vault, but more important and lying on its own on the top shelf, as O'Donnell had said, was a sealed white envelope. O'Neill removed it and put it into his pocket. He closed the safe door and, as the lock reset itself, he suddenly became aware of another sound, the single squeak of a pram wheel.

Fear threatened to paralyse O'Neill, his throat was so tight that he could hardly breathe. He knew that Kell was behind him but the question was, how long had he been there? There was no alternative, he had to brass it out. He put the key back in the slot and watched the door swing open again hoping that Kell would believe that he was just trying out the key. He gave a grunt of satisfaction and turned round to feign surprise at the sight of Kell and Nelligan in the doorway.

'I found it,' said O'Neill, holding up the card.

'So I see,' said Kell evenly and without smiling. 'Where?'

O'Neill told him the truth.

Kell looked over his shoulder at Nelligan and said, 'I thought you searched O'Donnell's desk?'

'I didn't look there,' confessed the big man with a hangdog expression.

'No matter,' said Kell quietly. 'The main thing is we have it.' He held out his hand and O'Neill walked over to drop the card into it. 'Anything interesting in there?' Kell asked, fixing O'Neill with a stare.

'I didn't really have time to look. Would you like me to look now?' asked O'Neill with a casualness that was a long way from being genuine. As Kell searched his face he felt the blood pound painfully in the stump of his arm.

'Later will do,' said Kell. 'We have things to talk about.' Kell looked up at Nelligan and said, 'Leave us.'

Nelligan parked Kell's pram at the head of the oval table and left the room. O'Neill sat down at the other end and faced Kell.

'The McGlynns have asked for a meeting,' said Kell.

O'Neill felt his stomach turn over. The McGlynn brothers, Dominic and Sean, were leaders of the Irish National Liberation Army in Belfast, a sect that had pursued its own war against the British after falling out with the IRA some years before, but their success in attracting the most violent of extremists to their banner had been offset to a great extent by constant internal feuding and disputation over leadership. In more recent times the McGlynns, through psychopathic ruthlessness, had established themselves at the head of what O'Donnell had constantly referred to as 'that festering sore'. In many ways the McGlynns and Kell were alike but the brothers lacked Kell's brains and political intuition.

'Have they now?' said O'Neill softly.

'They want an alliance,' said Kell.

O'Neill rubbed his hand against his forehead but said nothing while he considered the thought of Kell and the McGlynn brothers running the organisation.

'What do you think?' asked Kell.

'The same as O'Donnell always thought,' replied O'Neill. 'If we ever joined with that lot we'd end up losing the sympathy of our own. They are a liability.'

'True,' murmured Kell. 'Still it's always nice to know

what everybody's thinking, eh, Martin? No harm in listening to what they have to say.'

O'Neill looked at the smile on Kell's face and thought of a spider reasoning with a fly. 'When?' he asked.

'Thursday. I'll send a car for you.'

O'Neill found Liam Drummond and said that he was ready to return to Cladeen.

As they left Belfast O'Neill sensed that Drummond was itching to say something but was not sure what O'Neill's reaction might be. Eventually he said, 'I told you, didn't I?'

'Yes, you told me,' agreed O'Neill.

'You can't run the organisation on fear,' said Drummond.

O'Neill silently declined the invitation to agree.

'I said . . .'

'I heard you.'

'Are you feeling all right, Mr O'Neill?' asked Drummond with a sidelong glance.

'An hour ago I blew a twenty-year-old's brains out.'

'But that little bastard betrayed you and . . .'

'Shut up.'

As the miles passed O'Neill began to regret having snapped at Drummond. The man was one of the best; he had been with the organisation for as long as anyone could remember. By way of making amends he said, 'You've heard that the McGlynns want to talk?'

Drummond's reaction told O'Neill that he had been forgiven. The driver threw back his head and snorted. 'Those cretins! They've forgotten that Kell has a long memory.'

'What do you mean?' asked O'Neill.

'The bomb,' said Drummond.

'What bomb?' asked O'Neill.

'The one that took Kell's legs off. It was made by the McGlynns' father, Seamus. Everybody thought that it was just one of those things, but not The Bairn. He was convinced that McGlynn had mis-set the fuse deliberately. He never said so publicly at the time, but privately he swore to get even one day and when The Bairn makes that kind of promise . . .'

'What did McGlynn have against Kell?'

'You know how it is when you're young. McGlynn was a hero until Kell came along and started upstaging him all the time. You could put it down to simple jealousy.'

'That's useful to know,' said O'Neill. He was delighted to have found that there was some obstacle to the frightening prospect of Kell forming an alliance with the McGlynns.

'Is Kell going to speak to them?'

'On Thursday,' replied O'Neill.

Drummond smiled wryly and said, 'If I were a McGlynn . . . I'd take a long spoon.'

Kathleen knew that something was troubling O'Neill but did not ask what. He would tell her in his own time as he always had done in the past, she decided, and got on with washing up their dinner things. Despite being several years younger than her brother she had acted as mother to the O'Neill family since the age of fifteen when Mrs O'Neill had died. Apart from Martin, there had been two other children, Maureen and Claire, both younger than herself and both of whom had now married and gone to live abroad, one to Canada and the other to Australia.

The family had been steeped in nationalism for as long as any of them could remember and their father, although more active with a bottle than with anything else during his own lifetime, had never let them forget the exploits of their grandfather who had fought in the Easter Rising of 1916 and had been executed by the British in the aftermath.

Despite the considerable demands put on her by domestic chores and responsibilities Kathleen had not only coped but had achieved academic success too. Three years after her brother had taken his degree she herself had graduated from the same university with a degree in modern languages and, while her brother's political beliefs had become for him the most important thing in life, she had become a teacher and now taught French and German in a Catholic High School.

Maureen and Claire O'Neill had been simple, uncomplicated girls who had sought nothing more from life than husbands, security and children, as indeed had many of Kathleen's contemporaries. It was partly for this reason that Kathleen valued her friendship with her brother so highly; they were intellectually compatible. But it was a friendship that had cost her dearly in terms of lost social life for, as Martin had risen within the IRA, she too, as a loyal sister, had become a legitimate target for harassment.

A friendship with a fellow teacher at the High School that had looked like blossoming into romance and marriage had foundered when an ultimatum had been issued concerning the activities of her brother and Kathleen had refused to disown him. She had lost count of the number of young men whose ardour had cooled on hearing that she was Martin O'Neill's sister.

'I've got a problem, Kath,' said O'Neill.

'Can you tell me?'

'There's an envelope in my pocket. I took it from the Long House.'

'Do you mean you stole it?'

'I took it from the safe. O'Donnell ordered me to get it before anyone else did.'

'Meaning Kell?'

'Meaning Kell,' O'Neill agreed.

'What's in it?'

'I don't know.'

'You're not making much sense,' said Kathleen.

O'Neill stopped staring into the fire and turned to face

Kathleen. He said, 'O'Donnell ordered me to hand it over to the British.'

'You can't be serious.'

'I wish I wasn't.'

'But why?'

O'Neill shook his head.

'Can't you open it?'

'I'm considering it.'

Kathleen watched O'Neill as he returned to looking into the fire. She said, 'You look as if you have some notion about what's in the letter.'

O'Neill smiled and said, 'You always could see through me. O'Donnell loathed Kell as much as I do. I think he may have been planning to hand Kell to the British on a plate so that we would be rid of him for good.'

'You said yourself that Kell could destroy the organisation,' said Kathleen.

O'Neill nodded and said, 'But betrayal is another matter. He *is* the commander.'

'And if you hand over the letter you will be a traitor?'

O'Neill nodded.

'You must open it,' said Kathleen firmly. 'It may not be what you think.'

'You're right,' agreed O'Neill. 'Hand me my jacket will you?'

Kathleen laid O'Neill's jacket over his knees and switched on the standard lamp behind his chair. She resisted the urge to help while she watched him struggle to open the sealed envelope by holding it between his knees and pushing his thumb under the flap. She picked up the empty envelope from the floor while O'Neill flattened out the paper with his palm and began to read.

Kathleen saw the colour drain from her brother's face but did not interrupt until the tension became unbearable. 'Is it what you feared?' she asked.

'No,' replied O'Neill as if in a daze. 'It's something quite, quite different.' He handed the papers to her.

Kathleen felt her jaw drop as she read the contents. Her shock changed to protest. 'But this cannot be true,' she said, 'We would have heard something. Did you see the date on this? It's nearly three weeks old.'

O'Neill nodded. 'I know, but O'Donnell didn't think it was a hoax.'

'Why did he hide it? Why did he want this to go to the British?' asked Kathleen.

'I'm thinking, I'm thinking,' murmured O'Neill.

Kathleen poured whiskey into a glass and handed it to O'Neill as he continued to stare into the embers of the fire. At length he said, 'I think I understand. It's too big. If we were to take this on there would be civil war and we would lose. When the smoke cleared and the blood was washed away Ireland would be more divided than ever. O'Donnell must have realised that and decided to keep us out of it. Kell on the other hand . . . would go for it.'

'But it has to be some kind of hoax,' protested Kathleen.

O'Neill thought before replying. 'Maybe not,' he said. 'It's just possible that the British have managed to keep the whole thing quiet to give themselves time.'

'But if O'Donnell turned the offer down?'

'Maybe he didn't,' replied O'Neill. 'Maybe he was stalling for time. Maybe he told them he was trying to raise the money. Maybe he *was* trying to raise the money. We don't know anything for sure.'

'Either way, won't they get in contact with Kell?' asked Kathleen.

The thought chilled O'Neill. 'You're right,' he said. 'We have to get this information to the British.'

'I'll drive into the city in the morning,' said Kathleen. 'It's late. Get some sleep.'

O'Neill nodded but said that he was going to finish his

whiskey before going upstairs. Kathleen said good-night and took the letter up with her.

O'Neill finished his whiskey and poured another. It was the one thing that seemed to deal effectively with the constant nagging pain from the stump of his arm and he needed to be able to think clearly and without distraction.

It was two a.m. when he thought that he heard a sound on the gravel outside. Alarmed, he got up from the chair and walked to the window to be reminded yet again of the need for two hands as he tried to see out against the reflections from inside the room. He switched out the light and returned to the window. There was nothing to be seen but, once more, he thought he heard the sound of something moving outside on the gravel. This time he was sure.

O'Neill turned to go to the kitchen where he kept his pistol in a drawer but almost immediately he realised that it was too late. He was furious with himself for being such a fool. The sounds from the gravel at the front had been made deliberately as a distraction. Someone was coming in the back!

The door leading to the kitchen burst open and O'Neill saw a man standing there framed in the moonlight. He was holding an automatic weapon and it was pointed at his stomach. Another man squeezed past and switched on the room light.

'What the hell is this?' exclaimed O'Neill as he recognised one of them as the one who had come into Kell's room while he had been searching for the key to the Council Room.

The man did not reply but motioned with the muzzle of the gun that O'Neill should move towards the fireplace. The other man, whom O'Neill did not recognise, opened the front door and stood there as if waiting for something. The sound of squeaking wheels told O'Neill exactly what everyone was waiting for. He watched helplessly as Nelligan manoeuvred Kell into the room and closed the door.

'What in the name of God is going on, Finbarr?' O'Neill asked bravely.

Kell stared at him as if he were a stain on the carpet. 'Show him, Reagan!' he hissed.

The man who held the gun used it to knock the lampshade off the standard lamp and reveal a microphone that was taped to the stem.

'Every word,' said Kell like a death sentence. There was a smug look on Kell's face that heralded an orgy of gloating. He turned to Nelligan and said softly, 'What did I always say? Never trust an intellectual.'

'Treacherous bastard!' snarled Nelligan.

'I'm no traitor, Kell. I've always done what's best for the cause.'

Kell let out a humourless laugh and looked to the others for support. They obliged. 'You plot to give information to the enemy and you're no traitor?' he sneered.

'Kevin O'Donnell was my commander. I was obeying his orders.'

'O'Donnell!' snorted Kell. 'That weak-kneed jelly! He spent so much time on the phone warning the British it's a wonder they didn't include him in their Honours List!'

When Nelligan's dutiful laughter had died down the smile faded from Kell's face and it became a mask of venom. 'Where is the letter?' he spat.

'I'll get it,' said O'Neill, making a move towards the stairs.

Kell nodded to Reagan who swung the butt of his carbine into O'Neill's stomach with full force. O'Neill collapsed on to the floor, his face twisted in pain.

'Will you never learn to stop taking me for a fool?' asked Kell in a deathly whisper. He looked up at Reagan and snapped, 'Get upstairs and bring down that schoolteacher bitch!'

Reagan was back within seconds. 'She's gone, Mr Kell!'

'What do you mean "gone"?' rasped Kell.

'Her window's open. She must have climbed down on to the roof of the shed and got away.'

'Jesus! Am I completely surrounded by idiots? She can't have gone far. Find her! Bring her back!' Kell looked down at O'Neill who was still lying on the floor. 'Meanwhile our friend here can tell us what was in the letter,' he whispered. 'Can't he, Nelligan?'

The big man moved out from behind Kell to stand over O'Neill. From where O'Neill lay he looked twelve feet tall.

Knowing that she would not get far on foot and in her night-dress Kathleen had not tried to escape but had hidden herself in the hut at the foot of the garden among various garden tools and sacks of peat and fertiliser. It was her one hope that Kell's men might overlook that possibility and leave the house without discovering her. Beyond that she had no plans at all. She had already almost given the game away when moonlight through a dirty window-pane had silhouetted a rat moving along the handle of the lawnmower. But revulsion had paralysed her throat and prevented her breath from leaving her in anything more than spasmodic gasps. In her hand she clutched the letter from the Long House. She held it tightly as she tried to bury herself deeper into a pile of hessian sacks in the corner.

'I'm waiting,' said Kell, his voice filled with soft menace.

O'Neill had recovered from the blow to his stomach but now fear was making him feel sick. 'All right, I'll tell you,' he said, acknowledging that resistance was pointless.

When he had finished O'Neill saw Kell's face darken with anger. His eyes seemed huge behind his spectacles. Nelligan kept looking towards him to see what his reaction should be.

'You seem to think that I'm a complete imbecile, O'Neill,' said Kell in tones that cut into O'Neill like a razor-blade. 'Did you really think that I would swallow this preposterous crap?'

O'Neill was taken aback for he had not considered for a moment that Kell would not believe him when he spoke the truth.

Kell looked at Nelligan and rasped, 'Show him the error of his ways!'

Nelligan lashed the back of his ham-like fist across O'Neill's face and sent him sprawling again. This time O'Neill landed heavily on the tender stump of his left arm and let out a cry of pain. Kell homed in on it like a shark and said with mock concern, 'Mr O'Neill's wound seems to be troubling him . . .'

Nelligan took his cue and kicked O'Neill viciously in the stomach before pinning him to the ground with his knee and punching the stump of his severed arm repeatedly. He seemed oblivious to O'Neill's screams and looked only to Kell to find renewed vigour in his master's approval.

O'Neill's agony ended mercifully in unconsciousness. He was no longer in Cladeen. He was sixteen years old and leaning on a fence at the farm in Valeena where he and the family had spent their last summer holiday together. The sun was shining and the grass was green. He could feel the warmth of it on his back as he waited for Maureen, the girl from the village, to come across the field. He could see her; she was wearing the white dress that he liked so much and her hair was bouncing on her shoulders as she moved. She was smiling and her eyes were filled with the frankness of young love. God, it was so good to be young and in love. Life was so good, so full of . . . icy-cold wetness and pain . . . excruciating pain.

'He's coming round,' said Nelligan after dousing O'Neill with cold water.

'Give him more of the same,' spat Kell.

'Stop it! This is what you want!' said Kathleen coming in through the door. She threw the letter at Kell and pushed Nelligan out of the way to kneel down beside her brother.

She cradled his head in her arms and said, 'I'm sorry, I couldn't bear what they were doing to you.'

'You always were around to wipe my nose,' gasped O'Neill through his pain.

Nelligan moved in to separate them but first looked to Kell for approval. Kell dismissed the notion as being unimportant with an impatient wave of his hand and returned to being engrossed in the letter. Nelligan stood back to watch as Kathleen continued to administer to O'Neill's needs.

Reagan and the other man returned from their fruitless search for Kathleen and stood sheepishly by while Kell continued to read, fully expecting to receive the brunt of Kell's wrath when he was ready. Instead The Bairn remained fully preoccupied with something else. There was silence in the room while Kell, having finished reading, stared into space for a long time. After a while he suddenly appeared to become aware of the others in the room again and smiled. 'Well, well, well,' he said softly. 'So our intellectual friend wasn't lying after all. I think we owe him an apology, Nelligan.'

Nelligan grinned unsurely.

'Take them to the Long House,' Kell snapped.

Reagan led out Kathleen and O'Neill at gun-point. Kell did not bother to look up as they passed for he was deep in thought again.

'Are we going back too, Mr Kell?' asked Nelligan cautiously when he and Kell were alone.

'No,' replied Kell. 'I want to speak with Harrigan in England. Get him on the phone.'

The meeting with the McGlynn brothers took place in the Council Room at the Long House on Thursday. Nelligan and Reagan and two others stood, stony-faced, behind Kell as Dominic and Sean McGlynn were escorted into the room with two of their henchmen in attendance.

'Good to see you, Finbarr,' said Dominic McGlynn.

'And you, boys,' replied Kell softly. 'To what do we owe the pleasure?'

'To come straight to the point, Finbarr, we've been thinking that the time is right for us to bury our past differences and join forces again.'

'And what brings you to that way of thinking?' asked Kell evenly.

'O'Donnell's death,' said Sean McGlynn flatly. 'O'Donnell was a man we could never get on with, but you, Finbarr, well, you are different. We think alike. We know all this political pissing around is useless. We should be giving the British what they understand best.'

Kell stared at the McGlynns for a moment then his face relaxed into a smile. 'Well, boys,' he said, 'it so happens, you could not have come at a better time.'

The McGlynn brothers exchanged glances and visibly relaxed as did everyone else round the table. 'Whiskey for our guests, Nelligan,' said Kell.

'You sound as if you have something in mind, Finbarr?' said Dominic McGlynn accepting his glass.

'Indeed I do,' smiled Kell. 'Listen carefully.'

When Kell had finished everyone tried to speak at once in an atmosphere that had become electric. Kell held up his hand and the noise subsided.

'But have you checked it out?' asked Dominic McGlynn.

'Of course I've checked it out. What do you take me for?' snapped Kell.

'And?'

'The place is tighter than a drum. No one is saying anything but no one has seen him in the last three weeks.'

'Don't you have anyone on the inside?'

'A domestic. The official story is that we have made some kind of death threat and that's the reason for the low profile.'

'But why didn't they ask the British for the money?' asked Sean McGlynn.

Kell smiled and said, 'It's always easier to deal with friends than enemies.'

Dominic McGlynn, who had been keeping quiet, said softly, 'If we had him we could bargain for anything we wanted.'

'Exactly,' said Kell.

'Where do we come in?' asked Sean McGlynn.

'Money,' said Kell. 'You boys have always had to make your own arrangements for "funding".' Kell paused and smiled.

'The banks?'

'The banks,' agreed Kell.

'But we could never get that much,' said Dominic McGlynn.

'No,' replied Kell, 'But I was thinking, if you were to hit four banks simultaneously you could get quite a bit.'

'Four?' protested McGlynn. 'That would stretch us to our limit. It would need every man we had in the field at the same time.'

'This is going to stretch all of us to our limit,' said Kell.

'And what are your men going to do?' asked Sean McGlynn.

Kell shook his head and said, 'We've lost O'Donnell, and O'Neill has turned out to be a traitor. We're in a mess. The best we can do at the moment is to create a diversion for you boys, if you let me have the details.'

'Where are you going to get the bulk of the money?' asked Dominic McGlynn.

'The Americans,' replied Kell.

'But they always keep a tight grip on the purse strings,' argued McGlynn.

Kell nodded and said, 'Maybe this time I can persuade them different.'

The room fell to silence while the McGlynn brothers whispered briefly to each other.

'Well?' asked Kell. 'Are you in or out?'

'We're in,' replied Dominic McGlynn.

Nelligan poured more whiskey.

'How do you get in touch with them?' asked Sean McGlynn.

Kell smiled. 'We place a message in the personal column of the London *Times*,' he said.

'Saying what?'

' "Sean will cross the Rubicon".'

Along the passage, in the same cell where he had shot the traitor, Martin O'Neill looked up as keys rattled in the lock and Liam Drummond came in carrying a tray with bread and tea on it. 'I was wrong,' whispered Drummond as he put down the tray.

'Wrong?'

Drummond nodded. 'Kell has joined with the McGlynns.'

FIVE

IT WAS RAINING WHEN AVEDISSIAN ARRIVED at the hospital and the wetness made the stonework black. The whole building had an air of gloom about it. Avedissian picked his way through a muddle of ambulances parked outside the Accident and Emergency Unit and paused outside the swing doors to shake the water from his coat before entering. Once inside he stopped again at a barrage of directional signs and found the one that he was looking for. It read, Dr S. Harmon, Consultant. A & E.

The highly polished corridor led along past a waiting room with perhaps twenty people inside and somewhere nearby a child was crying loudly in defiance of a nurse and its mother who were trying to pacify it. A teenage boy lay on a trolley outside the X-Ray Department with his right foot bare and a large swelling round his ankle. Nurses moved quickly to and fro across the corridor, their feet squeaking on the linoleum.

Avedissian came to the door he was looking for and knocked once. He understood a muffled sound from within to be an invitation to enter and stepped inside.

Harmon turned out to be a thin man in his forties with jet black hair which gave him a very dark beard shadow. He looked at Avedissian over half-framed glasses and released the 'record' button of the dictation machine he had been using. 'Yes?' he asked.

'I'm Gillibrand,' said Avedissian.

'Sit down. I'll be with you in a moment.'

Avedissian found the man's tone neutral and difficult to analyse. In it he detected neither friendliness nor hostility. He sat down and looked across to the window while Harmon finished dictating his letter, not that there was much to see for the view comprised the building next door. An occasional figure passed the window opposite and by the time Harmon had finished recording Avedissian had counted two nurses, and three patients wearing dressing-gowns.

'. . . We would therefore anticipate a degree of stiffness in the joint for some time to come. Yours etc.' Click. 'Welcome to Belfast,' said Harmon accepting the documentation that Avedissian handed to him. He flicked through it briefly then tossed it into the wire tray on the corner of his desk. 'I know you're not Gillibrand,' he said. 'This twaddle is for administration,' he added, nodding to the paperwork.

Avedissian could now feel animosity in the air.

'I'll be perfectly frank with you,' said Harmon. 'I resent outside interests telling me how I should staff my department. I resent it deeply.'

'I can understand that,' said Avedissian.

'In Belfast we get the kind of cases that haven't been seen since Korea. I've got a waiting list a mile long of doctors who want to work here and I land up with a registrar who hasn't seen a Casualty department since medical school.'

Avedissian stayed silent while the lecture continued.

'I don't know why you are here, Gillibrand . . .'

'Neither do I,' interrupted Avedissian who was beginning to tire of being dressed down by a man who, but for circumstances, would have been his peer rather than his superior.

'Are you serious?' asked Harmon.

'Yes.'

Harmon let out a long sigh and said, 'God, how I'm sick of

secrets and intrigue and . . .' His hands sought the air as he searched for words. 'Charades. Some days I can't move for men in grey suits hiding behind plastic ID cards.'

'What do you mean?' asked Avedissian.

'For the past month every A & E unit in the province has had an Intelligence presence.'

'I would have thought that normal under the circumstances,' replied Avedissian.

'Oh, I don't mean just the usual police interest in who's coming and going. There is something else going on. Something has happened, or is about to happen, and they're listening. I've no idea what it is they're after and I don't think I want to know. I just wish that they would stay out of my road.'

'Maybe it's connected with O'Donnell's death,' suggested Avedissian. 'They could be listening for information about the new hierarchy.'

Harmon nodded and said, 'That might have been true but for the fact that this all started before O'Donnell died. But as you have brought up the subject I suppose you know that we are all sitting on a powder keg?'

Avedissian admitted that he had heard rumours about the new IRA leadership and the possibility of a show of strength.

'The last time we went through this we finished up with four bin liners full of assorted limbs,' said Harmon.

Avedissian screwed up his face.

'I wish the bastards could come down here after their bloody bombs go off. I'd like to see them stand in the middle of that room out there and talk about their "struggle for freedom" among the blood and broken lives. They would have to shout above the screams, mind you. Who knows? They might even find the sound memorable.'

Avedissian nodded his agreement but reserved judgement on whether Harmon's words had a political basis or whether indeed they had come from the heart. He would decide when he got to know the man better.

'Well, Gillibrand, or whatever your name is, how does the prospect of assembling human jigsaw puzzles appeal to you?' asked Harmon.

'It doesn't,' replied Avedissian. 'It fills me with disgust.'

A momentary flicker of surprise registered on Harmon's face. It was followed by a slight pause as if he had been forced to make some kind of reappraisal. He said quietly, 'It does me too. I'm glad you didn't see it as "a challenge". I've had too many buggers here who see it all as "a challenge". No people, just challenges.'

Avedissian smiled as he warmed to the man. 'Belfast on the c.v. equals another ten grand stateside,' he said.

It was Harmon's turn to smile. 'Exactly,' he said.

A nurse put her head round the door and apologised for interrupting before saying that Harmon was required in the Admission Suite.

'Join me,' said Harmon getting up.

Avedissian pulled on a white coat and felt good as he did so for he had come to believe that it was something that he would never do again. But his pleasure was tinged with apprehension. It had been a long time. Could he still cope?

'In at the deep end, eh?' said Harmon as they walked along the corridor together.

'Might as well,' replied Avedissian.

After a brief introduction to the nursing staff Avedissian was left to ask a man in his thirties how he had come to have fallen off the ladder in the first place.

As the day progressed Avedissian found himself dealing with a perfectly manageable procession of cuts and breaks and sprains. Harmon warned him that it was the lull before the storm but, even if it was, thought Avedissian, he was grateful for it was giving him precious time to ease himself back into medicine.

The first real pressure on him came in the late afternoon when six people who had been involved in a bad car accident were admitted. Two were dead on arrival and the other four were very badly injured. A cursory examination by Harmon to establish where priority lay left Avedissian to deal with a young man in his twenties suffering from severe chest and lower limb injuries. The man arrested as Avedissian worked on him and it was a very long ninety seconds before Avedissian's attempts to revive him were rewarded and the patient's heart was restarted.

Although his own pulse was racing and self-doubt had threatened him from all angles Avedissian had outwardly remained cool and professional throughout and Harmon had noticed. He looked across and said, 'Welcome to A & E.'

Avedissian acknowledged the comment with a nod but there was no time for conversation. He still had a lot to do to stabilise the boy's condition and there was another patient waiting.

'There's a drug overdose on the way,' announced the unit sister. 'Female, 42. Librium.'

'Thank you, Sister,' said Harmon without looking up. 'Prepare to wash her out will you.'

There were to be two more drug overdoses, three more car accidents, a scalding and the aftermath of a 'domestic dispute', as the police put it, before Avedissian felt able to sign off and leave the night to the duty housemen.

He climbed the stairs to his small room in the medical residency and flung himself down on the bed. He was tired, in fact he was exhausted, not just with the work, although that had been considerable, but mainly because of the mental stress that he had been under. The fear that he might have lost all his old ability as a doctor had proved to be unfounded but it had been no easy task laying it to rest.

Now he began to feel good. The truth was that it had been a very long time since he had felt so good and the austerity of his surroundings could do nothing to diminish the feeling. It would not have mattered had it been a deep, dark dungeon instead of a dingy, Victorian turret room in peeling NHS green. Bryant had been right. A & E was exactly what he needed. Belfast was doing for his self-esteem what Llangern had done for his body.

When his mind had calmed Avedissian's thoughts turned to food and he went to eat in the hospital staff restaurant before returning upstairs to begin reading. Harmon had thoughtfully furnished him with copious reading matter on the various aspects of military medicine and he began with a tome on the treatment of gunshot wounds.

Tension grew in the city as the days passed with still no move from the IRA to justify the rumours that had been circulating in the pubs about what they would do to avenge the death of Kevin O'Donnell. The more optimistic began to suggest that O'Donnell's death had been a bigger blow to the IRA than had previously been thought while the more realistic just waited. The weather did little to help for it was warm and uncommonly humid as if a still, wet cloud were pressing down on the city. It shortened tempers and made skin glisten at the slightest effort.

Avedissian ran his forefinger round the inside of his collar as he came on duty in the afternoon. There was an unpleasant, sour smell of sweat about the department which had persisted for days despite competition from anaesthetics and disinfectant. 'What have we got?' he asked the duty sister.

'Not much. One sprained ankle and a broken thumb.'

The day continued routinely with troughs and peaks of activity until nine in the evening when Avedissian was thinking about calling it a day. As he took off his coat an ambulance drew up outside and the attendants carried in a woman who had obviously been badly beaten. As it was Harmon's day off and the houseman was busy with another patient Avedissian decided to stay and deal with the woman himself.

Her face was swollen and barely recognisable under a halo of beautiful red hair that was matted with blood along her forehead. Avedissian examined her limbs gently for broken bones but found no evidence of any damage other than severe bruising. He sent her to the X-Ray Department with a nurse in attendance and waited for the results.

Avedissian's optimism that the woman's injuries appeared to be a great deal more dramatic than they actually were was confirmed by an X-Ray report which confirmed that she had no broken bones and was free from damage to her skull. She had, however, taken a bad beating and was only now beginning to recover consciousness. She tried to speak and a nurse shushed her and told her to rest. This only made the woman anxious and even more determined to speak. The nurse tried again to soothe her but to no avail.

'All right,' said Avedissian to the nurse. 'Let her speak.'

While the woman tried to form words Avedissian asked the nurse quietly, 'Do we know who she is?'

'She had no handbag and no identification,' replied the nurse.

'Do we know why she was beaten up?'

'No, it was an anonymous treble-nine call.'

'What else?' said Avedissian under his breath. An unwillingness to 'get involved' was more in evidence in Belfast than anywhere else in the United Kingdom.

'I must speak . . . to . . . British Intelligence . . .' said the woman with obvious and painful difficulty.

'I'll ask the constable to come in, shall I?' said the nurse.

Avedissian was about to agree when the woman put her hand on his arm. 'No police . . . Intelligence . . . Bryant . . .'

Avedissian went cold at the mention of Bryant's name. 'Wait a minute,' he asked the nurse who was heading for the door. She paused with her hand on the handle.

Avedissian bent close to the woman and whispered, 'What do you know of Bryant?'

'I'm . . . Kathleen O'Neill . . . Martin O'Neill's sister . . . have important information . . . must tell Bryant.'

The name O'Neill meant nothing to Avedissian. He left the woman's side for a moment and walked over to the nurse. 'She says she's Kathleen O'Neill. Mean anything to you?'

The girl shook her head.

'She said something about being Martin O'Neill's sister.'

'Now that means something,' said the nurse. She told Avedissian that Martin O'Neill was a leading IRA man.

Avedissian returned to the woman and said, 'Can't you tell us what it is? You need rest and sleep.'

'No . . . must speak to Bryant . . . tell him . . . it's about the . . . missing person.'

Avedissian shrugged and turned to the nurse. 'Better call the security number.'

The nurse dialled a number, handed him the phone and said, 'It's ringing.'

'This is Dr Gillibrand, A & E at the General. I've got a woman here who says that she's Martin O'Neill's sister. She wants to speak to someone called Bryant about a missing person.'

In less than fifteen minutes a black saloon drew up outside A & E and Bryant got out accompanied by three other men. Bryant stared straight ahead but the other two looked about them constantly.

'Well, Dr Gillibrand, this is a coincidence. And how are things in the Emerald Isle?' murmured Bryant after making sure that no one else was within hearing range.

Once again Avedissian noted the sneer in Bryant's voice whenever he used the term 'Emerald Isle'. 'I'm coping,' he said.

'Good. Where's the O'Neill woman?'

'She's in here,' said Avedissian, pointing to a closed door. 'But she's very weak. She's been badly beaten.'

Bryant grinned as if Avedissian had said something that had amused him. 'Really?' he said quietly. 'Now isn't that a shame.'

Avedissian said, 'I think it would be best if you could leave off questioning her till the morning.'

The grin left Bryant's face in an instant and he hissed at Avedissian, 'When I want your "professional" advice, Doctor, I'll ask for it. Take me to her.'

Avedissian held his tongue and led the way. He was about to enter the room behind Bryant when Bryant stopped and turned. He said to Avedissian, 'Wait outside please.'

'She is my patient,' insisted Avedissian as loudly as he dared.

Anger flashed in Bryant's eyes. 'Let's not take the game too far, Doctor,' he hissed.

'It's not a game to her,' whispered Avedissian equally angrily. 'You do anything to harm her and I'll bring the whole house of cards tumbling down and screw the consequences!'

For a moment their eyes were locked in a contest of wills then Bryant relaxed and assumed a smile. 'All right, Doctor,' he replied. 'Five minutes, no longer, I promise.' With that he closed the door and Avedissian turned to face a puzzled nursing staff who were obviously wondering what had been going on.

'Bloody bureaucrats!' he murmured.

'You sound just like Dr Harmon,' said one of the nurses.

True to his word Bryant came out of the room after five minutes. He seemed very pleased with himself as he approached Avedissian and the nurses melted away. 'Well,' he said, 'Christmas has come early this year and Santa Claus has just been very good to us indeed.'

Avedissian waited for Bryant to explain but he did not.

Instead he said, 'The O'Neill woman will have to be transferred out of here.' Avedissian opened his mouth to protest when Bryant stopped him. 'For her own good,' he said, 'and for the good of the hospital. What do you think the IRA would do if they found out that Kathleen O'Neill was lying here shooting her mouth off to the British? Or do you think that the fact that it's a hospital would put these bastards off?' Bryant gave a mirthless laugh and said, 'We'll send someone for her. She'll be looked after.'

Kathleen O'Neill was moved from the hospital at two in the morning. It was done quickly and quietly as if she had never been there, and too impersonally for Avedissian's liking. He stopped the attendants as they wheeled the trolley to the door and asked Kathleen O'Neill how she was feeling. Her deep green eyes were frightened but she said, with what Avedissian thought was great courage, 'I feel much better, Doctor. Thank you for your help.' Avedissian gave her hand a little squeeze and let her go.

The little convoy, sirens mute and roof lights in darkness, stole off into what was left of the night to the accompaniment of a clap of thunder and a jagged flash of lightning. The humid weather was coming to an end.

Avedissian watched from the darkened doorway of A & E as torrential rain began to bounce off the pavements and tumble into the gutters. Some deity had decided to wash the city clean. All Great Neptune's oceans, he thought.

Avedissian was reading the morning paper on Friday when his attention was caught by an article headed, 'Top Civil Servant in Death Plunge'. Sir Michael Montrose, a senior official at the Home Office, it was reported, had fallen to his death from the top floor of a building in Belgravia. Foul play was not suspected.

It was not so much the story that captivated Avedissian as the photograph that accompanied it. Sir Michael Montrose was the man who had headed his interview team at Cambridge. Avedissian remembered how little love lost there had been between him and Bryant and how Bryant had openly appeared to ridicule the older man. But why should he have taken his own life?

Avedissian found that he had little time to consider the possibilities before all hell broke lose. At the height of the morning shopping period an enormous bomb was detonated in the Shamrock Shopping Precinct. Although it was nearly a mile away from the hospital Avedissian and the others felt the ground shake beneath their feet and a trickle of plaster fell from the ceiling of the treatment room. One of the nurses crossed herself. Harmon cursed loudly.

Avedissian, like many of the others, stood stock still in the unreal silence that ensued, mesmerised by the thought of the aftermath of the event before the wail of distant sirens broke the spell and sent them all into frenzied activity.

A radio call was broadcast to recall all staff from leave and a request made for blood donors to stand by. Nurses prepared trays of dressings and instruments and stacked them in neat piles round the room. From another part of the city the sound of gunfire reached them and everyone knew that the truce was over.

Avedissian had never seen such terrible injury to human beings before on such a scale. The nearest had been a train crash many years before but even that paled into insignificance beside the horror before his eyes. Dreadfully mutilated people bled to death in the ambulances before reaching hospital, while others, half stupefied by shock but still with the misfortune to be conscious, stared at their own insides through gaping blast wounds in their stomachs. A boy with no legs tried to get up and run from the stretcher that brought him through the doors. A woman with no face left screamed continually through a gaping, misshapen orifice that had once been her mouth. The sound was like nothing Avedissian had ever heard before.

Avedissian worked on as if caught up in a nightmare. He felt icy cold and, at times, almost on the verge of detachment from reality as his mind baulked at accepting what his eyes were seeing. The thing that kept him going more than any other was the sight of Harmon, very much in control, talking to the nurses, encouraging them, deciding priorities, keeping everything on a cool professional level.

Avedissian already knew that Harmon could be an emotional man for he had heard him speak of this very kind of situation with passion. But here, in the midst of the real thing, he was in complete control of things, an inspiration to all around him. At that moment Avedissian admired Harmon more than any other man he had ever known.

As the time passed some kind of order started to emerge from the carnage and chaos. The dead were removed by the porters to the hospital mortuary, those stabilised for surgery were taken out on trolleys to join the queues outside the theatres while the remainder were still held in A & E on life support pending removal to Intensive Care.

Avedissian had lost all track of time. He was still desperately trying to stop the bleeding on a young boy whose arm had been severed too near the shoulder for standard procedures when the radio announced that two gunshot victims were on their way.

The new patients arrived in a convoy of police and army vehicles and were afforded scant respect by their attendants. Several dead bodies were in the trucks. Harmon and Avedissian verified that they were dead before they were taken away. 'And now the other side,' said Harmon as they came back into the treatment room.

'What do you mean?' asked Avedissian.

'This lot are the IRA,' replied Harmon, indicating the men lying on the tables.

One of the soliders who had heard what had happened at the shopping centre lost control and raised his weapon to fire at one of the wounded men. He was manhandled out of the unit by an NCO amidst shouting and chaos.

'What's been going on?' Harmon asked a police inspector.

'It looks like the IRA and the INLA tried to pull a joint operation. The IRA attacked the shopping centre while the INLA raided a number of banks in the city.'

'What happened?'

'Apparently it all went wrong. The diversion didn't work and the INLA were wiped out.'

Harmon looked around him at the pools of blood and pieces of human tissue that had still to be cleared up and whispered, 'A diversion . . . this was a . . . diversion?'

'I think you had better come,' said one of the nurses who had been attending one of the men on the trolleys.

The duty sister had cut away the man's blood-soaked clothing to reveal the extent of the damage. He had been hit twice, once in the shoulder and once in the left thigh. In both cases the bullet had splintered the bone but had still managed to exit.

'Army weapon,' said Harmon. 'If you're hit you go down and you don't get up.'

Avedissian attended to the other gunshot victim who had been less seriously hurt in that the one bullet that had struck him had done so at an angle and gouged out a channel of flesh from his left calf. But the severe bruising about his face and body said that he had been subject to a 'difficult' arrest.

When the place had finally been cleared Harmon sat down slowly on one of the benches and lit a cigarette. He offered one to Avedissian who declined and they both sat in silence before the duty sister came over to them with cups of tea. 'Will you marry me, Sister?' said Harmon, accepting the cup as if it were the Holy Grail. 'Join the queue,' said Avedissian.

*

Next day the newspapers found it difficult to strike the right balance in their reporting of the news, for the triumph of the security forces over the INLA had been so violently offset by the tragedy of the Shamrock Shopping Centre. Seventeen people had died, five were still on the critical list and forty-three had been injured, some destined to carry the scars and mutilations for the rest of their lives.

Church leaders made renewed pleas for an end to the violence but, as always, the men who would heed such pleas were not those who perpetrated it. Hardline Protestants threatened revenge for what they called the 'bloody outrage' and politicians said whatever suited them best politically. As usual the man in the street was confused and angry. Everything was back to normal in Northern Ireland after a lull in the proceedings.

Avedissian was off duty and alone in his room when there came a knock on the door. His invitation to whomever it was to come in met with no response so he got up and opened the door himself. Paul Jarvis was standing there.

'I don't believe it!' exclaimed Avedissian, both surprised and delighted.

'Life is full of surprises,' grinned Jarvis.

Avedissian invited him in and asked him to sit down on the one chair in the room while he himself sat on a corner of the bed. 'It's not much but it's home,' said Avedissian, looking around him.

'Not for much longer,' said Jarvis.

'Something is happening?' asked Avedissian.

'We are to meet with Bryant tomorrow. Your time here is over. That's what I came to tell you.'

Avedissian nodded and accepted the news with mixed feelings for, after his initial feelings of apprehension, he had come to enjoy working with Harmon. He had almost allowed himself to believe that he had returned to practising medicine again. 'I'd better tell Dr Harmon,' he said.

'I think you'll find that he has been informed,' said Jarvis. 'He had to be warned so that a replacement for you could be found.'

'Of course,' said Avedissian quietly. 'Have you come from Wales or your base?' he asked Jarvis.

'Neither, I was given three days' leave. I spent it in Edinburgh with my girlfriend.'

'Annie,' said Avedissian.

'You have an excellent memory,' said Jarvis.

'It improved when I gave up the gin,' said Avedissian.

'Oh yes, I'm sorry about that.'

'Why sorry?' asked Avedissian.

'I'm afraid it was me who took your bottle at Llangern.'

'I see . . . I suppose I should thank you really.'

'You were in a bit of a mess,' agreed Jarvis.

'So what are we going to learn tomorrow?' asked Avedissian.

'I know as much as you. I was just asked to inform you tonight and pick you up tomorrow.'

Avedissian invited Jarvis to stay and eat dinner with him but Jarvis declined, saying that he had to report back. He would see him in the morning at ten o'clock.

Avedissian returned to the A & E department and sought out Harmon. He found him in his office working through a pile of paperwork with an air of frustration. 'Bloody nonsense!' he snorted, putting down his pen as Avedissian came in. 'Reports, reports, endless bloody reports. Nobody is going to read the damned things; they're going to file them and forget about them!'

Avedissian smiled and said sympathetically, 'It's the way of the world.'

'You've been told?' said Harmon, reading the look on Avedissian's face.

Avedissian nodded. 'I'm quite sorry to be going,' he added.

Harmon took off his glasses and said, 'I never thought that I would be saying this, but I am sorry to lose you. Things worked out fine . . . Dr Avedissian.'

'You knew?'

'Not until a few days ago, but there was always something familiar about your face. Then I remembered the case. I didn't remember all the details so I went and looked them up.'

'I see.'

'If it's any comfort, I have every sympathy with you.'

Avedissian got to his feet and said, 'Thank you, Doctor. It was kind of you to say so.' He held out his hand.

'I meant it,' said Harmon taking Avedissian's hand. 'I can't ever offer you a job, of course, only my best wishes for whatever your future has in store. Good luck.'

Avedissian left the room and had a last look round the unit. then he went upstairs to gather his things together before eating and settling down for an early night.

Jarvis arrived promptly at ten and Avedissian got into the car beside him. He found the drive through the city streets depressing for it reminded him of his own time in Belfast with the military. All these years, he thought, and so little had changed. A whole generation of children had grown up thinking of guns and uniforms as the norm. There was no escaping the bigotry of the graffiti, which was everywhere. Here in Ireland the enemy was your neighbour.

The car slowed and turned into an entrance bounded on both sides by high black railings. A wrought-iron gate swung open in response to an infra-red device operated by the driver and they passed through to follow a semi-circular driveway up to a low Georgian building with ornate lampposts on either side of the front entrance. 'N.I. Land Archives District 7' said the plaque on the wall.

Avedissian and Jarvis were left to wait in a small back room which looked out on immaculately kept gardens after being asked if they would like coffee, an offer that both accepted. The coffee arrived and they sipped it in silence while they continued to look out of the window.

'Mr Bryant will see you now,' said the woman who had brought the coffee.

Avedissian and Jarvis left their cups and saucers on the window-ledge and followed the woman through to a much larger room where Bryant was sitting behind a long mahogany desk.

'The waiting is over, gentlemen,' said Bryant. 'I'm going to tell you why we need you.'

Avedissian and Jarvis looked briefly at each other before giving their full attention to what Bryant had to say.

'A few weeks ago a child was abducted and has not been seen since. We would like you to help us get him back.'

Avedissian was confused. 'But the police?' he began.

'Were never informed,' said Bryant.

Jarvis was as puzzled as Avedissian. 'I'm sorry, I don't understand, sir,' he said.

Bryant opened one of the desk drawers and brought out a photograph of a family group. He turned it towards Jarvis and Avedissian and held his forefinger to one of the children. 'This is the child,' he said.

Avedissian felt his jaw drop and sensed Jarvis share his disbelief. 'Are you seriously telling us that one of the royal children has been kidnapped?' he asked.

'I am,' replied Bryant.

'But how could something like that be kept secret? . . . And why?' asked an incredulous Jarvis.

'Because of the repercussions,' replied Bryant.

'I don't understand,' said Avedissian. 'What repercussions?'

'In the absence of any information to the contrary the IRA would be blamed and the backlash would be unstoppable.'

'Civil war, you mean?' said Jarvis.

'I do. Hard-line loyalists would swarm into Catholic estates and the streets would run red.'

'You said, "In the absence of any information to the contrary". Does that mean that you don't know who took the child?' asked Avedissian.

'Correct.'

'Then it could have been the IRA?' said Jarvis.

Bryant shook his head and said, 'No, we know it wasn't them.'

'How?'

'Because they have been asked for the ransom.'

'*What*?' exclaimed Avedissian and Jarvis almost together.

'The kidnappers asked the IRA for the ransom, not us.'

'But why?'

'Presumably they thought the IRA would be easier to deal with and might want him just as badly to use as a bargaining measure.'

'But surely the IRA wouldn't touch it for the reasons you mentioned? There would be civil war.'

'The new leadership seems to think it's worth the risk,' said Bryant.

Avedissian, who had found himself being lulled into accepting everything that was being said, suddenly felt a sense of incredibility well up inside him. 'But how could something like this be kept secret?' he demanded. 'People must know the child is not there?'

'Officially, there has been a death threat made against the royal children. Security has been tightened and the family are maintaining a low profile, cancelling public engagements etc. Only a few trusted servants know that the child is really missing and they have been sworn to secrecy.'

'But there must be a limit to how long you can keep this up?' said Avedissian.

'Of course. That's why we must get the child back as

quickly as possible now we know about the ransom demand.'

'How do you know about the demand?' asked Jarvis.

Bryant pressed a button on the desk and sat back for a moment in silence. At length the door opened and the woman who had met Avedissian and Jarvis on their arrival came in accompanied by another woman, who walked slowly as if she were stiff. It was Kathleen O'Neill.

'I think you two have already met,' said Bryant to Avedissian.

Avedissian got up and smiled at Kathleen who smiled back and said that it was nice to see him again. He enquired about her health and noted that the bruising to her face had subsided a good deal. Jarvis was introduced to her and they all sat down again.

Bryant said, 'It was Miss O'Neill who gave us the information about the ransom demand to the IRA. Apparently they were offered the child for some twenty-five million dollars just after he was taken but their leader, O'Donnell, hesitated for presumably the reasons that have been mentioned. But now there has been a change in the leadership. Kell is in command and he wants to bargain for the boy.'

'How does Miss O'Neill know all this?' asked Jarvis.

'I am Martin O'Neill's sister,' replied Kathleen O'Neill.

Bryant read the look on Jarvis's face and said, 'You are obviously wondering why we should believe a single word that the sister of one of the most wanted men in the province says?'

'Frankly, yes.'

'Apart from the information that Miss O'Neill has given to us about the ransom demand she also told us of a new alliance between the IRA and the INLA. She warned us that the INLA were going to hit the banks last Friday and which ones. She was largely responsible for our success in damn nearly wiping them out in their attempt to raise money for the ransom.'

Avedissian turned to Kathleen O'Neill and asked simply, 'Why?'

'My brother, like Kevin O'Donnell, wanted the IRA to have nothing to do with this business. In fact O'Donnell ordered him to give the ransom note to the British but Kell found out.'

'What happened to your brother?'

'Kell had him shot before my eyes,' replied Kathleen, looking down at her knees.

'But you managed to escape?'

'I was to be shot too, but the man detailed to do it had other plans for me first.'

'He was the one who beat you up?'

'Yes. After he had raped me he fell asleep. I managed to knock him out and get away before he came round.'

'You've had a horrific experience,' said Avedissian softly.

'I dare say the O'Neill family have been responsible for some horrific experiences of other people in their time,' said Bryant coldly.

'So what happens now?' asked Jarvis.

'Two days ago the IRA placed an ad in *The Times* indicating their willingness to negotiate with the kidnappers. Our people will stay close.'

'Where will the IRA get the money?' asked Avedissian.

'Certainly not from the banks,' said Bryant with a cold smile. 'It will have to come from outside interests.'

'Meaning?'

'NORAID,' replied Bryant. 'Misguided, interfering American clowns.'

'But that much?' said Jarvis. 'Twenty-five million?'

'It's an all or nothing operation,' said Bryant.

'And where do we personally come into it?' asked Avedissian.

'We have assembled a rescue team comprising people of

every skill known to man. Drivers, climbers, parachutists, you name it, we have it. It will be their task to recover the child. When they have done their job the boy will be handed over to you two for the return home, while everyone else guards your rear, so to speak. It will be your job, Doctor, to look after the boy's health.'

'And me?' asked Jarvis.

'You will be the link between the team and Avedissian.'

'When do we start?' asked Avedissian.

'Soon.'

'And until then?'

'You will all remain here.'

'Miss O'Neill too?' asked Avedissian.

Bryant smiled and said, 'Her too. So far her information has proved invaluable to us. There is probably a lot more she can tell us about Kell and his people. There is a suite of rooms on the second floor where you will be comfortable. If there is anything else you want, no reasonable request will be denied.'

SIX

AVEDISSIAN FOUND HIMSELF DRAWN to Kathleen O'Neill. At first he managed to convince himself that his concern was medical and then, as the bruising disappeared, that it was pity he felt for her. But while it was true that she had lost more than anyone should at the one time, for she was to receive a new identity and leave the only country that she had ever known, it was also true that Avedissian felt a strong personal attraction towards her. As her injuries healed he was struck by how beautiful she really was. He knew about her hair and deep green eyes but the soft lines of her face, which had been obscured by the swelling after the beating, were a revelation and afforded her an air of serenity that he found totally captivating.

It was also clear that Bryant and Jarvis did not share his regard for Kathleen, apparently crediting her with the sins of her family. In her absence Bryant always referred to her as the O'Neill woman. Paul Jarvis was ever civil but made no overtures of friendship towards her.

Although not permitted to leave the precincts of the building the limits of their 'house arrest' did allow Avedissian, Jarvis and Kathleen the use of the garden, something that Avedissian and Kathleen made full use of while Jarvis tended to confine himself to using a small gymnasium on the top landing in his continual quest for fitness.

Avedissian's attempts to get Kathleen to speak of her family background and the philosophy behind her regard for her brother had been largely unsuccessful. He tried again as they walked together in the garden. 'You wouldn't understand,' she said, to Avedissian's annoyance.

'Why not?' he asked.

'You have no understanding of our history.'

'History!' exclaimed Avedissian. 'It's always "history".'

'It's important.'

'I would have thought that the future was a damned sight more important,' said Avedissian.

'A nice, comfortable view,' replied Kathleen.

'I want to understand. I really do,' said Avedissian.

Kathleen smiled and said, 'Let's stop talking politics shall we?'

Avedissian hesitated for a moment then agreed. He said, 'Tell me about your teaching. You are a teacher aren't you?'

Kathleen spoke readily of her job at the High School. She was obviously fond of children and her career had clearly been important to her, maybe even as important as his had been to him. Her enthusiasm made him wonder if she had yet faced the fact that it was probably over. But to point this out was something that Avedissian found he had no heart for. Instead he smiled and laughed at the tales of the High School and its pupils. 'You never married?' he asked when there was a lull in the conversation.

'No. You?'

'She died.'

'I'm sorry.'

Avedissian found himself taken unawares when Kathleen started asking him about his own life and career. Up until then she had been content to let Avedissian make all the running in their talks and he had come to accept that as the norm. Now he felt the need to become evasive and did not enjoy the feeling.

'Did you always want to be a doctor?'

Avedissian considered taking the easy way out and saying yes but did not. For some unaccountable reason he felt that he did not want to lie to Kathleen. 'No,' he replied, hoping that the inquiry would stop there. 'That came later.'

'Later than what?'

Avedissian took a deep breath and said, 'I was in the army.'

Kathleen looked at him with surprise on her face. 'But not here?'

'Yes, here. I was an officer in the Paras.'

Kathleen looked away and they continued their walk. They had come to the rose bushes and she stopped to examine a giant yellow bloom before she asked, 'How did you like that?'

'I didn't,' replied Avedissian.

'So you became a doctor?'

'Yes.'

'Good for you.'

Avedissian was left with the feeling that he had learned nothing about Kathleen from the exchange. They returned to the house, unaware that Bryant had been watching them from a first floor window for some time.

Seeing Avedissian and the O'Neill woman walking together in the shrubbery had given Bryant an idea. Kathleen O'Neill had been his biggest stroke of luck since taking on the Irish problem and she could not have happened at a better time. Perhaps she could still be of use.

The triumph over the INLA at the very inception of a new IRA-INLA pact had made Bryant look good and it had vindicated his view that the fight should be taken to the enemy, not the other way round. Waiting to be hit first before retaliating was a schoolboy concept, a stupid *public* schoolboy concept. That was the trouble with the Service, he reckoned, it was full of old fools like Montrose who had never really left their bloody public schools. Still... Montrose was no longer a problem. If he could pull this operation off successfully he could circumvent the lot of them and rise to the very top, then they would have to do things his way. He asked to see Kathleen O'Neill.

'You wanted me,' said Kathleen O'Neill putting her head round Bryant's door.

'Come in. Sit down,' said Bryant in what Kathleen thought were much warmer tones than usual. 'It's about your new identity...'

'There's a problem?'

'Not exactly,' said Bryant, obviously stalling.

'Then what?'

'I wondered how you would feel about helping us further?'

'I've told you all I can.'

Bryant raised his hand and said, 'Yes, I know, it's just that I've had an idea.'

'Go on.'

'You know just how important it is that we get the child back safely and without anyone knowing? Important for Ireland as much as anything?'

Kathleen nodded.

'Our people will need all the help they can get in bringing this off.'

'Where do I come in?'

'You know a lot of faces in the IRA. If you were on the spot it could be a tremendous help.'

'You mean I should go with the doctor and Captain Jarvis wherever it is they are going?'

'In a word, yes. The fact that you're a woman is also to our advantage.'

'How so?'

'A child travelling with a man and a woman is much more

111

inconspicuous than a child travelling with two men,' said Bryant.

Kathleen swithered and said, 'I'd like to know what the others think.'

'We can ask them.' Bryant picked up the phone and asked that Avedissian and Jarvis join them.

Avedissian thought that it was a good idea. Jarvis said merely that it made sense.

'Well?' asked Bryant.

'I agree,' said Kathleen.

'When is something going to happen?' asked Jarvis when the hubbub had died down.

'Almost immediately,' replied Bryant. 'We know roughly where the boy is. You, Jarvis, will be leaving tonight, the other two tomorrow afternoon.'

Jarvis asked where he would be going.

'The United States,' said Bryant.

'How do I make contact with the team?' asked Jarvis.

'I will brief you when we are alone,' replied Bryant. He turned to the others and said, 'The operation will be conducted on a need-to-know basis. No member will be told anything that he or she does not absolutely need to know. It's safer that way. You can't be betrayed by someone who doesn't even know who you are or what you're doing.'

'But . . .' began Avedissian.

'When the time comes you will be contacted,' said Bryant, discouraging any more questions about procedure.

'And if something goes wrong?' insisted Kathleen.

'You will be given a telephone number to call. Now you really must excuse me.'

Avedissian and Kathleen said goodbye to Paul Jarvis just after nine and came indoors to eat on their own. By mutual agreement they moved the table closer to the window where they could see the garden in the twilight of what had been a long summer's day. Avedissian found himself taking continual sidelong glances at Kathleen and was caught doing so on one occasion. 'Is anything wrong?' she asked.

'I was just thinking how well you had recovered from your injuries,' replied Avedissian settling for the half-truth.

'Thanks to you,' said Kathleen. 'I'm grateful.'

'I did very little,' said Avedissian.

Kathleen walked across the room and Avedissian noticed that the stiffness had left her limbs. She exuded the kind of exciting sensuality that seemed to him to be peculiar to certain women in their early thirties when experience, personality and an understanding of men combine to endow them with an attractiveness that captivates men of their own age and can prove almost irresistible to boys on the verge of manhood. The Indian summer of Kathleen O'Neill, thought Avedissian.

'What are you thinking about?' asked Kathleen, returning to the table with wine glasses.

'I was wondering when you were last truly happy,' replied Avedissian.

Kathleen looked surprised but did not fend off the question. 'I suppose it must be ten, maybe twelve years. I've had the occasional day, of course, but for a period of sustained happiness or contentment, which I assume you meant?'

Avedissian nodded.

'It is certainly all of that. Why do you ask?'

'I wanted to know.'

'Trying to find out if I have a conscience?'

'Maybe, I don't know. I just wanted to ask you.'

'I suppose, being a doctor, you sleep the sleep of the just every night with a conscience whiter than arctic snow?'

'I am a struck-off doctor. They say I murdered a child. My wife committed suicide in the aftermath.'

'My God,' said Kathleen. 'I had no idea. How awful.'

'Perhaps I shouldn't have said that all at once. Your jibe about my conscience got through.'

'Will you tell me?'

Avedissian told Kathleen O'Neill of the past three years.

'So happiness is not a prominent feature in either of our lives,' said Kathleen when he had finished.

Avedissian smiled and refilled their glasses. 'To the future,' he said, holding up his glass.

'To the future,' replied Kathleen.

They had finished their meal and were drinking coffee when Bryant came into the room with some papers in his hand. 'Dr and Mrs George Farmer,' he announced. 'Going on holiday to the States with their son David.'

'But who . . .?'

'David is the son of one of our people. You will meet him at the airport. He will fly out with you and enter the States on your passport then someone will take him from you and bring him back across the Atlantic. But, to all intents and purposes, Dr and Mrs Farmer will have entered the States with their son David. No one will be surprised when they leave with him.'

'Only it will be a different boy,' said Kathleen.

Bryant nodded and said, 'Is there anything you would like before I say good-night?'

Avedissian, who had always replied no to this question before, said, 'Yes, yes there is. I'd like a bottle of Gordon's gin, a supply of Schweppes' tonic and one . . .' He paused to look at Kathleen who nodded. 'No, two crystal glasses.'

'I'll see what I can do,' said Bryant. 'Anything else?'

Kathleen shook her head. Avedissian said that there wasn't.

'How did you find out that the boy was in the United States?' Kathleen asked Bryant.

Bryant touched the side of his nose and said, 'Need to know . . . remember?' He left the room.

114

Five minutes later one of the staff entered with a tray carrying all that Avedissian had requested. Kathleen accepted her drink and said, 'What shall we drink to this time?'

'Let's just drink,' said Avedissian.

In an hotel suite, less than five miles from where Avedissian and Kathleen sat with their drinks, Finbarr Kell raised a tumbler to his lips and took an angry gulp. 'Where is he, damn it?' he hissed, looking at his watch for the third time in as many minutes.

'He should be here by now,' said Nelligan unhelpfully. It only annoyed Kell more.

'I know he should be here by now!' he snapped. 'The plane landed two hours ago.'

Kell was approaching his irritable worst and it was at times like this that his disability rankled most. He wanted to pace up and down and vent his frustration through physical action, but instead, he had to wait in nail-biting inertia, trapped inside a legless torso.

The response to his insert in *The Times* had been a directive to send an agent to Amsterdam to receive further instructions and, to this end, he had activated a man with no previous record or history of sympathy with the Republican movement. He had activated the Tally Man.

To the world at large Malcolm Innes was a respectably dull accountant in his late thirties whose thinning hair and anonymous features had made him ideal for the purpose. Malcolm Innes was the man who lived up the street from everyone. Malcolm Innes was also the man who had left his brief-case in a public place on three separate occasions with devastating consequences. Malcolm Innes was the invisible man who, in the past, had come up behind five known traitors in the crowd and left them with an ice pick in the kidneys. Malcolm Innes was the Tally Man.

To Kell, at the moment, Innes was a link in a chain that was currently under strain for he was more than an hour late. His plans had allowed for a margin of ninety minutes at the most, for the Americans were due at eleven and he had to digest the information that Innes was bringing before they arrived.

As Kell could have predicted, the Americans had gagged on hearing the sum involved. They always preferred to deal in small sums at intervals rather than entrust control of large sums to the organisation itself, a constant bone of contention but one the IRA could do little about. If the Americans, who had insisted on crossing the Atlantic to discuss the present operation before making any commitment, arrived to find Kell without the facts at his fingertips it would give them the excuse they would be looking for to pull out. He would look like a bungling amateur and the Americans would take the first plane back. Kell threw back his glass and handed the empty to Nelligan. 'More,' he said.

As Nelligan refilled the glass a knock came at the door. Kell held up his hand and they both waited. A further three taps followed by another pause then two more.

'Thank Christ,' said Kell and Nelligan opened the door to admit Malcolm Innes.

Innes entered the room clutching his brief-case and wearing a harassed expression. He took off his glasses to wipe some drops of rain from them.

'Something's wrong?' said Kell anxiously.

Innes shook his head. 'No,' he said. 'I just got stopped at Customs. I've never been stopped before but tonight of all nights I get the full treatment. They even took the lining out of my case.'

'They didn't have a reason to, did they?' asked Kell suspiciously. 'If I thought for one moment . . .'

'No, no,' Innes assured him. 'Unless you call ten cigars and a bottle of advocaat a "reason".'

Kell relaxed visibly. 'Bols,' he said.

116

'It's the absolute truth, Mr Kell . . . Oh I see,' said Innes, unprepared for Kell's joke and sudden change of mood.

Kell checked his watch and said, 'We've got thirty minutes. Start talking.'

Nelligan handed Innes a drink and the man took a hasty gulp to wash down two indigestion tablets before starting to speak. 'I got into Schiphol on time and heard myself being paged on the public address system. I was directed by telephone to a particular taxi on the rank outside and the driver took me to a rendezvous about five miles from the airport. After about ten minutes . . .'

'They were waiting to see if you were followed,' interrupted Kell.

'. . . green Mercedes drew up alongside and a transceiver was passed in through the window of the cab. We conducted the conversation by phone.'

'Did you see who was in the Mercedes?' asked Kell.

'No, it had tinted windows.'

'But they could see you?'

'Yes.'

Kell smiled distantly and thought for a moment in silence before asking Innes to go on.

'They want the ransom paid by credit transfer.'

'How?'

'An account is to be opened at this bank,' Innes handed Kell a slip of paper, 'and the money paid into it.'

'An account in whose name?' asked Kell.

'It doesn't matter but a confirmation password has to be agreed with the bank so that a check can be made that the money has been deposited.'

'Then what?'

'A second password has to be agreed with the bank for the transfer of the money. When we have the child we give them the password and the money can be transferred into whatever account they please.'

'What's to stop us grabbing the brat and not giving them the password?' grinned Nelligan.

'I feel sure they have considered that possibility, Nelligan,' said Innes coldly. 'They didn't strike me as being amateurs.'

'Indeed they are not,' said Kell quietly with a smile that only he appeared to know the reason for. 'But then again . . . neither am I.'

Innes continued, 'You are to have a man in Chicago within three days. He is to check in to Room 303 at the Stamford Hotel. It's been reserved.'

'Then what?'

'He will be contacted and taken to see the boy. The exchange is to take place within twenty-four hours after that.'

'Where?'

'They will decide that.'

'Of course,' said Kell softly as if something was amusing him.

'They are calling the shots,' said Innes.

'Of course they are,' said Kell with an even broader smile. His eyes, magnified by the strong lenses of his glasses, blinked with the mesmerising regularity of a lizard as he considered what he had heard.

'There will, of course, be the problem of getting the boy out of the country after the hand-over,' said Innes.

Kell looked at him as if he were some kind of mental defective then said, 'Well, I'm sure our American friends can help there, don't you think?'

'If you say so, Mr Kell.'

At eleven precisely the coded knock came to the door again and three men were admitted to the room. There were handshakes all round and the three introduced themselves as Shelby, Bogroless and Roker. Kell, still holding a tumbler of whisky, offered the Americans a drink. Shelby, their leader, a short dark man wearing a grey suit and a yellow silk shirt that threatened to burst under the strain of his stomach, nodded to Kell's glass and said, 'I'll have a drop of Irish, too.'

His assumption had been wrong. Kell turned to Nelligan and asked him to ring down for a bottle of Jamieson's. He raised his glass slightly in the direction of the American and said, 'Scotch.'

The American made a joke about Kell's taste in whisky and Kell pretended to share in the amusement for he was sizing up his guests. The request for Irish whiskey had been noted and the man classified by Kell as a Yankee Paddy, Kell's own derogatory term for Americans drawn to the romanticism of the idea of Old Ireland.

But it didn't matter what they were, only the money mattered. It was just a question of how best to deal with them. As the conversation continued it became clear that one of the others, Bogroless, fell into the same mould as Shelby. The third man, Roker, was not so easy to assess. He was not a Y.P. He was too quiet, too withdrawn, a bit like Innes really, a bit like an accountant. Chances were that's what he was. Kell decided that he was the one with the brains.

Shelby said, 'Commander, you have requested our co-operation in securing a great deal of money, an enormous sum of money in fact.'

'A free Ireland doesn't come cheap,' said Kell.

'You really believe that that is what it could mean?' asked Shelby.

Kell, adopting the rhetoric of the patriot, started selling the plan to the Americans. The longer he spoke the more he could see that he was convincing Shelby and Bogroless of the feasibility of the operation but he was worried about Roker. Roker had sat throughout with a complete lack of expression save for a cold, hard gaze that had never left Kell for a moment.

'Frankly, Commander, the sum of money involved is too large. Don't you have some other way of financing it?' asked Shelby.

'Twelve of our gallant lads went down in just such an attempt last Friday,' said Kell. 'Including a dear personal friend.'

'We heard,' Shelby sympathised. 'A tragedy, a tragedy.'

Bogroless nodded in agreement. Roker continued to watch Kell, apparently unmoved by what he had heard.

'I understood that it was INLA men who attempted the raids,' said Roker, speaking for the first time.

'Indeed it was,' said Kell. 'This operation is so important that we had decided to put aside our differences and work together. It's that big.'

Shelby said with an air of unease, 'Actually, Commander . . . it is just possible that we could raise such a sum but it would involve an all or nothing effort including a great deal of borrowing. Not to put too fine a point on it, it would bleed NORAID dry. If the operation failed there would never be any more . . .'

'This will be the last operation for all of us,' said Kell.

'That's what you have to convince us of,' said Shelby. 'Do you really believe that the British would pull out of Ireland in exchange for the boy?'

'Yes, I do.'

Roker interrupted. He had a cold featureless voice that matched his appearance. He said, 'Mr Kell, there is a school of thought that says that the British wouldn't stand for this and there would be a bloody civil war in Ireland instead of the triumph you suggest. What do you say to that?'

'I think that they are right,' said Kell to everyone's obvious surprise. Even Roker permitted himself a raise of the eyebrows. Are you telling us that you would plunge Ireland into civil war deliberately?' he asked.

Kell shook his head slowly and smiled indulgently as if

120

teaching a class of infants. 'No,' he said. 'A lot of people are missing the point. The British have covered the whole thing up. That works in our favour, don't you see? If the British agree to our terms then the boy could be returned to them without the press and the public ever knowing. They could save face as well as get their brat back and we all know how much that means to the British.'

The Americans saw the sense in what Kell was saying. Shelby said, 'You mean the world at large would never know that they had given in to blackmail?'

'Exactly,' said Kell, as if a pupil had finally managed to get something right.

'What are the arrangements for the ransom?' asked Roker.

Kell told him.

'If we were to agree we would have to be involved at all stages and we would keep control of the money until we were completely satisfied,' said Roker.

'We could work together,' said Kell.

'Excuse us a moment, Commander,' said Shelby. The three Americans moved to the adjoining room of the suite and talked in whispers while Kell, Nelligan and Innes waited.

'What was that about losing a dear friend in the INLA, Mr Kell?' whispered Nelligan quietly.

'Shut up,' hissed Kell.

The Americans returned. Shelby stood in the middle of the floor flanked by Bogroless and Roker. 'We agree,' said Shelby. 'We'll finance it.'

'Then this calls for a celebration,' said Kell. 'Nelligan! The glasses.'

It was decided that Roker would handle negotiations on behalf of NORAID and Innes would be sent to the States to represent the interests of the IRA. Kell suggested that Innes return with the Americans to their own hotel so that he and Roker could finalise details about the exchange.

'To a free Ireland,' proposed Shelby with the final toast of the evening. Kell smiled and raised his glass.

When the Americans had left, Nelligan asked if Kell wanted any more whisky. Kell shook his head and said, 'We've got work to do. I want to speak to Harrigan in England and then I want to see Reagan. But first, phone the Long House . . . find out if the woman has called.'

Avedissian found that he could not sleep. He tossed and turned for a while before getting up to look out at the garden. It was bathed in moonlight and pale shadow, like a scene from another planet where no man had ever trod. The flowers had lost their colour and the trees their true form to become abstracts in a dream. There was no sound . . . save for a slight scraping sound, that came from behind him! He turned round and saw the handle of the door turn slowly.

Avedissian tip-toed quickly across the room to press himself to the wall beside the door and wait for it to open. His pulse rate was rising rapidly. As a shadowy figure entered the room Avedissian reached out his arm and circled it round the figure's neck in a head lock. What he touched was silky and soft and smelled sweetly of a perfume he recognised. 'Kathleen!' he exclaimed. He relaxed his grip and felt on the wall for the switch.

'No, don't put on the light.'

'I'm sorry, I didn't realise . . .'

'It was my fault. It was a silly thing to do.'

'Are you all right? Did I hurt you?' whispered Avedissian, still holding her shoulders.

'I'm fine. I just feel stupid that's all.'

'But why? Why did you . . .?'

Kathleen looked up at Avedissian so that he could see her face in the moonlight coming from the window. 'It's silly. I couldn't sleep. I thought we might talk, then I realised that you would probably be sleeping so I thought I would look in on you quietly to see.'

Avedissian smiled in the darkness and told her that he hadn't been able to sleep either. He had been looking out of the window.

'May I join you?'

'Of course.'

'It's peaceful,' murmured Kathleen.

'Just what I was thinking,' agreed Avedissian. 'But when there is nothing to distract you all your past mistakes return to haunt you.'

'The accusation of silence,' said Kathleen.

'But now we each have a confessor,' said Avedissian.

Kathleen smiled and pointed to a cat that was stealing across the lawn in pursuit of some unseen prey. They paused in their conversation to watch it then, when it had disappeared into the bushes, Kathleen said, 'Me first?'

'If you like.'

'I wouldn't know where to begin, "Father", for I am guilty of so many things. I feel sometimes as if I have lived my entire life as a victim of circumstance. A willing victim for I did nothing to change it.'

'Does that make you guilty of anything?' asked Avedissian.

'I think so. I think if you see harm being done and do nothing to prevent it it's almost as bad as doing it yourself, perhaps even worse because then you can pretend that you're entirely innocent.'

'Are you talking about your brother?' asked Avedissian.

'I suppose so. Don't get me wrong, I'm for a free Ireland as much as he ever was. I want to see an end to all the injustices of the North and I want to see the British out. It's just that I lack conviction when it comes to the crunch.'

'I don't understand.'

'When Martin came to me, as he always did when he

123

needed someone, I was always there, but not because, as he imagined, I shared his enthusiasm for what he was doing but simply because he was my brother and I loved him.'

'That doesn't sound so bad to me,' said Avedissian.

'But it was. Don't you see? I let him think that I agreed with him that there was no other way to achieve our ends, because my head told me that he was right, and still does. It's just that my heart always told me that it was wrong and it was a dreadful sin. I never told him that. I never tried to convince him that I might have been right. I just opted out and played the dutiful sister.'

'You are doing something positive now,' said Avedissian.

'I'm just a victim of circumstance again.'

'You needn't have agreed to come along,' Avedissian pointed out.

Kathleen looked at Avedissian and smiled distantly. She said, 'You are a nice man, Avedissian. What kind of a name is that anyway?'

'Armenian grandfather,' replied Avedissian.

'And what sins are you guilty of?' asked Kathleen.

Avedissian shrugged. 'Arrogance when I'm winning, weakness when I'm losing,'

'You sound like the human race,' said Kathleen.

'It's just a question of degree.'

Kathleen shivered and Avedissian put his arm round her. He did it unsurely and there was an instant when she stiffened, but it passed. She relaxed and laid her head against his chest. 'It's been a long time since anyone held me,' she said.

'I'm sorry. That shouldn't be.'

'You do find me attractive?' Kathleen asked, sounding vulnerable.

'More than attractive. You are beautiful.'

'I'm thirty-four years old.'

Avedissian kissed her hair and repeated what he had said.

'You see, there has been no one to tell me that for such a long time.' Kathleen looked up and Avedissian brought his mouth down on hers, kissing her gently and feeling her lips part, warm and moist.

Kathleen drew away slightly and put her hands against Avedissian's chest. 'I'm going back to my room now,' she whispered. 'Thank you for talking to me.'

Avedissian smiled and whispered, 'Good-night, Kathleen O'Neill.'

He watched the door close and turned again to have a last look at the garden before returning to bed. It had started to rain, a few spots at first, then steadily. He got into bed and listened to the sound of the drops striking the leaves. Somewhere in the night an owl hooted but Avedissian felt warm and comfortable and out of its reach.

SEVEN

THE RAIN PERSISTED THROUGHOUT the following day. It made Avedissian and Kathleen huddle down into their collars as they walked the short distance from the airport bus to the steps of the TWA Boeing 747. David, to their relief, seemed completely at ease with them, something that Avedissian put down to Kathleen's winning way with children. They had had only an hour with him and his real parents in a room at the airport but it had been sufficient. The boy was happily clutching Kathleen's hand as he scaled, what were for him, the giant steps to the rear entrance.

Almost at the same time the three Americans who had met with Kell were boarding by the front steps. As 'Ambassador Class' passengers they would be unlikely to come into contact with the Farmer family who were more ordinary passengers, not that it would have mattered. They didn't know each other. Fate's little joke would have been lost on both parties.

Two hours out across the Atlantic David fell asleep and Avedissian and Kathleen could talk without distraction. Kathleen asked, 'Do you think we're going to the States because the kidnappers are American?'

Avedissian shrugged. He had been thinking along the same lines himself but had to confess that he had not reached any conclusion. He said, 'That seems logical but there could be other reasons. The kidnappers may know that the Irish could only fund this thing with the help of American money. They may have decided to set up shop close to the bank, so to speak.'

'So they could be any nationality.'

'I suppose so.'

'Why Chicago?' asked Kathleen. 'Wouldn't it have been more sensible to use a city on the East Coast?'

'My guess is that they are taking no chances. Chicago is in the middle. That gives them options to move north, south, east or west with equal predictability.'

They stopped talking to allow a stewardess to ask them if they wanted anything to drink. Both said no.

'I wish we were on the way back,' said Kathleen ruefully as the captain made a slight course correction.

Avedissian smiled. 'Do you know what I wish?' he said. 'I wish that we really were Dr and Mrs Farmer travelling with our son David for a holiday in the States.' He put his head back on the seat cushion and closed his eyes. He was pleased to feel Kathleen take his hand and squeeze it.

The flight landed on time in Chicago and they were met by a woman who took charge of David. She wished them well before disappearing into the throng on the main concourse. It happened so quickly that Kathleen was visibly surprised. She looked wistfully after the child as he vanished among the arms and legs of the airport crowd.

'No problem with goodbyes,' said Avedissian.

'I suppose not,' said Kathleen.

They took a yellow cab to their hotel and saw immediately why it had been chosen. It was enormous. Kathleen had to strain her head back to look up at the huge tower block. 'Identical rooms for identical people,' she said.

The edge of excitement that had been so much in evidence at the start of their journey had been dulled by the long flight and the knowledge that they were now in for another period of waiting. Their instructions, given by

Bryant before they had left Belfast for London Heathrow, were that one of them was to stay in the hotel at all times. The other had to check back at intervals of no longer than two hours.

'Hungry?' asked Avedissian when they had finished unpacking what little belongings they had.

'Just tired,' replied Kathleen.

'I want to stretch my legs,' said Avedissian.

'I shan't go out,' she assured him.

Kathleen was fast asleep when Avedissian returned from a brief walk in the streets around the hotel; he had enjoyed the exercise but had found the humidity oppressive and was glad to return to the air-conditioned comfort of the room. He tried to make as little noise as possible in taking a shower.

There was no message for them throughout the following day and they grew nervous with the waiting. Each had been unwilling to leave the other so they had spent almost the entire day talking in their room. It had not been unpleasant but always, at the back of their minds, they had known that they were waiting for something to happen and the seeds of frustration had been sown.

At seven in the evening Kathleen had just finished saying, 'They might keep us a bit better informed,' when the phone rang and their excitement grew. Avedissian answered. It was Paul Jarvis.

'Meet me in the bar of the Regency Hotel at seven-thirty,' said Jarvis. 'It's three blocks west of where you are.'

An American woman in her thirties was holding court in the bar of the Regency when Avedissian and Kathleen arrived. Her spreading buttocks slid around the bar stool as she emphasised every comment with extravagant hand gestures.

Her audience, mainly older men, were hanging on every

word, not that what she had to say was important; it wasn't, just loud, but Avedissian could see that she was flirting with each of them in turn.

A slightly built man in his early forties sat next to her and, at intervals, the woman would take a cigarette from the pack on the bar in front of her and have it lit by him, then she would turn away. The long-suffering husband, thought Avedissian.

Avedissian ordered gin and tonic for Kathleen and himself and five minutes later they were joined by Paul Jarvis.

Avedissian had deliberately picked a table well away from the crowd so that they could talk without being overheard. 'Does the team have the boy?' he asked.

'Not yet,' replied Jarvis.

'But you know where he is?'

'Not exactly.'

'But . . .'

'I understand from Bryant that the plan is to take the boy from the IRA after the exchange has taken place. He thinks it will be easier than dealing with both the kidnappers and the Irish at the same time. There's also the question of NORAID. We don't know what kind of a presence they are going to put up. There's a lot of money involved.'

'What do you want us to do?' asked Avedissian.

'First I've to give you these.' Jarvis handed Avedissian a sealed envelope and said that it contained airline tickets for the two of them and the boy. Avedissian put them safely away in an inside pocket.

'What about the kidnappers?' asked Avedissian. 'Do you know who they are?'

'Every lead has petered out into nothing as if a whole bunch of red herrings had been prepared in advance. Whoever they are, they are certainly no amateurs. They are almost too good to be true.'

'What about the Irish?' asked Avedissian.

'That's our trump card,' replied Jarvis. 'We know who their contact man is and we know where he is. If we stick with him he is going to lead us to the child. His name is Innes and he is staying at the Stamford.'

'How did you get on to him?'

'Intelligence from Bryant in London.'

'Then you have been in contact with London?'

'Of course,' said Jarvis. 'Nothing is done without Bryant's say so.' He turned to Kathleen and asked, 'Have you ever heard of this man Innes?'

Kathleen nodded. 'Malcolm Innes. They call him the Tally Man. He looks as if he wouldn't harm a fly, but he's dangerous.'

'Can you describe him?'

Kathleen gave Jarvis a description.

'That's the man all right,' agreed Jarvis. 'Is there anything else you can tell us about him?'

Kathleen shook her head and said not.

'Are there any more IRA here?' asked Avedissian.

'Not overtly,' said Jarvis with plain meaning.

'But you think there might be?'

'What do you think?' said Jarvis.

Avedissian nodded then asked, 'Has Innes been contacted by the kidnappers yet?'

'Yes, that's why I called you. He was contacted by phone this afternoon and told to attend a baseball game this evening.'

'Then the exchange could take place tonight?' said Kathleen.

'I don't think so,' replied Jarvis. 'There hasn't been time to finalise the ransom details. It's my guess that NORAID or the Irish have asked to see the goods before they do business.'

'So the child could be at the stadium?'

'Perhaps, or maybe it is just being used as a crowded meeting place. Innes may be taken somewhere else after contact is made.'

'Are you going to be there?' asked Kathleen.

'We all are,' said Jarvis. 'We know where Innes will be sitting but we don't know who will be with him. I want you, Miss O'Neill, to have a look at the faces round about. Tell me if you recognise any of them.'

Kathleen nodded and Avedissian asked what he was supposed to do.

'Just be on hand,' replied Jarvis.

Under instruction from the NORAID man, Roker, not to do anything without keeping NORAID informed, Malcolm Innes had gone to a pay-phone in the street and called the number that he had been given. He told Roker of the contact that had been made and gave him details of his seat ticket for the game.

'Nothing else?' asked Roker.

'Nothing,' confirmed Innes.

It was true when he made the call but, as he left the hotel to attend the game, a bellboy handed him a pair of binoculars and an envelope. Innes opened it in the cab. It contained a piece of white card with a code on it. It said 'Section J, Seat L–17'. He examined his own ticket and saw that it was in a different part of the stadium. So that was it, he would be allowed to see the boy across the stadium using binoculars.

Innes edged his way through a crowd at a popcorn stand and climbed the steep banking to reach his row. He excused himself and a line of knees turned to the left to let him past. He had just settled into his seat when he felt a hand on his shoulder and a voice said in his ear, 'You came well equipped.' It was Roker.

Innes half turned and saw that Roker was referring to the binoculars. He told him how he had come by them.

'Did they give you anything else?'

Innes showed him the card.

Roker whispered, 'Let us deal with this.'

'Don't interfere!' hissed Innes. The last thing that he needed was the antics of bungling amateurs.

Roker gripped his shoulder more tightly and leaned close to his ear. 'Now get this, Innes! It's our money! A lot of our people have gone into hock over this. If there is the slightest chance that we can get the boy without paying through the nose for him we are going to go for it!'

'These people are not amateurs!' insisted Innes. 'You could ruin the whole thing!'

'Just sit on your butt and wait!' hissed Roker, getting up and leaving his seat.

Innes looked to his neighbours to see if his whispered altercation with Roker had attracted attention. There was no sign that it had. A family of four occupied the seats to his left and a teenage boy and girl sat to his right. In front two middle-aged couples shared out food and drink while behind him a man was explaining loudly to his wife or girlfriend exactly why he thought that Johnson was a better pitcher than Schwarz.

The steepness of the stadium made Innes uneasy for he had never been at peace with heights and he was sitting on the top deck of a series of steeply banked tiers. It seemed a very long way down to the brightly lit diamond where the players were now being introduced.

A roar from the crowd followed every announcement of a name and each player ran on individually to acknowledge the cheers with a raise of his arm. Innes put the glasses to his eyes and focused on one of them as he stood in line, shuffling nervously and chewing gum with monotonous regularity. He picked out the chain round his neck and could see that it carried a St Christopher medallion.

Out of the corner of both eyes Innes could see that all

attention was now being concentrated on the diamond. He put the glasses back to his eyes and raised them slowly to section 'J'. Seat L–17 was unoccupied as were the two seats on either side. Four or five rows behind the empty seats and slightly to the right three men were moving along the row. Innes could see that one of them was Shelby, the man who had led the NORAID delegation in Belfast. He cursed under his breath, then he became aware of someone entering the row behind him and glanced back. It was Roker returning.

Almost imperceptibly, darkness had closed in on the stadium, shutting out the world in the interests of the game. The crack of the bat sent a ripple of excitement round the tiers and set the tiny, bright figures down on the diamond into motion. The hitter, running at full tilt, slid safely into second base and the ball slammed into the catcher's mitt to kill the moment. The ball was returned to the mound in a lazy arc where the pitcher snatched it from the air and spat out a stream of tobacco juice into the dirt. He adjusted his cap and prepared to throw again.

From a position well behind Innes, Jarvis was watching him intently. Avedissian and Kathleen sat beside him. 'Do you recognise the man sitting behind Innes?' Jarvis asked Kathleen.

'I've never seen him before,' she replied.

'Do you think he's one of the kidnappers?' asked Avedissian.

Jarvis shook his head and said, 'No, or they would have done something by now. They're both waiting for something or someone. He's either NORAID or another IRA man.'

A roar from the crowd greeted the first home run of the game and Innes was momentarily lost from view as people leapt to their feet to applaud. As they settled Avedissian leaned towards Jarvis and whispered, 'Innes is not looking at the game!'

'What do you mean?'

'He's watching the crowd on the other side of the stadium.'

Jarvis looked at Innes and traced his line of sight. He could now see what Avedissian meant. Innes was looking at a section of the crowd on a lower tier. Jarvis raised his own glasses and tried to emulate the angle of Innes's binoculars. He found the empty seats. 'They are waiting for someone to arrive on the other side,' he said to Avedissian. 'Take a look at row "L".'

Avedissian looked, then passed on the binoculars to Kathleen.

Jarvis asked Kathleen to look at the crowd in the area of the empty seats to see if there were any faces there that she recognised. She looked but saw no one familiar.

'Keep looking!' said Jarvis, sounding anxious.

'Do you think they might try a snatch if the kidnappers bring in the boy?' asked Avedissian.

'It's possible,' replied Jarvis. 'It depends on how far in advance Innes was told where the boy would be and whether he or his NORAID cronies have had time to set up something across there.'

'You said the kidnappers were clever,' said Avedissian.

'That's what puzzles me,' replied Jarvis. 'This would be a silly mistake.'

'There's someone coming into the empty seats,' said Kathleen. She handed back the glasses to Jarvis.

Jarvis saw the figure of a man wearing a dark blue lumber-jacket and a baseball cap edge his way along the row and sit down. He was alone. 'I don't understand it,' said Jarvis, checking anxiously on Innes and finding that he was still looking across to the same place. 'There's no sign of the boy.'

Avedissian took a look at the man in the lumber-jacket. He had taken a packet of peanuts from his pocket and appeared to be watching the game intently. Avedissian looked at the man's cap then looked again for it did not carry the logo of either of the teams that were playing. It had a plain blue shield on it with the cipher, F–B9. 'The cap!' he whispered urgently to Jarvis. 'Look at his cap!'

Jarvis looked and understood immediately. He swung the glasses round to find section 'F' in the stadium and homed in on seat B9. There, sitting beside a woman wearing dark glasses, was a little boy. He was wrapped up warmly and seemed to be very tired. In his lapel he wore a small enamel badge with a Union Jack on it.

'Jesus wept,' muttered Jarvis. He passed the glasses along the line.

Avedissian heard Kathleen draw in her breath sharply. 'What's the matter?' he asked anxiously.

'There's a man looking at us!' she replied.

Jarvis looked and saw what had alarmed Kathleen. A man wearing a black overcoat and sitting three rows behind the woman and the boy appeared to be looking directly back at him through field glasses. His first impulse was to tear his own glasses away from his eyes but then he realised that the man was not looking at him at all. He was watching Innes. He was looking to see if Innes had noticed the seat code on the baseball cap . . . and he had not.

'We've got time!' Jarvis whispered urgently to Avedissian.

'What do you mean?'

'They will have to keep the boy there until Innes tumbles to the code on the hat. Maybe we can get to him before that happens!'

'Snatch him back ourselves, you mean?' said Avedissian, filled with apprehension.

'Only if we get a real chance,' replied Jarvis. 'We can't take any risks with the boy's safety. But we can get round there and take a look at the situation.'

Avedissian agreed.

'For God's sake, be careful!' urged Kathleen.

'We'll leave our seats one at a time,' whispered Jarvis. 'Make as if you are going out for a beer. We don't want to alarm our friends across the way.'

Avedissian waited until Jarvis had been gone for a few moments before getting to his feet casually and starting to edge his way along the row. As he got to the end of the row he looked back at Kathleen and smiled. 'Be careful,' she mouthed.

Avedissian found Jarvis waiting for him in the gallery behind the tier. Together they ran along it as far as they could before stopping when they came to a blank wall. There was a stairway beside it. They took the steps two at a time and descended to the tier below to look for the way ahead but there did not seem to be any. This section of the stadium appeared to be completely isolated from the next at all levels by a concrete partition.

'There's a door!' said Avedissian, pointing to a blue door set in the wall near the back edge of the gallery. They ran over to it but only to find that it was locked. Jarvis cursed and a voice behind them asked, 'What are you looking for, buddy?'

They turned to find a security man standing there.

'We've just seen an old army buddy of ours. We're trying to get to him,' replied Jarvis with what Avedissian thought was admirable presence of mind. What was more, Jarvis had said it in a convincing American accent. Avedissian thought he understood why Jarvis had been chosen for the job.

'You'll have to go down and round the outside,' said the guard. 'Just explain to the guy on the gate and he'll let you through if you show him your tickets.'

'Oh come on, man, that'll take forever,' pleaded Jarvis.

The guard swithered, rubbed his chin while Jarvis smiled

disarmingly at him and then gave in. He unhooked a bunch of keys from his belt and found the one for the blue door. 'Don't you ever say I did this,' he called after them as they passed through to the next section.

Jarvis ran up to the edge of the gallery and put the glasses to his eyes. Avedissian followed. Both men were breathing heavily. 'Are they still there?' asked Avedissian anxiously.

There was a pause then Jarvis replied. 'Still there. We can do it!'

They continued their run along the second gallery, swerving to avoid a fat woman coming towards them with a glass of beer in either hand and carrying several packets of popcorn between her teeth. She turned to protest but could say nothing for fear of losing the bags.

They made good progress, albeit in slalom style, as they weaved in and out to avoid cross traffic moving to and from the toilets and food stands. There had been no barrier between the last two sections; Jarvis prayed that there would be none between them and the final one where the boy was. His heart sank as he saw the concrete divide loom up.

'There must be a door in this one too,' reasoned Avedissian. 'You check one level up. I'll go one down.' He raced down the stairs to find another unbroken wall and cursed his luck before turning on his heel to climb back up again. He reached the level where Jarvis was and saw that Jarvis had found a door. He was trying to budge it with his shoulder.

Avedissian could see that Jarvis was attracting some attention so he hung back. He saw Jarvis put his foot to the lock in exasperation then someone said loudly, 'This guy's got a problem.' Jarvis threw himself against the door again but only succeeded in drawing a bigger audience. 'Somebody should call a cop,' suggested a fat man.

The mention of police made Jarvis abandon his attack on the door and run back to the gallery where he found

Avedissian. 'No luck,' he said as they raced back down the stairs.

'I saw,' replied Avedissian. 'We'll have to go round the outside after all.'

'There's no time,' insisted Jarvis. 'There has to be another way.' He hurried to the back wall of the stadium and looked over. There, two metres below, projecting from the outside wall, he saw a concrete ledge. It was narrow but it was a possibility. He said so to Avedissian.

Avedissian looked over and felt unwell. At this level they were still thirty metres above the ground. One slip and they would be dead. 'I don't know . . .'

'We can do it!' said Jarvis, deciding the issue by getting on top of the wall and lowering himself out on to the ledge. With a quick look behind him to ensure that no one was watching from the stairs, Avedissian followed.

Both men stood on the ledge, their bodies spreadeagled against the smooth face of the stadium wall. 'All right?' asked Jarvis. Avedissian grunted in reply.

Jarvis began to move along the ledge. Avedissian waited, pressing his cheek to the rough surface and considering all the things that could go wrong. He could fall and break his neck. Someone might spot them up there and call the police. The thought of a Hollywood style drama involving police and firemen frightened him into action. He started to move.

The ledge was not smooth underfoot for, over the years, it had accumulated a heavy coating of concrete dust and debris which made Avedissian painfully unsure of his footing. He tried to clear the way ahead by brushing it lightly with his leading foot but Jarvis stopped him. 'You'll attract attention below!' he warned. Avedissian took his chances with the uncleared ledge.

The blood was pounding in Avedissian's ears by the time they had passed the extent of the concrete partition and could once more get a firm grip on the top of the gallery wall. He permitted himself a look at the ground below but immediately wished that he hadn't when his senses began to reel. He closed his eyes for a moment and once more pressed his face to the wall until he had recovered.

'Come on!' urged Jarvis, pulling himself up and over the gallery wall. He turned to offer Avedissian a hand but it was not necessary and both men dropped down into the gallery of section 'F'.

'What the . . .?' exclaimed a voice from the shadows of the stairway and a policeman moved forward into the light. He started to draw his pistol but Jarvis was on him before he could get it clear of the holster. He floored the man with two quick blows and caught him before he touched the ground, dragging him back into shadow, where he propped him up in a corner against the wall.

'We've done it now,' exclaimed Avedissian.

'Let's go.'

They ran to the top of the stairs then Jarvis laid a restraining hand on Avedissian's arm. 'No more running,' he cautioned. 'From here on we melt into the crowd.'

Moving as casually as they could in the circumstances they approached the area where they had seen the woman and the boy. Jarvis stopped at a hot dog stand that had no queue beside it and bought two. He handed one to Avedissian and said, 'We are just returning to our seats.'

They approached the head of the aisle leading to row 'B' and looked down, Jarvis casually taking a bite of his hot dog and pretending to be having trouble with the contents escaping from the side into the napkin. Avedissian looked at the seats and saw that he need not have bothered. The seats were empty. They were as lifeless as tombstones. The boy had gone. They were too late.

Jarvis put the glasses slowly to his eyes and looked over to where Innes had been sitting. Innes was looking directly back at him. For a few seconds the two men looked at each other across the floodlit diamond. 'Another couple of minutes, damn you,' Jarvis muttered under his breath.

Avedissian grew aware of some commotion behind them and knew that the policeman must have come round. He said so to Jarvis. 'Use the empty seats!' whispered Jarvis. Avedissian moved down the aisle and into the row where they had seen the woman and the boy. 'Sit apart,' said Jarvis behind him, already in the act of removing his jacket to alter his appearance as much as possible.

Avedissian relied on munching his hot dog to create an aura of innocence but his pulse rate was topping one hundred and thirty as two policemen slowly passed the end of the row and looked along it. One was rubbing his jaw.

A home run down on the diamond helped break the spell and Avedissian leapt to his feet with those around him, uttering what he hoped was a convincing, 'All right, all right!' The policemen moved on to look at the occupants of the next row and Jarvis shot a quick glance in Avedissian's direction. Avedissian raised his eyes to the heavens in reply.

The game ended and thirty thousand people became intent on leaving the stadium, but at that moment Avedissian loved them all for they were his guarantee of anonymity. As he moved along the row to the aisle Jarvis said that they should split up, Avedissian should return to the gate where Kathleen would come out. He would make his own way out. As they parted at the top of the aisle Jarvis said, 'I'll meet you in the park by the hotel. Tomorrow at ten in the morning.'

Kathleen had already emerged from the stadium and was waiting outside when Avedissian finally managed to get round the perimeter through the throngs of people. 'We were too late,' he said.

'Are you all right?' she asked anxiously.

Avedissian held her close, suddenly feeling the

after-effects of the intense strain that he had been under. He assured her that he was. 'God, I need a drink,' he muttered.

'Let's go back to the hotel,' said Kathleen. 'Unless we're supposed to do something else?'

Avedissian shook his head in reply.

Avedissian lay flat on his back on the bed and let out a great sigh of appreciation for the air-conditioned quiet of the room. It was an island in the sea, an oasis in the desert. Kathleen brought him his drink and sat down on the edge of the bed to ask, 'What happened at the stadium?'

Avedissian told her and Kathleen exclaimed, 'That was a crazy thing to do,' when he told her about climbing out on the ledge.

'It seemed a good idea at the time,' said Avedissian, but now he cringed at the thought of how the venture might have ended. 'God, I was so scared,' he confessed.

Kathleen smoothed the hair back from his forehead in a gesture of affection and Avedissian looked up at her. 'You have gentle hands, my lady,' he said softly. Kathleen bent down and kissed him lightly on the lips.

'When I looked down and . . .'

'Sssh . . .' whispered Kathleen and kissed him again.

This time Avedissian was aware of how warm her lips were. He responded by pulling her to him and searching her mouth with his tongue and was aroused by the fact that she did not pull away. He ran his fingers through her hair to cup her face between his hands and look at her questioningly. She just smiled.

Avedissian whispered, 'I want you.'

'I know,' replied Kathleen softly. She got up from the bed but did not move away. Instead she started to undress, looking at Avedissian all the time as she did so. When she had finished she stood there and asked in a whisper, 'Do you still want me?'

Avedissian held out his arms in reply and crushed her to him. 'I want you so much,' he murmured, feeling Kathleen's passion grow to match his own. 'I want to feel all of you, I want to be deep inside you, God, how I want you.'

As they lay in the silent aftermath, Kathleen opened her eyes and looked at Avedissian. He responded by leaning over and kissing her lightly on the shoulder.

'*Post coitus omne animal triste*,' whispered Kathleen.

'After love . . . all animals are . . . sad?' was Avedissian's unsure translation.

Kathleen smiled and nodded.

'I didn't know you were a Latin scholar?'

'There's a lot you don't know about me,' said Kathleen.

'I want to know everything.'

Kathleen gave a shake of the head and whispered, 'There won't be time.'

'But we'll make time. When this is over we can . . .'

Kathleen put her finger on Avedissian's lips. 'Don't talk of the future,' she said.

'But if I object to your preoccupation with the past and you object to mine with the future all we have left is the present,' said Avedissian.

'That's all we ever had,' replied Kathleen distantly. 'Kiss me.'

Avedissian kissed her.

There was a fountain in the park. Avedissian and Kathleen chose to sit beside it where they could see people approaching from all directions and settled down to wait for Jarvis. They had got there at ten minutes to ten so that by a quarter past, when Jarvis had still not appeared, they were beginning to get anxious. Avedissian got to his feet for the second time and strolled round the fountain to check his watch once more when he returned.

'Do you think something has gone wrong?' asked Kathleen.

Avedissian shrugged his shoulders and sat down again.

They were joined on the bench by an old man who unwrapped a plastic bag and began feeding bread-crumbs to the birds, apparently oblivious of everything else around him. As the pigeons started to gather round their feet Avedissian indicated to Kathleen that they should get up and start walking. They walked slowly round the fountain, courting the outer edge of a fine spray mist and using it as an antidote to the morning sun that was already very hot.

'There he is,' said Kathleen.

Avedissian looked and saw Jarvis walking towards them on the broad path that led up from the gate. 'About time too,' he muttered.

'I'm sorry I'm late,' said Jarvis. 'I had to make new arrangements.'

'About what?'

'About everything. The kidnappers contacted Innes early this morning and told him that the boy will not be handed over here in Chicago.'

'Then where?'

'Kansas City.'

'Why the change?' asked Kathleen.

'Maybe something spooked them at the stadium or maybe it's just a last minute change of venue to stop anyone planning a sophisticated double-cross. Now there won't be time. The exchange will be made tonight.'

'So we go to Kansas City?'

'It's no big deal,' said Jarvis. 'I've booked your flight and hotel. Here are your tickets.'

'How long will it take?' asked Kathleen.

'About an hour.'

'Do we all travel together?' asked Avedissian.

'I'm going first, you two travel later this afternoon. I'll contact you when you arrive.'

'Do you know where Innes is staying in Kansas City?' asked Kathleen.

'The kidnappers told him to check in at the Plaza Hotel. Our team plan to get there first. The room should be bugged by the time I get there. Why do you ask?'

'No reason,' replied Kathleen. 'Good luck.'

'The same to you. See you later.'

They watched Jarvis leave the park and hail a cab then Kathleen turned to Avedissian and said, 'Do you realise that by this time tomorrow it could all be over?'

'A nice thought,' replied Avedissian. On impulse he stopped at a flower seller and bought a single red rose to give to Kathleen. She smiled and said, 'Another nice thought.'

EIGHT

AVEDISSIAN LOOKED DOWN AT the great flat expanse of the mid-western United States and said to Kathleen, 'America's heartland.'

'Dorothy lived down there,' said Kathleen.

'Pardon?'

'*The Wizard of Oz*. Dorothy lived in Kansas.'

'Of course, how stupid of me,' replied Avedissian with mild sarcasm that made Kathleen smile. 'It was my favourite story when I was a child,' she said. 'An aunt gave the book to me one Christmas and it made a lasting impression.'

'With me it was "The Billy Goats Gruff",' said Avedissian.

'What an admission,' said Kathleen.

The sun was shining brightly when their plane swept into Kansas City International Airport but the weather did not feel as nice as it looked when they got down on the tarmac and felt the high humidity. Kathleen saw Avedissian run his finger round the inside of his collar and agreed. 'It's sticky,' she said.

Arriving as they had on an internal domestic flight they were through with airport procedure in a matter of moments and on their way into Kansas City by cab.

'You folks here for the convention?' asked the driver.

'Yes,' replied Avedissian, not sure of what he was agreeing to but feeling that it might be the safest answer.

'You both doctors?'

So it was a medical convention, thought Avedissian, how fortunate.

'Just me,' he replied.

'You guys have cost me a fortune over the years and I've still got my bad back,' complained the driver over his right shoulder.

'Backs can be a problem,' agreed Avedissian unhelpfully.

'That sign back there said "Missouri",' said Kathleen, changing the subject.

'Yes ma'am, Kansas City is half in Kansas, half in Missouri. Your hotel is in Missouri.'

The wail of a police car siren proclaimed their arrival in the city. An eruption of concrete into the sky confirmed it.

'Not many people about,' said Kathleen for the streets were practically deserted.

'Not many shops either,' said Avedissian.

'Folks moved out into the suburbs a long time ago,' said the driver. 'The shops went with them. Theatres, movie houses too. Nobody lives in town any more. Folks drive in in the morning and home again in the evening, no call for them to linger.'

Avedissian and Kathleen accepted the explanation in silence and found something depressing about the place. Kansas City looked as if some dreadful plague had destroyed all the inhabitants and left a series of towering concrete tombstones to their memory.

'Crown Center,' announced the driver, slowing and turning off the road along a drive lined with the flags of all nations. They hung limp and lifeless in the still, humid air.

Four miles to the south, in the Plaza Hotel, Innes and Roker waited for the kidnappers to contact them. Relations between them had been at a low ebb since the events at the stadium in Chicago. They were still arguing about it.

'We could have had the boy by now if you hadn't been so damned stupid!' said Innes.

'We had to try,' insisted Roker. 'It's our money! Don't forget it.'

'I'm hardly likely to. All you succeeded in doing was to let them know that we can't be trusted.'

'We don't know for sure that they knew we were going to try for the boy in the stadium,' said Roker.

'Of course they knew!' said Innes. 'They were watching us all the time. They must have been watching the zone round the empty seats too. They would have seen Shelby and these other two clowns as soon as they moved anywhere near!'

'We had to try,' repeated Roker.

'I just hope you've learned your lesson,' said Innes. 'Play it straight from now on or you'll blow the whole deal.'

'Don't lecture me, Innes!' said Roker angrily. 'If there's any more crap out of you I'm going to pull NORAID out of this whole damned thing! I never liked it from the start. In fact, if you ask me, that little bastard Kell is some kind of nut!'

Innes could see that he might have pushed the American too far. Whatever his personal feelings of frustration, he had to recognise that NORAID were the source of the money. Antagonising them was going to be counter-productive. In fact, if he personally wrecked Kell's plan by pushing Roker past the limit it was going to get him less than nowhere, it was going to get him dead.

The thought of Kell's wrath introduced an immediate note of conciliation to Innes's voice. 'I apologise,' he said quietly. 'We are all a bit edgy over this thing; it's so important to all of us. After all these years we're standing on the very verge of success and a free Ireland.'

Roker appeared to calm down too and they sat in silence ·
for a moment before the telephone rang. It was the
kidnappers.

'Do you have the first password?'

'One moment.' Innes turned to Roker and said, 'They
want the password.'

Roker took the phone and said, 'We didn't get a good look
at the boy.'

Innes bit his tongue. Roker was still playing the fool.

'You saw the child at the stadium,' said the voice calmly.

'He was too far away,' said Roker.

'You might have got a closer look if you hadn't planned to
double-cross us.'

Innes shot Roker a look that said, 'I told you so'.

'We'd still like to see him close up,' continued Roker.

'That will not be possible.'

'Supposing we refuse to pay?'

'Then we will sell the child back to the British. Make up
your mind. You've got ten seconds.'

Roker bit his lip and Innes held his breath. 'All right,' he
said. 'It's Account Number 4494552 in the bank you
specified. The inspection password is PARTHENON.'

'Thank you. We'll be in touch.'

The phone went dead and Innes breathed a sigh of relief.
'You really push your luck don't you,' he said to Roker.

'It was worth a try,' said Roker.

Ten minutes later the phone rang again and the same
voice as before said, 'Your deposit has been verified. We will
hand over the child to you this evening in exchange for the
second password.'

'What are the arrangements?'

'We will bring the child to you at the hotel at eleven
o'clock. Any attempt to double-cross us this time will result
in disaster.'

'How many people are permitted?'

'As many as you like,' said the voice. 'The boy will be carrying an explosive device, not large, just enough to blow his head off. When we have completed the transfer you will be told how to disarm it.'

'What's to stop you transferring the money and killing the boy anyway?' asked Roker.

'A dead child is of no use to either of us,' said the voice.

'Very well, we agree.'

'Until tonight then.'

Once more Innes let out the breath that he had been holding and said, 'You heard what he said about the explosives? For God's sake don't try anything.'

'I won't,' replied Roker with bad grace.

Jarvis arrived at the Crown Center Hotel at five-thirty and found Avedissian and Kathleen drinking coffee in their room.

'It's all set,' he said. 'The child is to be handed over tonight in the Plaza Hotel at eleven o'clock.'

'Then the team managed to bug Innes's room in time?' said Avedissian.

'It was perfect. Innes and a man called Roker, who seems to be handling NORAID's end of things, were contacted by the kidnappers this afternoon.'

Avedissian felt his stomach go light with excitement. 'So the team is all ready?' he asked.

'I don't know,' replied Jarvis looking worried.

'What do you mean?' asked Avedissian.

'I haven't been able to contact them.'

'Haven't been able to contact them?' repeated Kathleen in astonishment.

'I don't understand it either. The phone number I've been using has gone dead.'

'But everything depends on this,' insisted Avedissian. 'If the team aren't on the spot the IRA will get the boy!'

'You don't have to tell me that,' said Jarvis quietly and Avedissian backed off.

'Don't you have some other number? The London number? Can't you contact Bryant and tell him something's gone wrong?' he asked.

'I've tried. All the lines are dead.'

'The team were supposed to supply me with an emergency medical kit,' said Avedissian.

'We can only hope that you won't need it.'

There was absolute silence in the room for a few moments.

Avedissian looked at Jarvis and said quietly, 'You're the expert. What do you think has happened?'

Jarvis shook his head and said, 'Something major must have gone wrong. They must have had to change all the numbers. There's no other explanation.'

'Where does that leave us?' asked Kathleen.

'On our own,' said Jarvis. He looked at his watch and shrugged. 'Seven hours to go and we're on our own.'

'What can we do?' asked Kathleen.

'We can try to get the boy back on our own,' said Jarvis. Avedissian and Kathleen exchanged glances.

'Do you think that's really possible?' asked Avedissian.

'Let's count our blessings, shall we?' said Jarvis adopting a positive air. 'Innes's room is bugged and his phone is tapped. The receiver equipment is in my room at the Plaza and both systems are linked to a cassette recorder via a voice actuator.'

'A what?'

'A voice actuator. It just means that the recorder switches off again after thirty seconds of silence.'

'So you're not missing anything by being here?' said Avedissian.

'Precisely. If there are any more messages from the kidnappers or changes of plan they will be recorded for us, so our intelligence is good. It has been all along.'

150

'So what do you want us to do?'

I suggest we all go back to the room at the Plaza and wait for the exchange. We will hear everything that goes on in Innes's room so if we see an opportunity to rescue the boy after the exchange we can act on it. If not then we might be able to gather some information about what the IRA intend to do with the boy in the immediate future. It might be useful when we re-establish contact with Bryant.'

'Supposing we do see an opportunity to rescue the boy and we do it successfully. What then? How do we get away?' asked Avedissian.

'We are not completely without help in that direction,' replied Jarvis. 'Before I lost contact with the team I was told that two cars would be made available to us to get the boy away. I was just to call a local number and say where and when I wanted them.'

'And have you?'

'I've asked for one to be in the car park at the Plaza Hotel and the other to be left in the car park of the Rainbow Inn up on Rainbow Boulevard.'

'Why?'

'Just in case something stops us getting to the one in the Plaza. We shouldn't have all our eggs in one basket.'

'What's special about the Rainbow Inn?' asked Kathleen.

'It's next to the Medical Center, in case we have to go there in a real emergency.'

'You seem to think of everything,' said Avedissian.

'I had some prompting,' said Jarvis. He told them about the explosive device that the child would be carrying.

Avedissian screwed up his face and said, 'Do you think they're serious?'

'It's my guess they are. They couldn't afford to take a chance on being double-crossed.'

'Bastards,' said Avedissian.

'Clever bastards,' said Jarvis. 'But the boy should be in no danger just so long as the Irish play it straight.'

'This child may never be the same again when this is all over,' said Avedissian.

'What do you mean?'

'He's been through so much the scars may never leave him.'

'I never thought of that,' confessed Jarvis. 'I suppose all I've been thinking about is getting him back alive.'

'It's all we can do at the moment,' said Kathleen.

'So now we play it by ear,' said Avedissian.

Jarvis nodded and said, 'I think we should be getting back to the Plaza. Time's passing.'

There was very little to listen to on the recorder in Jarvis's room. The kidnappers had not been back in touch with Innes, and Roker had left shortly after hearing the details of the exchange. There had been a brief conversation between Innes and Roker about who would be present at the exchange. Roker had said that Shelby would definitely want to be present. Innes had asked why. 'To see what we have paid twenty-five million for,' Roker had replied. Innes agreed but asked that Roker keep the numbers to a minimum. As the tape went silent Jarvis switched off the machine and re-set it. 'Now we just wait,' he said.

Kathleen had been quiet for some time. She sat on one of the chairs, rubbing her forehead gently with the back of her right hand. 'Are you all right?' Avedissian asked her gently.

'Just a headache,' she replied.

'I'll nip down and get you some aspirins from reception,' said Avedissian.

'No, I'll go,' said Kathleen getting up. 'I could do with the walk. It's stuffy in here.' She got up and collected her handbag. 'Won't be long,' she said as she closed the door.

Avedissian watched Jarvis clean and check a gun and then fit a silencer to it. 'Please God you don't need that,' he said.

'Amen to that,' replied Jarvis.

They were both startled when the tape recorder suddenly switched itself on. 'Someone is phoning Innes,' said Jarvis, putting down the gun and picking up a headset. He placed it over his ears and sat concentrating on the floor while he listened. Kathleen returned while he was still monitoring the conversation and Avedissian put his finger to his lips when he saw her come into the room. A few moments later Jarvis took off the earphones and said, 'That was Roker. He and Shelby will be here in an hour. They've made arrangements to fly the boy out of the Downtown Airport in a private plane after the exchange.'

'The Downtown Airport?'

'Kansas City has two airports, the one you arrived at and a smaller one nearer the city. They plan to fly the boy west in a small aircraft and pick up a scheduled flight out of Los Angeles.'

Before either Kathleen or Avedissian had time to say anything a knock came at the door and all three froze. Jarvis got up quietly and hid the recording equipment out of sight then, picking up his gun, he walked over to the door and asked, 'Who is it?'

'Bellboy, sir,' came the reply.

'What do you want? I'm busy.'

'I have some keys, sir.'

Jarvis put the gun away and opened the door. He accepted a brown, Manila envelope and signed the paper that was held out to him. 'Just a moment,' he said and brought out some change from his pocket.

'Thank you, sir.'

Jarvis closed the door and said, 'The car keys. The cars are in place.' He examined the paper that had been in the

153

envelope and checked the numbers on the keys, then he put one set in his pocket and gave the other to Avedissian saying, 'You hang on to these. It's a white series "3" BMW with a blue triangle stuck in the windscreen.'

Avedissian put them in his pocket and said, 'Now you know where they're going after the exchange, are you going to make a rescue attempt?'

'We'll still have to play it by ear. We know what they plan to do but we don't know how many men are involved. That's the next big question.'

Innes checked his watch. Roker and Shelby would be arriving in thirty minutes. Providing these clowns didn't do anything stupid he was now only hours away from pulling off Kell's greatest coup. He checked his wallet to see that the contents were in order. Money, credit cards, plane ticket. He felt in the inside pocket of his jacket for his passport and found it. His travel bag sat on the floor beside the bed, already packed and waiting to be zipped.

He went to the bathroom and collected his toilet things, packing them into a brown leather case before adding it to his travel bag.

All that was left beside the basin was a slim plastic wallet which Innes now unrolled. From its pockets he removed a scalpel, tweezers, artery forceps, a syringe and a small glass bottle with an applicator. He left a series of needles, including two long hat pins, in their holder and gave a grunt of satisfaction. He had everything he needed. That just left the gun. He returned to the room and opened his brief-case to take out an automatic pistol. He removed the clip, checked it and reinserted it with a satisfying click, then screwed a silencer into the muzzle before looking along the barrel. 'Clumsy things,' he muttered under his breath.

Roker and Shelby arrived on time. Shelby, in particular, seemed excited for he was sweating profusely. Innes could see the wetness seeping through his jacket near the armpits. Innes invited them to sit but Shelby could not settle. He fidgeted constantly and finally got up to pace about the room. 'I can hardly believe it,' he murmured.

'Believe what?'

'That a child, a British royal child, is going to walk through that door in less than half an hour.'

'You'll believe it when it happens,' said Innes.

'This is a moment in history,' said Shelby. 'We are going to go down in history as the patriots who brought freedom to Ireland.'

'Providing nothing goes wrong,' said Roker.

'What's to go wrong?' asked Shelby. 'We're playing it straight from here on in.'

'Glad to hear it,' said Innes drily.

'Don't you have anything to drink?' Shelby asked.

'Afterwards,' said Innes.

Fragmentary conversation died away completely as the time grew near. There was silence in the room when a knock came to the door at three minutes past eleven. Innes, Roker and Shelby got to their feet before Innes said, 'Come in.'

The door opened and a little boy stood there accompanied by a man wearing a light raincoat. The man prompted the boy with a hand at his back and the child stepped unsurely into the room. The man followed and closed the door behind him. He waited with his back against it while Shelby moved towards the boy and stooped down to touch him almost reverently on the shoulder. 'Hello,' he said gently. The boy remained silent.

Shelby turned to the others and said, 'Hell, I don't know what to say to a royal boy. What *do* you say?'

'The boy has had a shock,' said the man at the door. 'He has temporarily lost his voice.'

'What the hell do you mean?' demanded Shelby.

'It's not uncommon and it won't last long,' said the man evenly.

Shelby ran his hands over the boy and was impressed that he did not shy away. He turned again and said with a half laugh, 'I'll say this for him. He's got dignity, yes sir, real class. Haven't you, little feller?'

The child did not flinch but continued to stare at Shelby.

Shelby stood up and turned to Roker and Innes. 'I suppose this *is* the right boy?' he asked with an embarrassed grin. 'It's crazy but it keeps occurring to me that none of us has ever seen him before . . . in the flesh, I mean . . . it's crazy when you think about it . . . pictures are OK but . . .' Shelby reached inside his jacket and pulled out a revolver. He levelled it at the man standing by the door and said triumphantly, 'I see you changed your mind about the explosive device. The boy is clean. I just frisked him.'

The stony expression on the face of the man at the door did not change. He shook his head slowly and said, 'There was no change of mind. The boy is wired.'

Shelby was embarrassed. 'What the hell do you mean?' he demanded weakly.

'May I?' asked the man, gesturing to the child.

'Go ahead.'

The man bared the left side of the boy's neck and pointed to a very recent scar. 'He has an implant.' He checked his watch. 'If I do not return within twenty-five minutes, you can scrape him off the wall.'

The sweat was pouring down Shelby's face. He dabbed at it angrily with a handkerchief. 'Well,'' he mumbled. 'You can't blame a guy for trying.'

The man said nothing.

'And if you are back within twenty-five minutes?' asked Roker.

'You will be called and asked for the password. The

device will not be triggered. When the money has been transferred you will be directed to a nearby clinic where the device will be removed.'

'What's to stop you just running off with the money?' demanded Shelby to the embarrassment of the others.

'As you've been told before. A dead child is no good to anyone. We like to keep our customers happy.'

'Just who is "we"?' asked Roker.

'That need not concern you,' replied the man. He looked at his watch. 'Time is running short.'

A knock came at the door. Innes acted immediately to calm the others. 'It's all right, take it easy,' he soothed. 'Who is it?' he called out.

'Your whiskey, Mr Innes,' said the voice.

'A little celebration,' smiled Innes. 'He's a bit early that's all. Come in!'

A waiter entered and put down a tray bearing a bottle of Irish whiskey and a number of glasses on the table while life stopped around him. 'Will that be all, sir?'

'Not quite, Reagan,' said Innes. 'The fat one is yours!'

The waiter took the silenced pistol that he had been holding under the tray and fired three times into Shelby. At the same time Innes fired twice at the man by the door and watched him slump to the ground.

'What the hell . . .?' exclaimed Roker, unable to believe his eyes. 'What in Christ's name did you do that for? Just what the hell do you think you are doing?'

Reagan took off his waiter's waistcoat and flung it in a corner before securing Roker to a chair while Innes held his gun on him.

'Fasten the boy too,' said Innes.

When both were tied firmly Innes put the barrel of his gun under Roker's nose. 'Now,' he said softly, 'I want that password.'

'You are mad,' stammered Roker, but he was afraid.

'The password!' Innes pushed the tip of the silencer so that Roker's face was forced up and to the left.

'Get lost,' said Roker.

'There's no time for heroics,' said Innes to Reagan. 'The brat is going to explode in fifteen minutes. Get the stuff from the bathroom.'

Reagan returned with the implements that Innes had prepared and Innes saw the fear in Roker's eyes. 'Now then,' said Innes, 'I've got acid for your eyes and needles for your nails. What's it to be?'

'You're crazy!' spluttered Roker, shrinking as far back as he could which was hardly any distance at all.

'Nails, I think,' said Innes, removing one of the needles from the wallet. 'Stick something in his mouth and hold him steady!' he said to Reagan.

Reagan looked about him and saw Shelby's handkerchief lying beside his body. He picked it up and forced it roughly into Roker's mouth then he held Roker's hand firmly on the arm of the chair while Innes inserted a needle under the nail of the index finger and pushed.

Roker's eyes rolled in agony. His skin paled and sweat ran down his forehead in a river.

'For Christ's sake, keep him conscious!' said Reagan.

'Don't tell me my job,' replied Innes, pushing the needle further under the nail.

Roker's head began to roll on his chest and Innes stopped. 'The gag!' he said to Reagan. 'Take it out.'

Reagan removed the handkerchief.

'The password!' demanded Innes in a whisper.

'All right . . . all right . . . it's . . . ARCHIMEDES . . . but . . .'

Innes smiled and said, 'That's all I wanted to know.' He pulled out one of the long hatpins from the wallet and searched for the right space between Roker's ribs. As Roker's eyes filled with horror at the realisation of what

Innes was about to do Innes pushed the pin through his heart.

Innes checked his watch and looked at the child. 'Ten minutes to go. We've got time to phone from here.' He picked up the room phone and dialled a series of numbers. 'This is Mr Innes, account number 6671081. I want to have some money transferred from account number 4494552.'

'That is a password tranfer,' said the voice. 'At the tone, give the password.'... BLEEP.

'ARCHIMEDES.'

There was a long pause. 'I'm sorry,' said the 'have a nice day' voice. 'The voice print is unacceptable to our computer.'

Innes felt the bottom drop out of his world. Paralysis threatened his throat. 'What do you mean?' he croaked.

'I'm sure there's some simple mistake, sir, but the computer is saying that the voice authorised to give that password . . . is not yours.'

'Sweet Jesus Christ,' said Reagan, who'd been listening at Innes's elbow. 'Now you've done it.'

Innes put down the phone as if in a dream and looked at the corpse of the man who had been authorised to give the password. 'A mistake, that's all,' he murmured, thinking of Kell. 'Just a simple mistake.'

'We'd better get out of here!' said Reagan, suddenly realising that time had been passing. As they left the room Reagan paused by the child and ruffled his hair. 'No hard feelings, son, eh? No hard feelings.'

Innes followed Reagan out the door but seemed totally preoccupied. 'Time to think,' he muttered . . . 'I need time to think.'

'Do something! For God's sake do something!'

'We can't. They'll kill the boy. We'll have to wait.'

Avedissian, Kathleen and Jarvis, who had had to listen to everything that had gone on in agonising impotence, sprang into life as they heard the IRA men leave. They raced along the hotel corridor and down the stairs to the room vacated by Innes and burst through the door.

The child was sitting in the centre of the room, his arms secured to the back of a chair. He stared silently at Avedissian who had entered first.

'Three minutes!' said Jarvis who had been keeping track of elapsed time since the kidnapper had spelled out the consequence of his failure to return. 'What can you do?' The tone of his voice reflected the despair that he felt.

Avedissian did not untie the boy for there was no time. He examined his neck on both sides and found the scar where the device had been implanted. 'Get out of here!' he snapped to Kathleen and Jarvis.

'But . . .' Jarvis started.

'Get out of here!' insisted Avedissian.

Both refused silently.

Avedissian saw the implements left lying by Innes and picked up a scalpel. He looked at the boy with pain in his eyes and said, 'I'm sorry. I'm going to have to do this. There's no other way. I hope one day you will understand . . .'

Kathleen came forward and cradled the boy's head in her arm so that his neck was exposed to Avedissian. The look on Avedissian's face told her of the agony he felt at not having any form of anaesthetic to offer the child. 'Do it,' she whispered. 'It's his only chance.'

'Two minutes!' said Jarvis.

Avedissian cut into the child's neck and blood welled up from the incision to flow down his chest and back. The child went rigid and started to shake in pain and terror but made no sound. Avedissian continued to cut through a haze of his own guilt and saw the implant come briefly into view before being obscured by blood again.

'Give me these forceps will you?' he asked Jarvis who had gone pale. Avedissian had to point to what he wanted from the floor.

'He's passed out,' said Kathleen.

'Thank God,' said Jarvis.

'I've got it!' said Avedissian.

'With one minute to go,' said Jarvis. 'Give it to me!'

Avedissian handed him the device, still in the jaws of the forceps, and Jarvis hurried over to the window. He stopped. 'Jesus!' he said, 'You can't open these windows. The air-conditioning!'

'The bathroom!' said Avedissian. 'Put it in the bath and shut the bathroom door!'

Jarvis took up the suggestion and slammed the bathroom door before throwing himself down on the floor to join the others. There was silence.

'Maybe they decided not to do it?' said Kathleen as the seconds ticked by.

Avedissian was busily trying to stem the flow of blood from the child's neck at floor level. Kathleen was still holding on to him, murmuring reassurance despite the fact that the child was unconscious.

'I don't think this thing is going to blow,' said Jarvis as the seconds became minutes. 'I'm going to take a look.'

'Be careful!' urged Kathleen.

'We can't just leave it there,' said Jarvis by way of explanation.

'How is he?' asked Kathleen, turning her attention back to the boy.

'All right at the moment,' replied Avedissian. 'The blood loss wasn't too bad but he may go into shock.'

Jarvis returned from the bathroom holding something in his hand. He tossed it a few inches into the air and caught it again. 'It's a button,' he said quietly. 'It's a silver button. Nothing more.' He sank down into a chair as his legs threatened to become too weak to support him.

Avedissian finished dressing the wound in the boy's neck as best he could then noticed that his own hands were shaking. He got up unsteadily and went to the bathroom to lean over the sink. His stomach turned over but he could not vomit. Instead his breathing became spasmodic and irregular as he re-lived the past thirty minutes. Kathleen came in and touched him gently on the shoulder. 'It's all over,' she murmured. 'You did the right thing.'

Jarvis opened the bottle of whiskey that Reagan had used to effect entry to the room and poured out three large measures. Avedissian gulped his own down and took comfort from the fire in his throat. 'Did you know?' he croaked accusingly at Jarvis.

'Know what?' asked Jarvis.

'That the child was not who Bryant said he was?'

'What?' exclaimed Jarvis with genuine surprise. 'What the hell do you mean?'

Avedissian looked at the boy and said, 'This boy is no royal child, he's a deaf mute.'

Jarvis and Kathleen stared wide-eyed at Avedissian. 'I don't understand,' said Kathleen. 'Of course he's the royal child. He's just lost his voice through shock. That's what the kidnapper said.'

Jarvis nodded his agreement. 'Take a look,' he said. 'See for yourself.'

'I've never met the boy or his family,' said Avedissian. 'Have you?'

'No,' admitted Jarvis. 'But I've seen photographs, TV reports, newsreels.'

'It's not enough,' said Avedissian. 'Many young children look the same when you know them superficially. You have to know them personally before particular characteristics become memorable. I'm a paediatrician, I know children. I know how they behave and I am telling you that this child has not suffered a temporary loss of speech. He has all the signs of being a deaf mute.'

'Are you saying that the kidnappers switched the child?' asked Kathleen.

Avedissian shook his head slowly and said, 'There are no kidnappers. There never were. It was a con. Bryant set it up.'

'But why?'

'Twenty-five million dollars?' suggested Avedissian.

'And the IRA?'

'Judging by what we heard, they must have known all along that it was a con. They played along for the money too. You must be able to do a lot of damage when you're given twenty-five million at the one time.'

'Especially if your name is Kell,' said Kathleen bitterly.

'So we are the only clowns in the circus?' said Jarvis.

'And him,' said Avedissian, looking at the child whom Kathleen was cuddling and keeping warm. 'Just look what the bastards have done to him.'

'Well, neither of them got the money in the end,' said Jarvis looking down at Roker's body. 'They killed him too soon.'

'What are we going to do?' asked Kathleen. 'We four seem to be the expendable ones in this game.'

'We'll have to get out of here!' said Jarvis. 'NORAID are going to start wondering why Roker, Shelby and the boy haven't turned up at the airport. In fact they're probably on their way here right now and, remember, they don't know that the boy was a trick! They don't know that it was the IRA who killed their men! They're going to think that the kidnappers tried some sort of double-cross and start hunting for them and the boy!'

'Maybe we should leave him,' said Kathleen quietly. 'He might be properly taken care of.'

163

'He might not be,' said Avedissian bitterly. 'It won't take long for them to discover that he's not who he's supposed to be and then what? How do they explain that away? Or maybe they don't. Maybe they just "rid" themselves of the problem.'

'What do you suggest?' asked Jarvis.

'We take him with us. We take him home and start finding out where the hell he came from in the first place.'

'How?'

'By asking Bryant,' said Avedissian through his teeth.

NINE

J ARVIS SEARCHED S HELBY'S BODY and removed his gun. He
gave it to Avedissian saying, 'You'd better have this.' He
then pulled the corpse away from the door and looked
around until he had found the room key. 'We'll lock it
behind us,' he said. 'That should give us a little extra time
before someone finds this mess.' He looked distastefully at
the needle protruding from under Roker's finger-nail then
said, 'Let's go.'

'The hotel has a side-entrance,' said Jarvis as they hurried
along the corridor. 'It'll be safer. Use the stairs,' he added as
Avedissian stopped at the elevators.

Avedissian, carrying the boy, who was still unconscious,
followed Jarvis through the swing-doors leading to the fire-
escape stairs while Kathleen held them open for him. They
met no one on the way down and Jarvis put away the gun
he had been holding ready in his hand.

The side-entrance to the hotel was used solely as a goods
entrance so there was no call for decor or furnishings in the
passages leading to it. Open pipework crowded the ceiling
and plain, white-washed walls lined their route. The hum of
ventilation machinery was loud in their ears but seemed to
do little to dispel the smell of food from the oppressively
warm air. The clangs of kitchen utensils and the sound of
voices were somewhere near but no one crossed their path.

As they came to the unimposing little side-door they

165

paused to catch their breath. Kathleen pulled the blanket back from the boy's face and looked at him. 'Poor little mite,' she said. 'How could they do it?'

The question had been rhetorical but it triggered off an idea in Avedissian's head. He suddenly bundled the boy into Kathleen's arms and said, 'I've got to go back! I won't be long.' He was gone before either Kathleen or Jarvis had had a chance to protest.

Avedissian climbed the stairs two at a time and was breathing hard by the time he reached Jarvis's floor and started running along the corridor. He tried the room door and found it locked; Jarvis still had the key. He drew back to the opposite side of the corridor and took a run at the door, crashing into it with his left shoulder. There was a splintering sound but the lock still held. It took two more attempts before the door flew back on its hinges and crashed open against the wall.

Avedissian could hear doors opening as people came out to investigate the commotion but there was no time to concern himself with that. He was only going to be a few seconds. He collected what he had come for and ran back along the corridor, brushing clumsily past a fat lady in dressing-gown and curlers who snorted her disapproval.

'What on earth did you go back for?' asked Kathleen when Avedissian re-appeared.

'The boy's future,' gasped Avedissian, still out of breath. 'Let's get out of here. I created a bit of a stir up there.'

Avedissian took the boy from Kathleen while Jarvis opened both inner and outer fly-screen doors. Jarvis looked out both ways before saying, 'It's all clear.'

They hurried towards an illuminated sign that told them where the exit from the underground garage was and stopped at the head of the ramp. Jarvis said, 'Wait here with the boy. I'll bring up the car.'

As they waited in quiet limbo, Avedissian looked up. The

air was still and warm and the sky laden with stars. A faint smell of blossom made him think of Cambridge in England. He was trying to recall the name of a piece of music coming faintly from an upper floor of the hotel when a sudden violent, but muffled, explosion rocked the building and shattered the peace of the night.

Black smoke billowed up from the garage and hung indecisively round the entrance like a great cloud in search of a breeze. Avedissian and Kathleen stared at the sight in disbelief, both unwilling to believe what they feared must have happened. But there was no escaping it: Jarvis must be dead. There had been a bomb in the car.

'What do we do?' asked Kathleen, her eyes filled with fear.

'We get away from here,' said Avedissian, unable to think beyond the moment.

They hurried along the lane and paused briefly to look back at the scene. The smoke was thinning. It drifted past the neon sign at the garage like a cloud across the moon. A group of people had now congregated at the head of the ramp and the sound of approaching sirens was becoming insistent.

As they watched, a long black saloon car entered the lane and three men got out. They seemed more interested in the sight of the man carrying the child at the far end of the lane than in what had happened in the garage below.

'They're NORAID!' said Avedissian. 'Let's move!'

'Where are we going?' gasped Kathleen as they raced down the side-street at the end of the lane.

'To find a cab!' answered Avedissian, his arms aching with the weight of the boy.

Kathleen risked a glance back and said in a voice courting panic, 'They're gaining!'

'Keep going!' urged Avedissian. He could see the lights of the main thoroughfare fifty metres ahead but knew that they were being rapidly caught. 'When we turn the corner, you take the boy!' he said.

They turned the corner and Avedissian bundled the boy over to Kathleen and said, 'Go and find a cab! I'll hold them off!'

Kathleen did as she was bid and Avedissian drew out the pistol that had been taken from the dead American. He waited with his cheek pressed up against the cold stone of the wall until he could hear the sound of running footsteps grow louder. For an instant he was back in Belfast, a long time ago. The fear in his stomach had a strange sexuality about it, danger, excitement, heightened awareness, a feeling only to be experienced on the very edge of disaster.

Holding the pistol in both hands and at arm's length, Avedissian stepped out smartly and dropped to one knee to fire at the approaching figures.

With the first bullet one of the running men pitched forward and fell to the ground. Avedissian heard a gun clatter from his grasp. The other man took panic in mid-flight and tried to stop too quickly. His arms and legs flailed in unsynchronised action as he sought cover from the totally unexpected. He loosed off a couple of wild shots in Avedissian's direction but was hopelessly off-balance. Avedissian held the gun on him and squeezed the trigger twice.

The street was silent. There were two bodies lying in it and no sign of the third man who had been in the black saloon.

Avedissian waited for a few moments, holding the gun in front of him, ready to fire at the slightest movement, but all was quiet. He put the gun away and hurried off to find Kathleen. He found her sitting in a yellow cab by the kerb, some two hundred metres from where he had left her. She was having a discussion with the driver about payment for waiting time.

'The Rainbow Inn,' said Avedissian, getting in the cab and putting an end to the conversation. Kathleen almost fainted with relief at the sight of him. 'Are you all right?' she whispered. Avedissian nodded in reply.

'You folks are English?' said the driver.

'We're visiting relations,' said Avedissian.

'And you are staying in the Rainbow Inn?' said the driver. 'Guess your relations ain't got much room.'

Avedissian silently cursed nosey cab drivers.

'Is the kid sick?' asked the driver.

'Just tired.'

'Well, it's late,' said the driver. 'Maybe too late for a little kid like that . . .'

'You know how it is, all the relations want to see him. It won't do him any harm.'

'Guess not.'

Avedissian was relieved to see the illuminated 'Rainbow Inn' sign come up on their right-hand side. 'Just drop us here,' he said to the driver.

'I can take you right into the parking lot.'

'This is fine.'

Avedissian gave the man the fare and a big tip and was glad to see the back of him. He looked around for inspiration and saw the sign of a fast food restaurant. 'In there,' he said to Kathleen. 'We have to talk.'

It was late and there was only a handful of people in the restaurant. They found a booth well away from the others and settled the boy in the corner. Avedissian checked the child's pulse surreptitiously and said, 'He's all right.' He bought coffee at the counter and returned to join Kathleen.

'We're in big trouble?' she said.

'I thought we might be able to check in at the Rainbow for the night but I've changed my mind. All NORAID have to do is ask the local taxi drivers about a couple with a child and they would find us. They're already going to find out about our "English" accents.'

'So what can we do?' asked Kathleen.

'I'll pick up the car from the car park and we'll drive somewhere.'

'What about the boy? Doesn't he need proper care at a hospital?'

'We can't risk it. We can't answer all the questions they would ask. They would call the police. I can look after him if I can get what I need.'

Avedissian left Kathleen and the boy in the restaurant and went to pick up their car. The parking lot seemed free of people when he got there but he stood for a few moments in the shadows to make sure. The fewer people who saw him the better. Satisfied that he was alone, he crossed quickly to the BMW and unlocked the door. The interior smelled of newness and leather. Outside, the lights of the Inn were reflected in the paintwork of the bonnet.

He inserted the ignition key and froze, sitting motionless for a moment, cold with fear as he recalled the pall of black smoke outside the Plaza Hotel. Surely the IRA could not have known about this car? he reasoned. It was conceivable that Innes had found out about Jarvis being at the same hotel but surely not about the other car he had parked at the Rainbow?

Avedissian could not turn the key. He let it go and pulled the bonnet release instead.

What was to be a reassuring look under the hood turned out to be the inspiration of a nightmare for there, strapped to the engine cover with bright yellow sticky tape, was a rectangular lump of something that looked like Plasticine.

The muscles in Avedissian's throat contracted and he held his breath as he traced the path of the two wires emanating from one end of the lump. One went to the ignition coil, the other to an earth point on the body. He saw the simple logic of it. If he had turned the key, power would have flowed from the battery to the coil and from the coil to the detonator in the plastic. He lowered the bonnet and walked away from the car.

Avedissian's mind reeled with the realisation that it had not been the IRA who had blown up Jarvis at all. It must have been Bryant's doing! It had been Bryant clearing up after a particularly dirty operation. No witnesses were to be left alive. He, Kathleen and the boy had been meant to die in whatever car they had chosen to use.

Avedissian heard the doors to the hotel open and, from the shadows, saw some men spill out onto the street.

'I could do with some fun,' said one of them loudly. 'These conventions bore me stiff.'

'Let's see what Kansas City has to offer,' said another. Both men had English accents.

'You're talking tomorrow, Miller,' said the first man. 'Better not get too well oiled. Still, if you're giving your usual gall stones talk it won't matter too much.'

'Bloody cheek!'

So that's who they were, thought Avedissian. Doctors here for the convention. Laughter broke out among them as one of the Americans in the party suggested what they might do for their night out.

'She picks it up with *what*?' exclaimed one of the party.

'As a gynaecologist I suppose I should display a professional interest!' said another.

'I'm a married man!' protested one of the Englishmen, provoking another round of laughter.

Avedissian thought of a risky idea, but he was desperate and if the hotel was full of out-of-town doctors it might work. The hotel seemed to be right next door to the medical centre – the chances were that it was a medical centre. He straightened his tie, brushed himself down briefly with his hands and walked in through the door of the Rainbow Inn, to find the lobby as crowded as he had hoped. He gave himself a few moments to acquaint himself with the geography of the place then approached the desk.

'How may I help you, sir?' said a middle-aged woman, with spectacles hanging round her neck from a heavy gold chain. Her smile looked as if it had been applied with her make-up.

'I'd like my room key,' said Avedissian sheepishly.

'The number, sir?'

'You're going to think this awfully silly,' said Avedissian with an embarrassed shrug and some emphasis on the Englishness of his speech, 'but the fact is . . . I've forgotten.'

The smile did not waver. 'Your name, sir?'

'Miller. Dr Miller,' replied Avedissian with an attempt at a smile. Please, God, Miller was not one of the delegates that she knew.

A scarlet nail traced a line down the room register and the woman said, 'You are in room 293, sir.' She handed him the key.

'Of course, how stupid of me,' exclaimed Avedissian. 'Thank you so much.'

'You are welcome.'

Avedissian headed for the stairs, half euphoric, half terrified that at any second the woman would call out behind him. His pulse continued to race as he let himself into room 293 and switched on the light. He found what he was looking for almost immediately: Miller's medical bag. It was under the dressing-table beside his suitcase, and a slim plastic document case that bore the logo of the convention. Avedissian opened the bag and examined the contents. 'God bless you, Miller,' he muttered. It contained everything that he needed.

The boy had come round when Avedissian got back to the restaurant. He was cuddling into Kathleen who was soothing him, but Avedissian saw him go rigid as he approached. There was terror in his eyes and Avedissian knew that he was the cause of it. He felt angry and impotent for there seemed to be no quick way to convince the child that he had done what he had done out of concern for his welfare. No child had ever looked at him like that before. It was something that he would remember.

'Where have you been? I thought something had

happened,' whispered Kathleen anxiously. 'Did you get the car?'

Avedissian told her why he had not got the car and saw her go pale. 'I don't understand,' she said. 'Why?'

'I suppose we were expendable, to use your word.'

Kathleen looked at the case that Avedissian had returned with.

'Medical. I borrowed it,' said Avedissian. He put his hand out gently to touch the boy's head but the child shrank from him and Kathleen had to reassure him again. 'I can't say I blame you, old son,' said Avedissian quietly.

'What do we do?' asked Kathleen with an air of hopelessness.

'We'll have to find somewhere for the night. I'll have to dress the boy's neck properly then we will have to make plans,' replied Avedissian. 'Let's get started.'

The boy, still terrified of Avedissian, would not come to him when he tried to take him from Kathleen. 'Just leave him,' said Kathleen.

'But he's too heavy,' said Avedissian.

'I can manage.'

Tension grew as they failed to find a cab until, in desperation, Avedissian said, 'There's a bus coming. We'll take it.'

The doors of the bus opened with a hydraulic hiss and they climbed on board. The driver was black; all the passengers were black. They regarded the three white interlopers with indifference.

'Kid's out late,' said the driver as Avedissian fumbled in his pocket for change. He ignored the comment and said, 'We want to go to the main bus depot.'

'Transfer at point four,' said the driver.

'Will you tell us?'

'Sure.'

The seats were hard, the lights were dim and there was an almost overpowering smell of diesel fuel. Overhead, advertising placards were interspersed with warnings spelling out the penalties for armed robbery. A notice near the driver declared that he personally carried no money; all fares were deposited automatically in a locked compartment to which he had no access.

The mention of money made Avedissian consider his own financial position. How much cash did he have? The answer did nothing to raise his spirits. But he did have a credit card.

They got off the bus and watched it draw away from the kerb.

'What was all that about the bus station?' asked Kathleen.

'A red herring,' replied Avedissian. 'Three white faces on an all-black bus. Just too easy to trace.'

They headed off in the opposite direction from the bus station and found the Blue Ranch Motel. It had seen better days, either that or it had always been seedy, but it had a 'Vacancies' sign above the entrance and all three of them were exhausted. The proprietor, attired in a vest that faithfully followed the rolls of flab about his middle, did not move as they entered but simply raised his eyes, giving the impression that their arrival was only going to be a very temporary interruption to his magazine reading. Avedissian could see that the lady on the cover was wearing a football helmet but little else.

'Number twelve, thirty dollars, pay in advance,' said the man, slapping down a key on the desk in front of him.

Avedissian paid and asked, 'Where do we find num . . .'

The man stabbed a forefinger to his right without looking up from the magazine.

'God, what a place,' sighed Avedissian when they had left the office and were making their way along the row of chalets. Kathleen could not argue. The smell of barbecue sauce, which seemed to pervade Kansas City, gave way to the scent of cheap perfume when they finally found number twelve and stepped inside.

They looked around, expecting the worst, but found it better than they had feared. Kathleen turned down one of the bed covers and looked at the linen. 'Good,' she said. 'I half expected to find it still warm.'

Avedissian drew the curtains and opened the medical case that he had taken from the Inn. He took out what he needed and laid it out in order on a bedside table. 'I want to look at the boy's neck,' he said quietly to Kathleen.

'It's not going to be easy,' she replied. 'But we'll try.' She smiled at the child and spoke to him all the time as she gently teased away the temporary dressing from his neck. At first he was uncertain but confidence started to grow in him. It lasted until it became clear that Avedissian was going to touch him again, then fear returned to his eyes and he drew close to Kathleen. She cuddled him and whispered yet more reassurance.

'It will have to be done,' whispered Avedissian.

Kathleen laid the boy gently back on the bed and took Avedissian's hand. She held it to her cheek in a gesture of trust for the child's benefit. The boy looked puzzled so she repeated the gesture, nodding as she did so.

It took some little time but the child eventually decided to give Avedissian another chance. He did not draw away when Avedissian made to examine his neck but his small body was rigid with uncertainty.

'Is it bad?' asked Kathleen.

'No,' replied Avedissian. 'The implant was just under the skin but I'll have to put in a couple of stitches to keep the edges together.'

'More pain?'

'A little, but nothing like last time.'

Kathleen held the boy while Avedissian did what he had to and then breathed a sigh of relief. 'It's done,' he said. He rubbed the child's hand and said, 'Well done. You were very brave.' The child stared at him blankly.

Avedissian took a bottle of red liquid from the table and poured some out on a spoon. 'This elixir will help him sleep,' he said to Kathleen. 'It tastes nice too.'

Kathleen encouraged the boy to accept it and was rewarded by a ghost of a smile. 'It's bed for you,' she whispered, giving the boy another hug.

When Kathleen had tucked the child safely into bed she returned to Avedissian. Now free of the need to play-act for the child's benefit, her face showed all the signs of the strain that she felt. 'What on earth are we going to do?' she asked.

'Our first priority is to get out of Kansas City,' replied Avedissian. 'We have to get away from NORAID. A couple with British accents and moving around with a child are not going to be too difficult to trace, and they must want us pretty badly.'

'If only they knew that the boy was not the royal child,' said Kathleen.

'Right now it wouldn't make that much difference,' said Avedissian. 'They think that we killed Roker and Shelby as well as the other two.'

Kathleen asked about 'the other two' and Avedissian told her what had happened during the chase. 'What a mess,' she sighed, nervously wringing her hands. 'It's all gone wrong.'

Avedissian found the comment strange but, at that moment, the boy moved in his sleep and Kathleen went to check on him. Avedissian watched while she settled him again. 'We'll try to make for Chicago,' he said. 'It has a big airport. Maybe we can slip through after a few days.'

'How do we get there? They'll be watching all the stations.'

'We'll have to get a car.'

'Hire one, you mean?' asked Kathleen.

'I've got a credit card.'

'Aren't we taking the same risk? A man with a British accent hiring a car?'

'We have to do something.'

176

'First thing in the morning?'

'Second. I have to go to the bank first.'

'The bank?' asked Kathleen in astonishment.

'I have to open an account,' said Avedissian.

'You're not making sense.'

'When I left you at the hotel for a few minutes, I went back to Jarvis's room and took the tapes from the recording machine.'

'Why?' asked Kathleen.

'Because somewhere on the tapes is the voice of Roker saying "Archimedes". That's what I meant when I said that I was securing the boy's future.'

It took a few moments for Kathleen to see the full implication of what Avedissian had said, but when it did dawn on her she exclaimed, 'Of course, that's brilliant! The password with the correct voice print! You can get the money!'

'I hope so,' said Avedissian. 'NORAID are not going to let the money lie in that account for ever but I think the deaths of both Roker and Shelby might slow them up with alternative arrangements. That and the fact that they must know by now that the money was not transferred after the exchange. They probably feel that there is no danger of anyone getting to it.'

'Sheer genius,' said Kathleen quietly but Avedissian got the impression that her thoughts were elsewhere.

'You know what?' she said.

'What?'

'I'm starving!'

Avedissian had to admit that he was hungry too. He could not remember when they had last eaten properly. 'I'll nip out and see what I can get,' he said, putting on his jacket. Before he left he removed the pistol from the pocket and handed it to Kathleen, asking if she knew how to use it. 'Lock the door behind me,' he said. 'If anyone insists on entering, shoot first, we'll discuss your options later.'

Avedissian was gone for about fifteen minutes. He returned with a selection of take-away food from a McDonald's restaurant to appreciative sounds from Kathleen. He could not help but notice the change in her mood in the past hour. For some reason she seemed to have been instilled with new hope.

'The coffee's a bit cold,' she said.

'I should have run faster,' said Avedissian quietly watching her.

Kathleen stopped eating and looked up. 'Oh, what a stupid thing to say!' she exclaimed. 'My mind was miles away. Forgive me?'

'You're forgiven.'

Kathleen came round to Avedissian's side of the table and sat down on his knee. She traced her finger-tips along his forehead and said softly, 'Whatever happens now, you are the most wonderful man I've ever known. It's the wrong time and the wrong place to say it but that is the plain unvarnished truth.' She kissed him lightly on the lips.

'We've not really had much say about times and places,' said Avedissian.

'No, but for what it's worth, I'm so glad I met you.'

'And I you.'

Kathleen crawled into bed beside the child in case he should wake up and panic during the night. Avedissian took the other bed and fell into a fitful sleep after savouring the quiet darkness for some minutes. His fear that he might not be able to sleep at all was overcome by sheer exhaustion. He had a great deal to think and worry about but his mind protested at any more anxiety in one day and insisted on rest. His sleep was, however, shallow and he woke at three a.m, puzzled by the sound of scratching.

The sound was not being made by an animal, he decided. It was too regular. Mice noises were intermittent. What was it?

Where was it coming from? Avedissian raised himself on one elbow to listen more intently. The noise changed to a gentle tapping. It was coming from somewhere near the door . . .

Silently Avedissian swung himself out of bed and found his jacket in the darkness. The gun was not in the pocket. He remembered that he had given it to Kathleen but he did not know where she had put it.

Another change in the noise and, all at once, Avedissian realised what it was. Someone had been etching the glass panel beside the door of the chalet with a glass cutter. The tapping had been to remove the etched area and allow access to the interior!

As the piece of glass was being removed Avedissian flung himself across the room, picking up the only weapon he could find on the way: the forceps he had used earlier when suturing the child's wound. A hand came through the opening beside the door to fumble for the lock, and Avedissian plunged the tips of the forceps into the back of it. He felt them go right through and heard the intruder grunt in pain before cursing him in an accent that he realised was not American.

Avedissian tried to capitalise on his advantage by letting go of the forceps to grip two fingers of the man's hand and pull them apart. His aim was to break one or other or both, knowing that the pain from such an injury might be sufficient to induce unconsciousness. He heard Kathleen at his back and shouted, 'The gun! For God's sake get the gun!'

As Avedissian struggled to get a better grip on the intruder's fingers the man suddenly smashed the remainder of the glass door panel with his other hand, sending a shower of glass into Avedissian's face and making him release his grip. The door was forced open and it hit Avedissian, who had been temporarily blinded by blood coming from the cuts on his forehead, and sent him reeling backwards across the room.

The door was closed and the lights went on. Avedissian managed to clear the blood from his eyes and opened them to see a thick-set man standing over him holding a gun pointing at his face. The man was sucking the wound in the back of his hand and staring at Avedissian with anger burning in his eyes.

Assuming him to be from NORAID Avedissian said, 'You don't understand! The boy isn't who you think he is! It was a trick!'

'Screw the brat,' rasped the man. 'Where are the tapes?'

Avedissian was stunned. From where he lay on the floor he stared at the man in blank astonishment. Again, the fact that the man did not have an American accent registered with Avedissian, but this time it meant more. The man did not have an American accent because he was Irish! 'Who the hell are you?' he asked.

'I'll not ask you again,' threatened the man. 'Where are the tapes?'

Avedissian's one hope lay in the fact that Kathleen was still in the bedroom and she had access to his gun. He knew that she must be listening and waiting for her chance. It was his job to stall as long as possible. 'What tapes?' he asked.

The man responded with a vicious kick at Avedissian's stomach which made him retch in agony. 'Don't give me that crap,' the man hissed. 'Kathleen! Get out here!'

Through his pain Avedissian heard the man call Kathleen by name and felt his anguish double. He saw Kathleen appear in the doorway and heard her say angrily to the man, 'I told you I would get them for you. Why did you have to come here?'

'Just get me the tapes!' rasped the man.

'I don't know where they are,' replied Kathleen. She came towards Avedissian and knelt down beside him, withering under the bitter accusation in his eyes. 'I'm sorry,' she whispered, 'more sorry than I can ever tell you, but you had better tell him where the tapes are.'

180

Avedissian looked at her long and hard then said with resignation, 'They're in the bedroom, in the cabinet by the bed.'

'Get them!' said the man to Kathleen and she got up.

As Kathleen left the room the man levelled his pistol at Avedissian and said, 'I win, you lose. I can't say it's been nice.'

Avedissian closed his eyes and waited for the end but it did not come. Instead he heard the full, flat sound of two silenced shots being fired. He opened his eyes to see the man slump to the floor in a motionless heap. Kathleen was standing in the doorway with the gun in her hand. She stared at the corpse.

'Who was he?' asked Avedissian quietly.

'His name was Reagan. He was one of Kell's men.'

Avedissian shook his head in confusion. 'But why?' he asked. 'Why did you do it?'

'I lied to you. My brother is not dead,' said Kathleen. 'Kell is holding him prisoner. Kell planted me on the British because he suspected that they were up to something. Originally I was just to confirm that a man called Bryant was involved in the child kidnap operation and find out anything else about it I could, but when Bryant himself saw that I could be useful in finding out even more about the IRA and NORAID, Kell instructed me to go along with it. I was to keep Reagan informed about Innes's progress and keep them in touch.'

'But the information you gave to Bryant was real,' said Avedissian. 'The INLA in Belfast were all but wiped out.'

'That was Kell's doing. He loathed the McGlynns. He saw his chance to set them up and convince Bryant at the same time that I was genuine.'

'How does Kell know Bryant?'

'Kell knows Bryant, Bryant knows Kell. That's the way things are at the top. They've probably never met each other but they know each other well enough. At that level it's like a big game. People's lives don't enter into it. The game is all important.'

'So Kell saw through Bryant's plan from the beginning?'

'More than that. He saw it as the perfect time to set up a scheme of his own.'

'To get the money, you mean?'

Kathleen shook her head. 'Not just that,' she said. 'Kell wanted Bryant to think that he had swallowed the royal child story for some other reason.'

'What reason?'

'I don't know, but the suggestion was that the operation might be even bigger than Bryant's.'

'You said that Kell was holding your brother?' said Avedissian.

Kathleen shrugged. 'Kell will kill him now,' she said. 'He was going to kill both of us until he saw how I could be useful. The bargain was that Kell would let Martin go if this operation was a success and he got the money. I thought the chance had gone until you told me about the tapes and I saw that I could still save Martin. I called Innes and Reagan when you were out getting the food and said that I would get the tapes if they would tell Kell not to harm my brother.'

'But Reagan decided to speed things up?'

'I foolishly told him where we were staying,' admitted Kathleen. 'And I nearly got you killed . . .' Tears came and Kathleen put her head against Avedissian's shoulder. 'Oh my darling,' she murmured.

Avedissian held her close, oblivious to the blood that was still running down his face from the cuts and said softly, '*Sshh*, you were the one who pointed out that you lived your life as a victim of circumstance. Let's say that this one was beyond your control.'

Kathleen looked affectionately at Avedissian then realised the mess that his face was in. She held it between the palms of her hands and said, 'I'll fetch a cloth.' She returned from the bathroom with a flannel soaked in cold water and began dabbing gently at Avedissian's cuts. 'They are not too bad when the blood has been cleared away,' she assured him.

'We'll have to get out of here,' said Avedissian.

'Can't we wait until morning?'

Avedissian shook his head. 'You said that there were two IRA men. We don't know where the other one is.'

'Innes, the Tally Man,' said Kathleen.

'He could be waiting nearby for Reagan to return, and when he doesn't . . .'

'I hadn't considered that,' said Kathleen. 'I had assumed that Reagan had come on his own.'

'Get the boy ready,' said Avedissian hauling himself to his feet. He picked up the gun that Kathleen had let fall to the floor and checked the clip. It was nearly empty. He picked up Reagan's gun and opted for that instead.

When they were ready to leave Avedissian switched out the chalet lights and opened the curtains a little to peer out. It seemed quiet enough but Avedissian was not convinced. He changed his mind about them all leaving together and told Kathleen to stay put with the child while he went out alone to take a look around.

Avedissian squeezed out of the smallest possible opening of the door and made for the nearest shadow in a crouching run. It was the area between their chalet and the neighbouring one. He paused for a moment before continuing along the row, looking for signs of life in the grounds of the motel. He found none and all the cars parked near the chalets seemed to be empty.

He was about to return to Kathleen to tell her that it was safe when he heard a car slow down on the road outside and turn into the grounds. He pressed himself back into the shadows to watch the new arrival pull up outside the front office. The driver got out and walked towards Reception. Avedissian's heart missed a beat for he recognised the man. It was the man he had seen at the stadium in Chicago. It was Innes! He had come to look for Reagan.

Avedissian was caught in two minds. His hand closed over

the butt of the pistol in his pocket. Should he kill Innes in cold blood when he re-emerged or should he return to Kathleen and the boy? He heard the sound of raised voices coming from inside Reception and moved to a position where he could see through the glass. Innes and the slob were arguing heatedly about something. The slob's wife joined him and Avedissian heard the word 'police' mentioned as the slob picked up the phone. He could see that Innes was still trying to reason with the man but with little success. There had been too many strange enquiries from people with foreign accents in the middle of the night and a bomb had gone off earlier at the Plaza Hotel.

Avedissian decided that he was not going to be given the chance to get Innes on his own and the thought of the police being called to the motel sent him scurrying back along the row. He paused outside each chalet to look through the windows of the car parked there. Then he saw what he wanted to see. One had been left with the keys in the ignition!

Avedissian climbed into the driving seat and turned the key. The engine turned noisily on the starter but did not fire. Sweat broke out on his forehead as he tried again, his foot stabbing at the accelerator, but still nothing. A face appeared at the chalet window but Avedissian was committed. He held his foot hard down on the pedal and tried again. The engine turned over with declining enthusiasm then fired with a roar of noise. At the same moment he saw Kathleen and the boy running towards him.

The car lurched forward and Avedissian leaned over to open the passenger door. Kathleen flung herself inside clutching the child to her. As Avedissian turned the car in a noisy and clumsy three-point turn he caught a glimpse of a man appearing at the chalet door; he was pulling on his trousers and yelling something after them.

They screeched out of the gate and Kathleen looked back to see Innes emerge from Reception. For a moment he was framed in the light from inside, then she saw him run to his car.

TEN

AVEDISSIAN HAD NO IDEA AT ALL where they were going, only that they were going there fast. He checked the dials on the facia and found the fuel gauge; it registered half full. That was the only one that mattered right now. His foot went down hard on the brake as they came to a large, green signboard and Kathleen had to slam her free hand against the dashboard to stop herself being flung forward. Her other hand held the boy.

'Fasten your belt,' said Avedissian.

'When I get a chance.'

Avedissian read the sign then wrenched the wheel over to the left and screeched off again down the slip road and out on to the inter-state highway.

'The speed limit is fifty-five,' said Kathleen as she saw the needle climb to eighty.

Avedissian, whose nerves were at fever pitch, wanted to snap angrily at Kathleen but saw that she was right. There was no point in attracting the attention of the Highway Patrol. He eased back on the pedal until their speed dropped to sixty and the tightness in his throat wore off. 'Can you see anyone behind us?' he asked.

Kathleen turned and looked. 'No, no one,' she replied.

They came to an interchange and slowed. 'If you were Innes what way would you guess at?' demanded Avedissian.

'East,' said Kathleen.

'I'd say west . . . so we'll choose neither.' Avedissian circled through the interchange and nosed the car out on to the north-bound carriageway.

'What's to the north?' asked Kathleen.

'Very little. We need breathing space.'

An hour had passed when Avedissian turned on the radio to break a silence that he was beginning to find oppressive. 'How is the boy?' he asked.

'Sleeping,' replied Kathleen.

The simple exchange of words served to lessen the tension in the car. Avedissian moved in his seat and altered the position that he had maintained rigidly for the past hour without realising it. Kathleen kneaded her fingers into the back of his neck and whispered, 'Is that better?'

'Much.'

'What do you think?' asked Kathleen, glancing behind.

Avedissian was reluctant to tempt fate but he replied, 'I think we're safe for the time being. I reckon we gave Innes the slip.'

Kathleen leaned forward and changed the radio station to something more soothing than the avant-garde jazz that was grating on her nerves.

'I've been thinking,' said Avedissian. 'If we can still get the money transferred, we can deal with Kell for your brother.'

'Do you mean it?' asked Kathleen.

'Assuming we get out of this alive, I don't see why not. But he's not getting it all. Some of it is for the boy.'

'Did I tell you that I love you?' said Kathleen.

'No,' replied Avedissian with a smile. 'You never did.'

'Well I do.'

'That could be a very mutual arrangement,' said Avedissian.

Another hour on the highway and Avedissian said, 'We need petrol.' He pulled off the freeway at the next service area and filled the tank. He was paying the cashier when he saw the reflection of a police car in the glass screen in front of him. He watched it crawl into the station like a cat stalking birds.

'There you go,' said the cashier handing him his change, unable to figure out what Avedissian was so intent on.

Avedissian took the money without diverting his eyes. He saw the patrol car creep past and park on the other side of the station outside a building marked 'Hank's Diner' in red neon. He pretended to count his change, but watched the two officers out of the corner of his eye as they got out of the car and stretched their limbs. They adjusted their caps and gun belts before walking towards the diner and opening the door. A blast of juke box sound escaped into the night before the door closed again behind them.

'Good-night,' said Avedissian to the cashier.

'Safe journey,' said the man with a puzzled look.

'I thought we were done for,' said Kathleen as Avedissian got back into the car.

'They couldn't have looked at the licence plate,' said Avedissian. 'I suppose cars get stolen all the time in Kansas City.'

'Thank God,' said Kathleen. They drove on.

Despite the sentiment Avedissian could not help but feel that they were pushing their luck to unreasonable limits. On impulse he decided to leave the freeway where they would be less likely to meet highway patrol cars. What they needed, he decided, was a place to lie low for a couple of days. Time enough for Innes and NORAID to lose the scent. Time enough for him to try for the transfer of the money.

'Do you know where we are?' asked Kathleen.

'Somewhere in Iowa.'

The night was ending. The comforting glow from the instrument panel, which had made it the centre of their world for the past few hours, was getting unfair competition from a huge sky.

187

'I've never seen anywhere so flat,' said Kathleen as she looked out at cornfields stretching to the horizon in all directions. Half an hour later the sun was up, bleaching the world yellow under a perfect hemisphere of blue.

Avedissian parked the car discreetly round the side of a diner near the outskirts of the city of Des Moines and Kathleen woke up the boy. 'Breakfast time, my prince,' she whispered in his ear. The boy awoke with a look of alarm on his face but it quickly disappeared at the sight of Kathleen although he reserved a more baleful look for Avedissian.

Kathleen took the boy to the toilet while Avedissian ordered food for them from a waitress who sucked the tip of her pencil before writing each item down on her pad. She read back the order and Avedissian nodded.

'We have washed our face and are feeling a lot better this morning,' said Kathleen, returning with the boy, who now seemed wide-awake and hungry. Avedissian smiled at both of them. 'Eat up,' he said. 'We'll all feel better.' He was right, they all did feel a great deal better with a large breakfast inside them.

'Are we going to stay in the city?' asked Kathleen.

'No, we'll skirt round it, I think. But I would like to go to the bank in the city. They must have a branch here and the sooner we do it the better. I want to go alone and I don't want to take the car into town in case we get spotted by some eager-beaver patrolman. That means we have to find somewhere for you and the boy to stay till I get back.'

'We could ask the waitress,' suggested Kathleen.

The waitress sucked her pencil while she thought and then said, 'Old Mrs Lehman, she runs a rooming house about two miles north of here. She can probably fix you up.'

'Sounds ideal,' said Kathleen, listening intently while the woman gave more detailed instructions on how to find the Lehman place.

Avedissian paid and gave the waitress a large tip for her

188

help. 'You're English aren't you?' she said as they went out the door. Avedissian wished that she hadn't.

They found the Lehman house without much trouble and Avedissian was pleased to find that it was well back from the road. The house itself was a wooden building, three storeys high and painted white, although it had been some time since the last painting and large areas were bare where the surface had flaked off. An old woman they took to be Mrs Lehman came out to meet them and Avedissian explained that they wanted a room for a couple of days to break their journey. They hated staying in the city.

'I feel the same myself,' said Mrs Lehman in a strong German accent. 'All that noise and fuss.'

They were shown to a bright, airy room on the first floor and were pleased with it. Avedissian paid in advance and brought in what little they had from the car. It consisted solely of what Kathleen had been able to grab with one hand when they left the motel in such a hurry, but they managed to disguise the fact from Mrs Lehman. Kathleen chatted to her downstairs while Avedissian pretended to carry up their 'luggage'.

'The boy doesn't say much,' said Mrs Lehman, noting that he seemed immune to all her attempts to make a fuss of him.

'He's very shy,' lied Kathleen. There was probably no need to be evasive but it had become a state of mind.

'We should be safe here,' said Avedissian when they were alone. Kathleen agreed as they looked out of the window to the waving fields of corn. It seemed unlikely that either NORAID or Innes could find them here. 'When will you go into the city?' she asked.

'I'll check on the bus situation with the old woman then go as soon as I can. If we can get it all done today we can lie low here for a couple of days then make for Chicago and a flight home.'

'Wherever that is,' said Kathleen ruefully.

Avedissian put his hands on her shoulders and said softly, 'We'll find somewhere and we'll be together. All right?'

Kathleen nodded and said, 'Go ask Mrs Lehman.'

'You have just missed one,' said the old woman when Avedissian asked about buses into the city. 'Next one is not for two hours. It stops at the end of the road.'

Avedissian thanked her and returned upstairs.

'Do you know what I'd like to do?' said Kathleen when Avedissian told her of the delay. 'Go for a walk. I feel as if I've been in prison for the last week.'

'We'll all go,' said Avedissian.

They walked along the dirt road leading from the house to a local farm, with the sun on their backs and a soft breeze drifting through the corn. The child, who had continued to cling to Kathleen at all times up till now, relaxed his grip on her hand for the first time and skipped a few paces ahead of them. Kathleen looked at Avedissian and smiled. 'I think he's getting over it,' she said.

'I'll get him some toys when I'm in the city this afternoon,' said Avedissian.

'What's going to happen to him in the long run?' asked Kathleen.

'It all depends on where he came from,' replied Avedissian.

'Where could he have come from?'

'My guess must be some kind of home or orphanage. I can't see any parents being duped into letting their child be used for something like this, can you?'

'I can't see any home or orphanage doing it either,' replied Kathleen.

'Sometimes the situation with children in care is a bureaucratic mess,' said Avedissian. 'The kids get bundled around from one branch of the social services to the next. If, as I suspect, the boy has no living relatives, he would be a real problem for them because of his handicap. Being a deaf-mute would not make him a good bet for adoption.'

'So you think that Bryant exploited some mix-up in the system?' asked Kathleen.

'Or created it,' said Avedissian bitterly.

'If it does turn out that he has no relations . . .' said Kathleen uncertainly.

Avedissian could see what was coming. 'Y–e–s?' he said with a smile.

'Do you think he could possibly . . . ?'·

'Why not?' said Avedissian. 'We're all in the same boat. Maybe we should stick together.'

Kathleen took Avedissian's arm and hugged it. Avedissian checked his watch and said, 'We'll have to start back.'

The bus was ten minutes late but Avedissian had been able to watch it coming for the last five minutes because of the dust cloud it had created in the distance. He climbed aboard and paid the driver, who asked him if he was staying at the Lehman place. Avedissian said that he was and the driver proceeded to tell him what a fine woman Rosa Lehman was and how she had two fine boys who had gone East to pursue careers in the professions. Lawyers, he thought, or maybe one of them was a doctor. He always did get mixed up between the Lehman boys and the Miller boys down in Twin Forks.

'Rosa's boys are both lawyers,' prompted one of the other three passengers on the bus. 'It's Johnny Miller who became the doctor.'

'Thank you, Martha,' said the driver without turning his head. 'You staying long?' he asked Avedissian.

'A couple of days.'

'You're English, aren't you?'

'Yes.'

'Don't get too many Englishmen in these parts,' said the driver. It had been a cue for Avedissian to say what he was doing there but Avedissian just looked out of the window and, to his relief, the driver did not pursue the matter.

The journey took forty minutes and Avedissian stepped out in the centre of Des Moines in the early afternoon. He asked the driver about a return bus and was given details of when and where he could pick one up. 'Have a nice day,' said the driver.

'You too,' said Avedissian.

He found the main branch of the bank he was looking for without much difficulty, for all the banks seemed to be clustered together in the heart of the city, and walked in through the impressively tall doors. It was cool inside the main banking hall, thanks to air-conditioning. It was just a question of approaching the correct window for his purpose. There seemed to be more than twenty and all were manned.

Seeing that he appeared indecisive, an armed guard approached Avedissian and asked if he could be of assistance. The words were polite but the face was stone.

'I want to open an account,' said Avedissian.

'Number fourteen, at the end,' said the guard, pointing with his finger.

'Thank you.'

'Welcome.'

As he walked across the floor to window fourteen Avedissian wondered if he were walking on real marble or whether it was just a very good imitation. The support columns in the hall appeared to be made of the same, endowing the place with an aura of Greek grandeur. A nation in search of a heritage, he thought, as he smiled at the lady in the window.

'How may I help you?'

'I'd like to open an account.'

'Checking?'

'No, deposit.'

The woman took a form from the collection to her left and started writing. 'How much would you like to deposit, sir?'

'What's the minimum?'

'A dollar.'

'A dollar,' said Avedissian.

The woman looked up briefly at him before exercising a professional control over her features and carrying on with the paperwork.

Avedissian said, 'Am I right in thinking that all details relating to this account will be kept confidential?'

'Yes sir . . . Your dollar is safe with us.'

Avedissian thought the teller was being impudent until he saw that she was pointing to the bank's logo. 'Do you have a branch in London?' he asked.

'London, England?'

'Yes.'

'I'll have to check.'

The woman went to confer with a colleague sitting at a computer terminal. Avedissian saw the colleague pick up a blue-covered book and flick through the pages before nodding and pointing to an entry.

'Yes sir, we do,' said the teller.

'Is it possible to have an account transferred between here and England?'

'I'll have to ask again.' She asked. 'Yes, sir, it's possible. When the time comes you just fill in the appropriate form and we will transfer the account.'

'I'd like to fill it in now,' said Avedissian.

'Now, sir? You want to transfer an account of one dollar?'

'I want to fill in the form just now. I don't want the account transferred till Friday. I'm expecting a large sum of money.'

The teller brought the appropriate form and Avedissian completed it. He handed it back saying,'Is there anything else I have to do?'

'No, sir, that's everything.' The teller handed Avedissian confirmation of his one dollar deposit and the all-important account number that he had come to get. 'Have a nice day.'

Avedissian stepped out into the sunshine and felt that

things were going his way. He paused at a news-stand and bought a paper before going to a nearby café and ordering coffee and doughnuts.

The story on page three destroyed his sense of well-being. His spine tingled as he looked at the photograph of the motel chalet where a man had been murdered. Police were looking for an English couple who had made their getaway in a stolen car. The description and licence number of the car were given. The worst news was that a gas station cashier had reported seeing an Englishman driving a car similar to the description a few hours after the murder. He had been heading north on the freeway.

Avedissian cursed his luck. NORAID, Innes, the police, they all knew now that he had headed north on leaving Kansas City. Avedissian read the story again and found some reassurance in the fact that there was no mention of the child. The slob at the motel had taken so little interest in them when they arrived that he had completely overlooked the fact that Kathleen had not been alone in the background. That made all the difference between a couple and a family. There was no description of either him or Kathleen in the story for the same reason, thought Avedissian.

The fact that the story was on page three also helped. Not everyone would see it. In fact a murder at a seedy motel in Kansas City might not have made the papers at all if it had not been for the fact of the car bomb explosion at the Plaza Hotel and the apparent murder of several other people. Police believed that the two events might be linked. The car bomb story itself had made page one. An Englishman had died and two Americans, and an unidentified man had been found murdered in one of the rooms. No theories as to reason or motive were offered.

Avedissian left the café and considered his position. He decided that they would have to leave the Lehman place sooner than they had intended for it was just conceivable that the waitress at the breakfast diner might be asked about an English couple and direct the enquirer to the house. They would have to find somewhere else. He checked his watch and saw that there would be a bus in fifteen minutes, and he still had things to do.

Avedissian sought out a large chain-store where he would be anonymous and bought a small Japanese cassette recorder then, remembering what he had said to Kathleen, he went to the toy department and bought a few things for the child before picking up some essential toilet articles and hurrying to catch the bus. This time he paid the driver and went straight to a seat at the back of the vehicle to discourage any questions or conversation.

Kathleen and the boy were playing together in the garden of the Lehman house when Avedissian got back. They both came to meet him when he appeared at the gate. For the first time Avedissian noticed that all trace of suspicion had disappeared from the boy's eyes when he looked at him. He was pleased.

'Did everything go all right?' asked Kathleen.

'I opened an account but we have another problem. They know we came north.'

'Who does?'

'Everyone.' Avedissian told her about the story in the paper. 'We'll have to move.'

Kathleen looked dejected. She said, 'Couldn't we stay here tonight? I don't think I could face another night like last night.'

Avedissian considered then agreed. It was against his better judgement but he wanted to stay too. He gave the boy the toys he had bought for him and saw him smile for the first time. It was a good moment.

As the boy played with a toy bulldozer Kathleen looked at him fondly and said to Avedissian, 'What are we going to call him?'

195

'He must already have a name,' replied Avedissian.

'But we don't know it. We'll have to call him something.'

'You choose,' said Avedissian.

'I already have,' said Kathleen. 'Harry.'

Avedissian smiled and said quietly, 'Why not . . . Our Harry.'

Avedissian left Kathleen and Harry in the garden while he went upstairs to their room. He got out the tapes that he had taken from Innes's room and plugged in the recorder to play them back. He searched through the first one, listening to snatches of conversation to establish where he was in the train of events. It brought back chilling memories.

He ascertained that the tape he was scanning had been for the room bug. The other cassette must hold the telephone monitor. He pressed the fast-forward button again then stopped it. He was listening to the torture sequence. 'The password!' demanded Innes's voice . . . 'All right . . . all right . . . it's ARCHIMEDES . . . but . . .'

Avedissian cued the tape backwards and lined it up to deliver the password alone. He removed the cassette and put in the other one to listen to the last telephone call made from the room. He wrote down the account number that Innes had asked for then changed over the tapes again.

There was no telephone in the room. He would have to ask Mrs Lehman if he could use hers.

'Of course,' said Rosa Lehman. 'It is a local call?'

Avedissian assured her that it was and she said that she would go speak to Kathleen outside until he had finished. 'Bless you,' said Avedissian. He looked at the framed photographs that the old woman kept on her dresser while he waited for the bank to answer. One man looked as if he might have been Rosa's husband. There were two of young men in college gowns. The lawyers, thought Avedissian. A woman's voice answered.

'This is Mr Avedissian, account number . . .' Avedissian

read from the paper in his hand, '5523408. I want to have the contents of account number 4494552 transferred into mine.'

'One moment, please.'

Avedissian's palms grew damp as he began to imagine the worst. A man's voice came on the line. 'How can I help you?' it said. Avedissian repeated his request and the man replied, 'This is an unusual request. I take it some arrangement has been made with the bank in this matter?'

'Yes,' said Avedissian with his heart in his mouth.

'Might I ask what arrangement?'

'A password transfer,' said Avedissian.

'I see . . . one moment, please.'

Avedissian now began to have visions of the bank stalling in order to trace the call. He considered putting down the receiver and putting an end to the tension that was becoming unbearable.

'We don't seem to have a record of any such arrangement,' said the voice.

'It was made with your branch in Kansas City,' said Avedissian, trying a last resort.

'Kansas City?' said the voice. 'You didn't say that. I assumed that this was a local arrangement.'

'No,' said Avedissian, walking a tightrope of nerves.

'One moment, please.'

Avedissian found the delay excruciating. The spectre of police cars already whining their way towards the Lehman place haunted him.

'Hello, caller?'

'I'm still here.'

'We have confirmed the arrangement with Kansas City and have a copy of the voice print. Are you ready?'

'Yes,' croaked Avedissian, for his mouth had gone dry. He fingered the recorder button in readiness.

'At the tone, give the password . . .' BLEEP.

Click . . . 'ARCHIMEDES.'

'Transfer is complete, caller. The money has been credited to your account.'

Avedissian put down the phone and felt weak at the knees. It had worked! It had actually worked! There was now twenty-five million dollars in the account he had just opened. He went outside but did not have to tell Kathleen for she read it in his face. She smiled.

They left the Lehman place after breakfast next morning after telling Rosa Lehman that they had had to change their plans and were heading south to St Louis, Missouri. She wished them well and waved to them from the gate as they drove off. They filled the car's tank at a local gas station and bought a route map at the same time, for it was Avedissian's intention to head north-west on country roads, the more remote the better. They had agreed that, whenever they had to stop for petrol or supplies, the child should be kept very much in evidence, thus promoting their image as a family on the move rather than an English couple who might provoke memories of the newspaper article.

The day grew hot and Harry began to get restless as they drove across seemingly endless deserts of corn. Occasionally they would see a farm vehicle in the distance or, more usually, a dust cloud thrown up by something moving along a far-off dirt road but, for the main, they were alone on the road.

'I think he's thirsty,' said Kathleen.

'Me too,' said Avedissian. 'We'll stop when we find some place.'

The vision of ice-cold Coke was snatched from them by the sound of tortured metal being turned against its will. Avedissian stopped the car and got out, fearing the worst. He was not disappointed. When he looked underneath the differential casing looked red-hot. Blue smoke was curling out from what Avedissian could see was a crack in the metal.

'The car is finished,' he said. 'We've lost all the oil from the rear axle. It's seized up.'

Kathleen and Harry got out to survey the useless heap of metal and stood in silence before it in the burning heat.

'Do you know where we are?' asked Kathleen quietly.

'Not really.'

'Maybe we can thumb a lift?'

'Maybe,' replied Avedissian but he was thinking of how little traffic they had come across on this route. That had been the whole idea. 'We can't just leave the car at the side of the road,' he said. 'The police will find it and identify it as the car from the motel. Innes and NORAID will be waiting for news of the car too. We could have them all down our necks.'

'What do you suggest?' asked Kathleen, looking at the cornfields. 'There's no place to hide it.'

'We'll get it off the road anyway. Anything that gives us a bit more time.'

Avedissian set the steering wheel and let off the brake. He put his back against the front grille and dug in his heels to get purchase before heaving. Sweat glistened on his face as the car edged slowly back. Kathleen and Harry helped by adding their weight to the wing until, with painful slowness, the rear wheels cleared the apron of the road and eased over the edge on to a slight downhill run.

'Heave!' groaned Avedissian, putting in a final effort to impart as much momentum to the car as possible. It rolled back about twenty feet into the corn and stopped for ever as far as they were concerned. 'Better than nothing,' said Avedissian, doing his best to disguise the path of the car's entry into the corn.

Half an hour passed without any vehicle coming along the road. The sun was now unbearably hot and thirst was becoming a fixation, then Avedissian had an idea. He got up from where they had been sitting at the edge of the road and said, 'Maybe we can drink the contents of the windscreen washer in the car.'

Kathleen watched as Avedissian waded through the corn to reach the car and released the hood to look for the screen wash bottle. He removed the cap and stuck in his fingers before putting them up to his mouth. 'Water!' he exclaimed. 'Plain water!'

The bottle was clamped to the wing valance with a metal band. Avedissian found an adjustable spanner in the back and released it. He brought the bottle over to Harry and Kathleen and they took turns at drinking. 'You're a genius,' gasped Kathleen after taking her turn.

'If I was I'd know how to get us out of this mess,' said Avedissian.

'Stop blaming yourself,' pleaded Kathleen. 'Somebody will be along soon. You'll see.

Avedissian smiled and Kathleen got up to look along the road. She put her hand to her eyes and stood on tip-toe saying, 'That just might be a dust cloud in the distance.' She was craning her neck as she spoke. She took a few steps forward without looking where she was putting her feet and tripped over a stone to go tumbling down the bank and into a shallow ditch. Avedissian sprang to his feet in alarm but Kathleen laughed and assured him that she was all right. She was sitting up in the ditch looking more embarrassed than injured.

'Out you come,' smiled Avedissian but the smile froze on his face as he saw something move in the dirt beside her. 'Look out!' he yelled but the warning came too late. The snake had sunk its fangs deep into Kathleen's leg and her scream rent the air. She rolled over in panic and Avedissian could see that the snake had not left her. It was preparing to bite again as he threw himself down the bank and struck out with the adjustable spanner that was still in his hand. The blow did not kill the snake outright but he managed to get a grip on it, holding it firmly behind the head so that it could not strike at him. He held it against a rock to bring down the spanner on its head and destroy it with all the fear and anger he felt behind the blow.

Kathleen was in a state of shock and trembling uncontrollably when Avedissian examined the wound. He did his best to clean it up with water from the screen bottle and encourage bleeding from the site of entry but knew that a great deal of the venom had got into her body. Harry was sitting on the edge of the ditch with terror in his eyes. Something terrible had happened to the lady who was kind to him. Kathleen caught sight of Harry and managed to control her fear and pain. 'It's all right,' she said, looking directly at him. 'Come!' She held out her hand and Harry came towards her uncertainly and took it. 'Just you sit there,' she said.

Kathleen turned to Avedissian and asked, 'Am I going to die?'

'I think it was some kind of viper,' said Avedissian. 'I don't think the bite will be fatal but you will have a lot of pain. We really have to get you to a doctor with anti-serum.'

'That sounded like the truth,' said Kathleen.

'It was,' said Avedissian. He got up and climbed up to the road to look along it in both directions. 'Please, God,' he murmured. 'Just one lousy car . . .'

ELEVEN

IT WAS TWENTY MINUTES before Avedissian's prayer was answered. At first he thought that his ears were deceiving him but the sound grew louder and louder until he could see the dusty farm truck coming towards them. He left Kathleen by the verge and stood in the middle of the road with his arms raised. The vehicle stopped and the driver, an elderly man wearing bib overalls, looked out of the cab. 'What's your problem?' he asked.

'My wife's been bitten by a snake.'

The man turned his engine off and got out to hurry over to Kathleen. 'We'd best get you to a doctor as soon as possible,' he said after offering sympathy. Avedissian and the farmer helped Kathleen into the cab then Avedissian lifted up Harry and got in himself. It was a tight squeeze and very hot inside.

They rattled along the flat ribbon of road in the heat and with the smell of manure from the heavily contaminated wheel arches in their nostrils. Kathleen seemed close to losing consciousness and Avedissian took her head on his shoulder to whisper encouragement.

'The boy doesn't look too well either,' said the farmer.

'He's thirsty,' said Avedissian. 'We've been out in the sun a long time.'

The man reached down behind his seat and brought out a bottle of lemonade. He handed it to Avedissian saying, 'Give him some.'

202

Avedissian held the bottle to Harry's lips and saw him drink with relish. The slaking of his thirst brought about an almost immediate improvement in his demeanour. Avedissian handed the bottle back.

'Maybe your wife would like some? You too?' asked the man.

Kathleen took some, then Avedissian. The lemonade was warm but, in the circumstances, it tasted better than anything Avedissian could ever remember.

'Looks like you folks have been having a bad time.'

'Our car broke down.'

'I didn't see it back there,' said the farmer.

'We walked a good bit, trying to find somewhere,' said Avedissian.

'That's easy to do in these parts,' said the man.

Avedissian could see that they were approaching a small cluster of houses. 'Where are we?' he asked.

'Alta Vista,' said the man.

Even with all that he had on his mind Avedissian saw the name as being incongruous. Alta Vista, High View, the ground seemed absolutely flat for as far as the eye could see.

They stopped at a clapboard house on the very edge of town and the driver got out and hurried up to the door, while Avedissian helped Kathleen out and made sure that Harry was with them. An elderly man came out from the house with the farmer. Avedissian waited at the gate until he reached them.

'Doc Feldman,' said the man. 'Let's get her inside.'

Avedissian stood by while Feldman examined the bite on Kathleen's calf. 'How long?' he asked.

Avedissian looked at his watch. 'Fifty minutes. Do you have anti-serum here?'

'Should do. Marty said it was a pit viper?'

'I couldn't argue,' said Avedissian. 'I wouldn't know one from another.'

'English?'

'Yes.'

Feldman brought out a tray from his fridge containing several small brown bottles and extracted one of them. He read the label, holding the bottle at nearly arm's length, and said, 'This is the stuff.' He filled a syringe and asked Kathleen if she was having much pain. The expression on her face gave him his answer. 'It's going to last for a while yet but this is going to improve matters,' he said and then injected the anti-serum.

Kathleen was settled in bed in a ground floor room, prepared by Feldman's housekeeper, and Avedissian said to Feldman, 'I can't thank you enough.'

'It's my job,' said Feldman. 'It has been for a long time.'

'How long?' asked Avedissian.

Feldman smiled and said, 'I came here forty years ago to escape from Boston. What brings you here?' he asked.

Avedissian gave him the story about being on their way to visit relatives when their car broke down.

'Is someone dealing with it?'

'No, not yet,' said Avedissian. 'The snake bite took precedence.'

'Of course,' said Feldman, looking intently at Avedissian. 'Would you like me to call Tyler's garage?'

'No!' said Avedissian, almost too quickly, for he had still to think of a good reason why not. 'It's finished,' he said. 'It's a rented car and it's just going to hold us up even more if we have to hang around for the recovery. I'll phone the car company and tell them where they can find it. They can make their own arrangements.'

'As you like,' said Feldman. He turned to look at Harry who was sitting on the floor outside the door where Kathleen was sleeping. 'Your son is very quiet,' he said.

'He is a deaf-mute,' said Avedissian.

'I thought so,' nodded Feldman. 'He's also very nervous.'

'It's been a harrowing day,' said Avedissian.

'I guess so;' said Feldman with a trace of uncertainty in his voice.

'Doctor, is there somewhere in town where we can stay until my wife is well enough to travel?' asked Avedissian.

'You can stay here,' replied Feldman. 'There's only me and Minnie, my housekeeper, all alone in this big house.'

'We couldn't presume, Doctor.'

'I'll be glad of the company.'

Deciding that the argument was over, Feldman got up and said that he would tell Minnie. Avedissian thanked him and, as Feldman went out, got up to have a look at something that had caught his attention when he had first come in. He was exmining it when Feldman returned. 'I haven't seen one of these for years,' he said, holding up an old laryngoscope.

'Are you a collector or a doctor?' asked Feldman.

'A doctor.'

'I see,' said the old man. 'Then we must talk. I don't often have the chance to meet my fellows.'

'What shall we talk about?'

'Why you have been lying ever since you set foot inside my house,' said Feldman matter-of-factly.

'I don't understand,' said Avedissian.

'I think you do,' said Feldman. 'I may be old but I'm not stupid. You have an English accent. Your "wife" has a different one and your "son" is as nervous as a stray dog. You say you are on your way to visit relatives but you are miles from the freeway, and if your relatives were local you would have said so. You abandon your car and presumably all your luggage, unless, of course, you never had any in the first place which is the more likely. You are not visiting relatives, "Doctor", or was that a lie too? You are running from something or somebody.'

Avedissian's shoulders dropped in resignation as he lost the will to argue. 'I am a doctor,' he said. 'That part was true.'

'And the rest?'

'You're right. We are on the run.'

'Perhaps you would care to talk about it?'

'I can't.'

'It's that serious?'

'I wouldn't know where to begin. What are you going to do?'

Feldman shook his head and said, 'I haven't made up my mind. The three of you make an unlikely gang. Where did you hope to get to?'

'Chicago,' said Avedissian.

'To leave the country?'

Avedissian nodded.

'We'll talk after dinner,' said Feldman. 'I need time to consider.'

Avedissian went in to check on Kathleen, and felt her forehead as she slept; she was warm but there was no sign of fever. All the indications were that the anti-serum had been given in time and that it was going to prevent the worst effects of the venom. In Avedissian's mind, Feldman had now become the bigger problem. If the old man should decide to call the police he would have to stop him or else it would be the end for all three of them. The vision of a life together would evaporate almost as quickly as it had arisen, a momentary mirage in a desert of loneliness.

But having to stop Feldman physically was the last thing he wanted to have to do. Apart from anything else, it would be best if Kathleen could stay here until it was certain that the anti-serum had been effective. If she were to get any worse during the night she might still have to go to hospital. Avedissian decided that, for the moment, their future lay in Feldman's hands.

Enforced idleness gave him time to think about the opposition. Both NORAID and Innes would have used the gas station on the freeway as their starting point after the story in the paper. It seemed reasonable to assume that they would have gone north at first until the trail had gone cold, and then retraced their steps, guessing at possible turn-offs. It was conceivable that one or the other had already traced their movements to the Lehman place. From there it would be back to guess-work. But the longer they stayed put in one place the more guesses the opposition would have. Every minute that ticked by could be bringing the enemy nearer.

Avedissian was about to close the bedroom door when he felt Harry tug at his trouser leg. The boy had spent the last hour being entertained in the kitchen by Minnie but had come through to check on things at intervals of never more than ten minutes. Avedissian picked him up and took him back into the room to look at Kathleen sleeping. The boy struggled slightly to be let down and Avedissian placed him back on the floor. He watched as Harry moved up slowly to the bed and touched Kathleen's hand gently. He turned to discover Avedissian's reaction and Avedissian smiled at him. 'You and me both,' he said quietly.

'How is she?' asked Feldman at his back.

'Sleeping peacefully,' said Avedissian.

Innes reflected on the day as he drove on through the gathering darkness. It had been well worthwhile having a talk to the cashier at the gas station. A bit of flattery and a ten-dollar bill and the jerk had remembered that the Englishman had seemed distracted on the night in question. It was not until the story had broken afterwards, said the man, that he had realised that it had been a police car coming into the station that had worried him.

To Innes this had been a gem of information, a golden nugget. If the Englishman had suffered a fright at the gas station the chances were that he would have left the freeway at the first available opportunity. He, Innes, would do the same. The jerk had also volunteered the information that 'a couple of other guys' had been asking about the Englishman that morning. They had wanted to know which direction he had gone off in. 'What did you tell them?' Innes had asked. 'North,' the man had replied.

Guessing at an average speed and knowing the time that the Englishman had left the gas station he had made an estimate of where he and the O'Neill woman would have been at around breakfast-time, assuming they had in fact left the freeway at the first turn-off. He had found the correct diner at the third attempt.

The waitress had been a bonus: not only had she known what direction the English folks had gone off in, she had known exactly where they had been going.

The Lehman woman had been a bit of a disappointment, however, with her story of St Louis, Missouri. There was just no way that the Englishman was going to head south through Kansas again in that car of his. The question was, which way would he be heading? A rough calculation of the mileage since the gas station on the freeway said that he must have been running low on fuel when he left the Lehman place. A local gas station perhaps?

The Englishman had been remembered at the second gas station he had asked at. He had bought a route map and was heading north. If he had bought a route map he must have been planning to travel long distances on country roads.

Innes slowed as he saw an obstruction ahead in the road. A break-down truck and a police patrol vehicle were blocking the way ahead. A patrolman stepped out in the road and waved him down. Innes opened the window and waited for the explanation.

'Won't keep you long,' said the policeman. 'We're just pulling a vehicle out of the field. Goddam joy-riders!'

Innes smiled and nodded. It was his policy to say as little as possible in an accent that would immediately mark him out as being different. Anonymity was to be courted at all times.

It was the reason he had been so successful over the years. No one ever remembered him.

He watched idly as the winch on the recovery truck hauled the car out of the field, then the smile faded from his face and his hands gripped the wheel tightly. This car had not been abandoned by joy-riders. He knew this car. He knew it very well. Perhaps its occupants were nearby . . . The patrolman waved him on.

Minnie put Harry to bed and then served dinner for Avedissian and Feldman. At any other time Avedissian would have enjoyed the meal, for the food was good and the company congenial, but the circumstances of his current predicament destroyed his appetite and weighed heavily on his mind. 'Have you decided?' he asked Feldman.

Feldman played briefly with his fork before saying, 'I'm not going to call the police. Whoever you three are, you seem to care about each other an awful lot so I just can't believe you've done anything too bad. When your wife is ready to travel I'll run you over to Ames and you can make your own arrangements from there.'

'Thanks,' said Avedissian. It came from the heart. His appetite returned and he ate what was in front of him with new relish. He did not even feel nervous when the phone rang.

Minnie came into the room and said, 'It's Marty, Doc.' Feldman left to take the call. Minnie cleared away Avedissian's plate and asked, 'How was it?'

'Best meal I've eaten in a long time,' replied Avedissian.

Minnie flushed with pleasure and said, 'Pity your wife wasn't well enough to enjoy it too.'

Feldman came back into the room. He waited until Minnie had gone out with the dishes before saying urgently, 'That was Marty, the man who brought you here. He said that the police have pulled a car out of a field a few miles down the road. They thought some kids had dumped it there after stealing it, but when they checked out the plates they found it had been taken from Kansas City by an English couple who are wanted for murder. They think that they must be in the area. Marty remembered that you were English. He rang to point that out. It is your car isn't it?'

Avedissian confirmed it.

'You killed someone?' asked Feldman as if unwilling to believe it himself.

'Only to stop him killing us,' replied Avedissian.

'Surely, if it was self-defence, you should give yourselves up and tell the police everything?' said Feldman.

Avedissian shook his head and said, 'Believe me. It isn't that simple. A whole lot of people want us dead. In some ways the police are the least of our worries.'

Feldman shrugged and said, 'The "least of your worries" could be here real soon.'

'We'll have to get out of here,' said Avedissian.

'If you must go, leave your wife and the boy.'

'They are in danger too,' said Avedissian. 'We'll all have to go.'

'How?'

Avedissian looked embarrassed. He said, 'I'm afraid I am going to have to ask for your car.'

Feldman shrugged in resignation and did not force Avedissian to elaborate on what he meant. He said, 'The keys are on the table by the door, I put gas in it this morning.'

'I'm sorry. I really am,' said Avedissian.

'I'll have Minnie get the boy ready,' said Feldman.

Avedissian woke Kathleen gently and found to his relief that she was not too sleepy from the medication. 'We'll have to go,' he whispered. 'Can you stand?'

Feldman and Minnie looked at the pathetic trio at the door and stood back to let them pass. 'I hope you know what you are doing,' said Feldman.

'I can assure you we don't have an alternative,' said Avedissian. 'Thanks for everything.'

As they walked down the path Feldman called after them, 'If it's any comfort, Minnie and I are going to bed now. We'll find the car gone . . . in the morning.'

Avedissian helped Kathleen into the back of Feldman's car and put Harry in beside her to cuddle up tight. He did not look back as they drove off.

Kathleen was lucid but felt tired. The snake bite and the subsequent anti-serum therapy had taken their toll in physical terms and the thought of yet another night of travelling on the run had brought her spirits to a low ebb. She had her arm round Harry but her head rested against the window and she gazed idly out at the night as they headed for the far edge of town.

Avedissian slowed as they came to a crossroads, and she idly took in the name of the bar on the corner, 'The Nitelite'. There was a man coming out of it. He was wearing a raincoat and looked, at once, strangely incongruous yet familiar. How ridiculous, she thought and then, as the man looked directly back at her, she screamed.

Avedissian was startled out of his wits and temporarily lost control of the wheel. 'What is it?' he demanded as he corrected the car.

'Innes! . . . It's Innes!' said Kathleen, verging on hysteria.

'Where? What are you talking about?'

'Coming out of the bar! It was him! I saw him!'

Avedissian found Kathleen's fear infectious. 'Did he see you?' he snapped.

'He looked right at me!' replied Kathleen.

Avedissian put his foot down and turned the headlights to full beam. 'Of all the rotten luck,' he muttered, swinging the wheel over to the right to recover a rear wheel drift. The road was narrow and winding and the car was wide and softly sprung. On corners it behaved like a three-legged cow in a sand pit. He cursed again as its rear end slid away from him and Kathleen and the boy were flung across the car once more. 'Can you see anything behind us?' he gasped.

Kathleen had to strain to turn her head, for the effort involved in just combating the erratic motion of the car and holding on to Harry had used up what little energy she had. The fact that she was desperately afraid had done nothing to help matters and now she felt exhausted and distinctly woozy. She looked out of the back window at the blackness. 'No, nothing,' she said. But, as she said it, she caught a momentary glimpse of a headlight beam somewhere behind them. She corrected herself and Avedissian pushed himself and the car even closer to their limit.

A wall loomed up at them out of the night and Avedissian hit the brakes and flung the wheel over in a last-ditch attempt to negotiate the bend. The front of the car refused to hold the line and they slid over the road and into the stonework. The impact crushed the near-side wing and deformed the wheel arch so that it was touching the tyre as he tried to drive on. A strong smell of burning rubber filled the car and Avedissian took his foot off the pedal. There was a bang as the tyre burst and the wheel started to run on its rim.

At the very last moment, as he was preparing to stop, he saw a farm track leading off to the left and swung the car off on to it. He limped up the track with all the lights off. The track terminated after thirty metres or so, outside a large barn. There seemed to be no other building near it. They were sitting in silence when they heard Innes's car roar past on the road.

'What do we do now?' asked Kathleen in a voice that suggested that she was barely in control of herself.

'Let's have a look at this place,' replied Avedissian. He still had the gun he had taken from Reagan so that put him on equal terms with Innes if it came down to that. It was

212

Kathleen and the boy who were the problem. If he could find somewhere for them to be safe, he would take his chances with the Tally Man.

There were two giant doors at the front of the barn and a smaller one at the side. Avedissian tried the small one and found it unlocked. He looked inside but could not see anything in the dark. 'Come inside,' he said to Kathleen. He closed the door behind them and felt on the wall for a light switch. The barn turned out to be a garage for heavy farm machinery. Two combine harvesters sat side by side like sleeping giants.

'Take Harry and get up into the cab of this one!' said Avedissian. He helped Kathleen mount the ladder and then pushed Harry up after her. 'Now keep well down!' he said. 'Whatever happens, keep down!' He returned to the small door and locked it from the inside. To get in, Innes would have to use the main doors, and that was exactly what he wanted. He memorised the position of the other harvester and then switched out the light to make his way to it in the blackness. He spoke to Kathleen as he felt his way up the ladder to the cab, trying to reassure her that things were going to be all right, but he got the feeling that he was fighting a losing battle. Kathleen sounded ill. She couldn't take much more.

Avedissian held the gun in readiness as he sat in the cab. When Innes opened the big doors in front of the harvesters he would be ready for him. He would be able to get a clear shot at him when he came through.

High above them the moon came out from behind some clouds. A pale shaft of moonlight came through a skylight on the barn roof and lit up the inside of the cabs with an eerie light. Avedissian looked at the instruments and pushed the gear-stick forward to give his knees more room.

'Are you all right?' he asked Kathleen.

'We're all right,' replied Kathleen but she sounded on the verge of exhaustion.

'Is Harry a problem?'

'We're holding each other,' said Kathleen.

'Hold on tight.'

Avedissian ran the palm of his hand over the large starter button that protruded from the panel in front of him. It was pleasingly round and smooth to the touch, then, somewhere in the distance, he could hear the sound of a car. He checked the gun again and said to Kathleen, 'It won't be long. Remember, keep down.'

Avedissian heard the car slow and knew that Innes had found the turn-off. He heard the car reverse a little and then heard the sound of its wheels on the gravel. The Tally Man had arrived.

'I think I'm going to faint . . ." said Kathleen weakly in the darkness.

'You mustn't!' hissed Avedissian. 'For God's sake, hold on!'

Avedissian heard Innes try the side door. It rattled loudly. Then he heard the sound of the main doors being unbarred and his pulse rate rose. One of the huge doors swung open and Avedissian watched its edge like a hawk. His eyes were accustomed to the darkness and it was lighter outside. The moment Innes emerged from the shelter of the door he would fire and keep firing.

Innes had pinned the door fully open against the outside wall. Avedissian kept his gun trained on the corner of the entrance that he must come round. He was concentrating so hard that he had all but stopped breathing when, to his left, he heard the sound of a sigh and then a thud and knew that Kathleen had passed out.

Innes had heard the sound too. His voice broke the silence. 'Let's stop playing games,' he said in a gentle but menacing Irish brogue. 'Just give me the tapes and we can all be on our way.'

It was a bargain that Avedissian would have been glad to make, even if the tapes had not been as useless as they now were, but one did not make bargains with people like Innes and live. He remained silent, still holding the gun trained on the edge of the doorway.

Suddenly he became aware of another noise to his left and, for a moment, he hoped it might be Kathleen coming round. But then, to his horror, he realised that it was Harry trying to climb down from the cab! Unable to hear or speak and left all alone with the unconscious Kathleen in the darkness the boy had been terrified and had left the cab to find someone.

Instinctively and uselessly, Avedissian shouted out a warning. A moment later he heard Harry lose his grip on the ladder and tumble to the ground and then had to watch in absolute agony as the child crawled away from the harvester towards the front door . . . and Innes. Innes grabbed him as he rounded the corner and it was all over. Avedissian put his hand to his head in anguish.

'I take it you would like the brat back alive?' asked Innes's voice from outside.

'Yes,' said Avedissian.

'Throw out the gun.'

Avedissian threw down the gun from the cab and Innes appeared, holding the child in front of his body. He switched on the barn lights and motioned with the gun in his hand that Avedissian should stand up. He then circled round cautiously to the other harvester and saw that Kathleen was slumped unconscious in the cab before returning his complete attention to Avedissian.

Avedissian could see the fear in Harry's eyes as he struggled in Innes's grasp but to no avail. 'The tapes!' said Innes.

'If I give you the tapes, will you let us go?'

'Just give me the tapes,' said Innes as if he were growing bored with the whole thing.

At that moment, Harry sank his teeth into Innes's hand. Innes cried out in pain and, raising the gun above his head, he brought it crashing down on the boy's skull with all the force he could muster.

Avedissian almost choked on the vomit that welled up in his throat for he knew that the child's skull could not possibly have

215

withstood such a blow. Sickness and anguish was replaced by anger. 'You bastard!' he almost screamed at Innes. 'You rotten bastard! May you rot in hell!'

Innes was breathing heavily. All trace of boredom had gone as he pointed the gun at Avedissian and snarled, 'Shut your trap and GIVE ME THE TAPES!'

Avedissian took the two cassettes from his pocket and made a last gambit for his life. He paused for a moment with the tapes in his hand.

'Down here!' snapped Innes.

Avedissian threw them so that they landed on the ground but inside the leading blade of the harvester. Then, as Innes reached out to retrieve them, Avedissian slammed his knee against the starter button in the cab and the machine, being in gear, lurched forward.

The great paddle wheel spun round and snatched Innes in by his arm. Such was the power of the harvester that the motor did not even notice the obstruction caused by a mere human body. It simply reduced Innes to a boneless pulp in seconds, spraying blood over the barn like sudden rain. Avedissian killed the engine and climbed down slowly from the cab.

Kathleen had come round but was disorientated. Avedissian caught her in his arms as she descended unsteadily from the harvester. 'Harry! Where's Harry?' she asked anxiously, then she saw the child lying in the doorway and, before Avedissian had had time to say anything, she broke free and went to him. She held him briefly before collapsing in tears. 'How could anyone? How could anyone?' she sobbed.

Avedissian put out the lights in the barn and tried to comfort her before saying softly, 'We have to go.'

'I don't want to leave him,' whispered Kathleen.

'We'll take him,' said Avedissian gently. He picked up Harry's body and carried him to Innes's car to lay him gently on the back seat. 'We're going to take this car,' he told Kathleen. 'It's not stolen.'

As they were about to leave, Avedissian had a sudden thought and got out of the car to fetch a jerry can of kerosene from the barn. He opened the doors of Feldman's car and doused the interior before laying a trail up to the barn doors and throwing the can inside. He moved Innes's car down the track a little before realising that he did not have any matches. He punched the car cigar-lighter into its socket and waited with mounting impatience until it had warmed up to red heat.

Avedissian threw the lighter at Feldman's car and saw it errupt in a burst of yellow fire, which raced up to the barn and started to engulf the building in a matter of seconds. He climbed in beside Kathleen and drove off.

'Why?' asked Kathleen.

'It's going to take the police a while to sort that mess out. They will identify the car and their immediate assumption will be that we died in the fire. Finding Innes's charred body will help to confirm that impression for they don't even know that he exists. By the time they work out that we're not there at all we should be out of the country.'

They drove through the night in silence, Avedissian concentrating on the road and Kathleen preoccupied with thoughts of Harry and of what might have been. As the first light of dawn streaked the sky in front of them Avedissian asked, 'Are you all right?'

Kathleen came out of her trance-like state and gripped Avedissian lightly on the arm. She said, 'Of course, but you must be exhausted.'

'I want to get as far away as possible,' said Avedissian. 'We'll drive all through the day then stay overnight before making for Chicago Airport tomorrow.'

'And Harry?' asked Kathleen softly.

'We'll find a place . . . a nice place.'

Avedissian took the car off the road just after they had passed through a copse of trees by a river and looked back. 'There?' he asked.

Kathleen saw the morning sun sparkle on the waters of the river as it moved sluggishly round a bend by the trees and said, 'Yes.'

Avedissian opened the boot of the car and found something to serve as a digging tool. He wrapped Harry's body in a rug that had lain on the back seat and carried him through the trees to put him gently down by the water's edge while he dug out a shallow grave.

Avedissian finished filling in the grave and stood up to watch Kathleen pick up a handful of earth and let it fall slowly through her fingers. Tears were running silently down her face.

'We'll have to go,' said Avedissian as gently as he could.

Kathleen nodded and turned away. Avedissian put his arm round her and they walked slowly back to the car.

They drove across Iowa into Illinois and on towards Chicago as they had planned and then, as night fell, they stopped in the town of Fenning and found a place to stay. There was a small-town pleasantness about Fenning that appealed to both of them as they strolled in the cool of the evening, ridding their limbs of the stiffness brought on by the marathon drive.

'Do you think there's still time to save Martin?' asked Kathleen.

'Of course,' said Avedissian, squeezing her arm. 'Innes was still trying for the tapes. Kell will be waiting to hear from him. He won't do anything until he's sure he has the money.'

People sat talking on verandahs or walked arm in arm down Main Street. Muted laughter drifted on the still air. Teenagers bunched on corners. 'It's another world,' said Kathleen.

'Not ours,' said Avedissian.

'Couldn't we make believe?' asked Kathleen.

'Why not?' smiled Avedissian. 'Just for tonight.'

218

They walked hand in hand down the street, pretending that that was what they did most evenings after dinner. 'How long have we been married?' asked Kathleen.

Avedissian thought then said, 'Twelve years. It's our anniversary next Wednesday.'

'Children?'

'Two. A boy and a girl.'

'Job?'

'I sell farm machinery.'

'What do I do?'

'You were a nurse in the local hospital until Janey came along.'

'Who's looking after Janey tonight?'

'Your mother. She comes round every Tuesday and Friday.'

'You're good at this game,' said Kathleen.

'We have to cut short our walk tonight.'

'Why?' asked Kathleen.

Avedissian stopped and turned towards her. He kissed her softly on the lips and said, 'Because I want to make love to you.'

The TWA Jumbo took its place in the queue to leave O'Hare Airport which, even at eight in the evening, was impressively long. The snake of predominantly Boeing aircraft, carrying the liveries of the world's airlines, crawled up to the head of the runway to take off in turn with what seemed like little more than seconds between them. As Avedissian felt the back of his seat begin to press into him he took Kathleen's hand and squeezed it. 'We made it,' he whispered. Kathleen nodded and closed her eyes. Silently, she said goodbye to Harry.

TWELVE

AVEDISSIAN TURNED HIS HEAD and saw that Kathleen was sleeping. The cabin lights had been dimmed and the whine of the engines had become for many a reassuring white sound in their subconscious. The slight moan from an auxiliary hydraulic motor made Avedissian look out of the window to see the trailing edge of the wing alter slightly as the captain made a course correction. There was a full moon on the port side. It caught the rivets along the top surface and created geometric shadows on the engine cowling. Avedissian closed his eyes and imagined what the moonlight must look like on the Atlantic seven miles below. He fell asleep.

Avedissian and Kathleen did not discuss a plan of action until they had cleared Heathrow and journeyed to Avedisian's flat by taxi. There was a greyness about London which at other times might have been depressing but after the heat of the Mid-West they found acceptable. On the way Avedissian noticed that the mere fact that it was not raining had encouraged quite a few women to pretend that it was still summer and reflect that attitude in their dress. He admired their spirit.

'How will you contact Kell when we get to Belfast?' he asked Kathleen.

'There are several pubs used by our people. I can get a message to him.'

Avedissian noted the phrase 'our people' and felt distanced

by it. He did not say anything but wished silently that Kathleen had not used it. They discussed where they would stay until the deal was made with Kell. Kathleen suggested that she had several relations whom she could trust but Avedissian argued, and Kathleen finally agreed with him, that they should trust no one. They would find an anonymous boarding-house.

'There is one thing,' said Avedissian. 'You know Kell. Do you think he will agree to a straight deal?'

Kathleen's face took on a pained expression and she replied, 'My heart prays that he will but my head tells me different. Nobody crosses Kell and gets away with it. Something tells me that even if he gets the money he won't rest until Martin and I are dead. For Kell it will be a matter of principle.'

'From what I've heard of him I was afraid that might be the case,' said Avedissian. 'So we're not going to let that happen.'

'What do you mean?'

'I mean we start taking care of our own future.'

'In what way?'

'Kell still thinks the tapes are the key to the money. We are going to exchange the tapes for your brother and then use the money to buy a new life for all of us.'

Kathleen's eyes opened wide in astonishment. 'You intend to double-cross Finbarr Kell?' she exclaimed in disbelief.

'You've just said that he intends to double-cross you.'

'But Kell! You don't know what you're saying!'

'He's a man.'

'You don't know him.'

'All I know is you can buy a lot of time and distance with twenty-five million dollars. What's the alternative? Running? Hiding? Watching our backs all the time? That's no life. It's time to stop being a victim of circumstance. It's time to fight for what you want.'

'It's crazy . . . crazy,' muttered Kathleen as she considered

221

what Avedissian was suggesting but, despite her fear of Kell, she could see that it made some kind of sense. If Kell intended to kill them even if he got the money, why give it to him in the first place? 'All right,' she agreed.

'I had to get rid of the gun before we got on the plane. I'm going to feel naked without one. Any ideas?' asked Avedissian.

Kathleen looked at Avedissian and wondered if he really appreciated what he was getting into. Few people in their right minds would ever dream of tangling with Kell, whatever the ordnance, and here was Avedissian wondering where he could get a gun. At that moment she loved him more than she thought possible. 'We can't risk buying one. Apart from that there's no time,' she said. 'But there might still be one in the cottage at Cladeen.' She told Avedissian of the cottage used by the IRA and where she and Martin had last been together. 'Martin had a gun in the dressing-table upstairs; he kept it as a second one in case of emergencies. If Kell's men did not search the place after we left and no one has used the house since then it will still be there.'

Avedissian asked how they would get there.

'We'd need a car.'

'We'll need one anyway. We'll rent one.'

'It would be best to go at night,' said Kathleen.

Avedissian looked at his watch and said, 'We can be in Belfast by this evening.'

'You need some proper rest,' said Kathleen.

'There's no time. But there will be when it's all over. How's the leg?'

'It's fine,' said Kathleen. 'Have I told you lately that I love you?'

'No,' smiled Avedissian.

'Well I do.'

Avedissian ran his fingers lightly through Kathleen's hair and said, 'I have to go out, arrange the tickets, go to the bank, get some odds and ends. Get some sleep. I'll be back soon.'

Avedissian picked up a newspaper on his way back to the flat and read it when he got in. It was strangely reassuring to find that the world seemed to be going on as normal. The more trivial the story the more Avedissian liked it and took refuge in its diversion. He did, however, find one article on Ireland and the Troubles. It reported that earlier fears of a new reign of terror in Belfast had been subsiding in recent weeks with an unofficial truce apparently having been declared by the IRA after the bombing of the Shamrock Shopping Centre. It was suggested that that particular outrage had been a one-off, a show of strength for the benefit of any doubters of the new régime and did not herald a new wave of violence.

Avedissian felt uneasy at the complacency of the article. He remembered what Kathleen had said about rumours of a Kell operation to outshine even Bryant's grandiose scheme. A chill ran through him when he thought of her assertion that no one crossed Kell and ever got away with it.

He turned the page and read of a TV star's addiction to heroin and moved on to a story about a cat being rescued from a church roof by the fire brigade. A brave pensioner's struggle with teenage muggers came next and then, as he prepared to skip over the children's section, he saw a photograph that caught his attention and paused. 'Another First for *Blue Peter*' read the story. Royal child to share his birthday celebrations with handicapped young people from all over the country. Avedissian looked at the child in the photograph and felt a desperate bitterness when he thought of Harry. The child in the photograph would never know what happened to his unwitting alter ego or why. But Bryant would, Avedissian promised himself.

It was raining when they got to Belfast and, for some reason,

Avedissian had known that it would be. The universal grey wetness was just as he had pictured it in his mind two nights before in Fenning. They picked up their hire car at the airport and headed for an area of the city liberally endowed with terraced boarding-houses. They picked one for no particular reason and booked in for the night. They would move to another next day using the same story. They were stopping off in Belfast for one night before driving south.

It was eight p.m. when they left for Cladeen, with Kathleen giving directions to Avedissian, who was having trouble enough with the rain proving too heavy for the wipers. Red brake-lights flared up ahead and were reflected many times over in the river of water on the screen. Avedissian slowed and saw that there was an army patrol up ahead. A soldier stood in the road, one hand resting on his shoulder-slung weapon and the other in the air to halt traffic.

It was an anxious moment for Avedissian who did not relish the prospect of an identity check but he was relieved to see that they were not the object of the army's interest. Traffic was being held up to allow a large military vehicle to reverse out from a lane. This over, the convoy continued.

Despite their agreement that the torrential rain could not last long, it did. It was still pouring down when they got to Cladeen and pulled into the little lane leading to the cottage. They were drenched within seconds of leaving the car and approaching the house on foot in case anyone should be staying there.

The cottage was in darkness and there was no sound from it save for the rain gurgling through the overloaded gutters. Kathleen signalled to Avedissian that he should follow her, as she led the way round to a back window near the ground. She tried it and it opened. Avedissian climbed in behind her and closed the window to stand, dripping water on the kitchen floor.

'This way,' said Kathleen. She led the way upstairs to the

bedroom and opened a drawer to withdraw an automatic pistol and hand it to Avedissian. He checked the clip and said, 'It's loaded.'

They came back downstairs and Kathleen paused to look at the living room. It was exactly as they had left it after that awful night. The lampshade still lay on the floor where it had been knocked off to expose the microphone. In her mind she could see her brother lying in agony on the floor while Kell's eyes burned with mad fury. The thought that she was getting ever closer to Kell made her desperately afraid. 'Let's go,' she said.

'Which pub are we heading for?' asked Avedissian as they reached the outskirts of Belfast.

'Try the Blind Horse in Lyndock Street,' said Kathleen.

'How do we get there?'

'Stop the car.'

Avedissian stopped and Kathleen took over the driving. They were there in ten minutes after weaving through Belfast's dockland. Avedissian did not like the look of the place. He would not have liked it had it been a bright summer's day but, near to closing time on a wet night, it made the dock taverns of East London look classy.

'What do I do?' asked Avedissian.

'Stay with me and keep your mouth shut, or that accent of yours could have you face down in the water.'

The inside of the pub was as dingy and run-down as the exterior and Avedissian found himself feeling relieved that they had got soaked in Cladeen. Their sagging clothes and matted hair brought them some kind of common denominator with the clientele.

Kathleen ordered and paid for the drinks. It made Avedissian feel uncomfortable but no one seemed to see anything unusual in it. They sat down on a bench seat and sipped Guinness. 'Do you see anyone?' Avedissian whispered.

'No.'

A few minutes later a small man in a dark, ill-fitting suit emerged from the gents' toilets. He had a cigarette in his mouth with nearly an inch of ash clinging to the end but still managed to cough without disturbing it. Avedissian felt Kathleen stiffen beside him. She whispered, 'That's Connell Murphy. He can get a message to Kell.' She got up and went to the bar, indicating with her hand that Avedissian should stay seated.

Avedissian watched Kathleen engage the man in conversation but was too far away to hear what was being said. He saw Murphy nod two or three times and then say something to the barman in response to something Kathleen had said. A whiskey was put down in front of him and Kathleen paid. The man downed it in one gulp and left the bar. Kathleen came back and sat down. She started to say something but had to pause for a loud bell that heralded closing time. Auxiliary shouts of 'Time' broke out before she could try again so they got up and left. 'I've asked him to tell Kell that I will be here tomorrow lunchtime,' said Kathleen as they returned to the car.

It was agreed that Kathleen would go alone to the Blind Horse to negotiate the exchange. Avedissian did not like the notion but conceded that it made sense. Kell could not risk harming her while he held the key to the money. But, even with that seemingly undeniable thought to comfort them, neither could sleep that night and morning came as a relief. The sound of milk and papers being delivered provided a welcome distraction from the fear inspired by thoughts of Kell. They spent the morning rehearsing what Kathleen should say in outlining conditions for the hand-over of the tapes. At eleven-thirty she left for the rendezvous.

Avedissian watched the progress of every minute on the clock. He calculated that Kathleen should be back by twelve-forty, having taken an agreed detour to ensure that she was not being followed. They would then move to another boarding-house and make final plans for their escape from Ireland, based on the information that Kathleen returned with.

Twelve-forty came and went as did one o'clock and one-fifteen, then there was a slight knock on the door. Avedissian snatched it open and found their landlady standing there. 'You did say that you were leaving today . . . Mr Farmer?'

'My apologies, Mrs Fagan. My wife had to go out and find a dentist this morning. She has terrible toothache. She should be back shortly and then we'll be on our way.'

'Just as long as I know, Mr Farmer . . . I really should be charging you for an extra day you know . . .'

Avedissian closed the door on the woman and checked the time again. Where was she? What had happened?

At one-forty-five the little tap came to the door again. Avedissian, his nerves strained to breaking point, cursed under his breath and took some money from his wallet to stuff into the woman's hand.

'Are you still there, Mr Farmer?' asked the voice, making Avedissian mutter again as he went to open the door. 'Here you are Mrs . . .' he had started to say when he saw the woman swept aside and the muzzle of a gun was whipped across his face. He staggered backwards and fell to the floor, an easy target for the boots that came thudding into him. He was dimly aware of being dragged out of the house and bundled into a car, but the lapses into unconsciousness were too frequent for him to plot any chain of events after that.

When he did come round he was lying on a stone floor in semi-darkness and had a raging thirst. He lay still for a moment, wondering whether or not he had any broken ribs but they seemed to be intact when he tried breathing a little deeper. He moved his jaw from side to side. It wasn't

227

broken. Gritting his teeth, he tried to get up, letting out an involuntary groan at the stiffness in his neck through lying in the one position for God knew how long.

A metal slit was hammered back in the door and eyes peered in. The slit closed and a few moments later bolts rattled and the door was flung open to allow a man holding a gun to enter. He motioned with the muzzle and said, 'Out, you bastard.' Avedissian was prodded and poked all the way along a corridor and then told to wait while another door was unlocked. He was thrown inside and the door closed behind him.

Avedissian was no longer alone. There were two other people in the room and one of them was Kathleen, her face stained with tears and racked with pain. 'Oh, my love,' he exclaimed in anguish as he crawled towards her, 'What have they done to you?'

Kell burned her till she told him where you were,' said the other person in the room, a thin, haggard-looking man with only one arm. 'I'm Kathleen's brother.'

Despite the poor lighting in the cellar Avedissian could see the marks left by cigarette burns on Kathleen's exposed breasts.

'I told them . . . I told them . . .' she murmured. 'I let you down . . ."

'Don't, don't say that,' whispered Avedissian. He was thinking of the length of time he had waited at the boarding-house and what Kathleen must have been going through. He closed his eyes and put his cheek against her hair. 'What happened?' he asked.

'They didn't even talk,' said Kathleen. 'As soon as I got to the Blind Horse Kell's men put me in a car and brought me here. All they wanted to know was where you were . . . and I told them.' More tears began to flow and Avedissian tried to comfort her.

The temperature in the room seemed to drop as a

persistent squeaking sound reached them. Avedissian looked at O'Neill and asked, 'Kell?' O'Neill nodded and the sound grew louder. Avedissian could feel Kathleen's body stiffen in fear.

The door opened and Nelligan, Kell's minder, manoeuvred the pram expertly inside. He turned it round on its back wheels alone so that Kell now faced the three of them. Nelligan stood behind like a rock with a gun.

'Well, well, well,' said Kell with syncopated precision. 'Isn't this nice.'

Avedissian felt a new kind of fear grow within him, for the monster in the pram seemed to radiate evil and malice. He found himself mesmerised by the huge eyes behind the glasses and the pale, hairless face.

'Now then,' said Kell with a smile that seared Avedissian like a soldering-iron. 'I want my money.'

'You would have got the tapes. What the hell did you have to do this for?' said Avedissian with much more bravery than he felt.

Kell fixed him with a long stare and said, 'I said money, not tapes.'

Avedissian stayed silent but felt his position crumble as Kell resumed his stare.

'When news of Miss O'Neill's generous offer reached me last night I thought it was about time to re-establish contact with our American friends and commiserate with them over a British trick that had fooled both of us. They told me that things were even worse than I thought. The British bastards had actually managed to get their hands on the money when they had thought it safe for the time being. But, of course, you and I both know that it wasn't the British who got the money, don't we . . . Doctor?'

Avedissian swallowed hard and said hoarsely, 'All right, Kell. I've got the money. Let us go and you can have it.'

The smile vanished from Kell's face and was replaced with

venomous anger. 'I can have it, can I?' he whispered. 'How kind.'

Avedissian was trying desperately to appear calm for he found Kell's anger almost tangible in the confines of the cell. He would never have believed that anyone could unnerve him so much.

'Where is it?' rasped Kell.

'It's in a bank,' said Avedissian.

'Then we must get it out of the bank,' said Kell with a wide-eyed stare.

'Like I said, you let us go and I'll give you the money,' said Avedissian.

Kell shook his head slowly and said, 'You just don't understand, do you? There is no bargain to be made. You will transfer the money unconditionally.'

'Do you think I'm mad, Kell?' snorted Avedissian.

'No, I think you're dead,' replied Kell with a chilling finality. 'You are all dead,' he added. 'The only question to be decided is how much pain you go through before I permit you to die."

'Then I've got nothing to lose by refusing to transfer the money,' said Avedissian with cold sweat running down his back.

'Tell me that when Nelligan is cutting bits off the O'Neill bitch and feeding them to the dogs,' said Kell.

'All right, Kell, you win,' whispered Avedissian.

'Of course I do, Doctor,' said Kell, the smile returning. 'In the end, I always do. But there's no hurry. Enjoy my hospitality until Nelligan and I get back from proving that fact to Bryant.'

'What do you mean?' asked O'Neill.

Kell adopted a patronising sneer and said softly, 'C'mon, Martin, you with your university education an' all.' He turned to Kathleen and said, 'And you too, school-teacher. Knowing what Bryant had set up for us, what would you say

230

would be the last thing on earth that he would expect us to be planning in the circumstances? . . . No? . . . All that education and no ideas?' The smile faded and Kell hissed, 'I'll show that bastard who's boss. I'll make him rue the day he ever crossed the path of Finbarr Kell.' He turned to Nelligan and said, 'We have work to do. It's going to be quite like old times, eh?'

Nelligan agreed, basking in the recognition of his master like a labrador dog. He wheeled Kell out of the room and the door was clanged shut. Those left in the room listened in silence until the squeaking of the pram wheels had faded away then Kathleen said, 'So we are all going to die.'

'We're not dead yet,' said Avedissian, but failed to convince even himself that they had a future. 'I wouldn't have believed it if I hadn't seen him for myself,' he added.

O'Neill knew what he was thinking and said, 'From what Kathleen tells me, Bryant isn't much better.'

'What did he mean by saying it was going to be like old times?' Avedissian asked.

'I'm not sure,' admitted O'Neill. 'But Kell and Nelligan used to work together in the old days before Kell was crippled.'

Kathleen was holding herself in pain and Avedissian suffered the agony of knowing that there was little he could do to help in the circumstances but try to comfort her verbally, something he could do with little conviction.

They were left alone with their thoughts and fears until their guard, a particularly sullen and uncommunicative individual, brought in some brown bread and a jug of water. He refused all requests for a first-aid kit or any kind of medication for Kathleen's burns. 'You get what I'm told to give you,' he snarled. 'Nothing else.'

Toilet arrangements in their cell comprised a single rusty can which, when combined with a total lack of ventilation in the cellar, ensured that their world stank by early evening when the guard changed. Avedissian knew that Kathleen's burns must soon become infected in the squalor.

Their new guard brought in tea and bread rolls. O'Neill knew the man: he was Liam Drummond, the driver who had taken him to and from Cladeen after the amputation of his arm, the man who had complained bitterly about Kell's earlier behaviour. O'Neill said, 'So you were right about Kell.'

The man's face filled with fear and he whispered hoarsely, 'For God's sake, Mr O'Neill, keep your voice down! I'm doing my job. I don't want no trouble.'

O'Neill could see how scared the man really was. He would have to proceed with great care if Drummond were to be of any use to them at all and it might be that he was their only chance. But Drummond still called him 'Mr'. How much influence did he have left with the man? 'My sister is hurt bad,' said O'Neill. 'Kell burned her. She needs medication. Can you get her some?'

'Be reasonable, Mr O'Neill,' pleaded Drummond. 'It's more than my life is worth to cross Kell. You know that.'

'Kathleen will die if the burns become infected,' said O'Neill. 'She's in terrible pain.'

'The plain truth, Mr O'Neill, is that you are all going to die when the Bairn gets back,' replied Drummond.

'Back from where?' asked O'Neill.

'England. He's gone operational.'

O'Neill looked incredulous but he could see that Drummond was serious and fought an immediate urge to ridicule the notion. 'On what operation?' he asked.

'I don't know, Mr O'Neill, honest to God I don't, but it's something big, something very big.'

'And Kell is doing it himself?'

'That's what they say. He and Nelligan are going to do it, just like they used to,' said Drummond.

'You said, "when Kell gets back". Does that mean he has already gone?'

'An hour ago.'

'Then you can get us some first-aid stuff and Kell will never know.'

Drummond looked uncertain.

O'Neill pushed a little harder. 'Go on, bring the boxes from the sick room.'

'I'll see what I can do.'

'And for Christ's sake, change this can, will you?' added O'Neill, nodding to their toilet.

Avedissian admired the way that O'Neill had handled the situation. The man obviously understood people and how to manage them; that implied a degree of sensitivity that he was relieved to find in O'Neill for he had had qualms about meeting the brother that Kathleen cared so much about. In view of O'Neill's past record he had feared that any kind of liking for O'Neill might be completely out of the question. Now he was not so sure and the strange thing was that there seemed to be something familiar about him, something he could not put his finger on.

Kathleen was now in too much pain to pretend otherwise and sat huddled in the corner holding herself, rocking backwards and forwards as if subconsciously trying to induce a trance to escape her agony. Avedissian and O'Neill had stopped trying to comfort her for their efforts seemed to be doing more harm than good and only upset her more. O'Neill came over to Avedissian by the door and whispered, 'If God would grant me one wish before I died it would be to take that evil little bastard's life.'

'You and me both,' said Avedissian.

O'Neill said quietly, 'I asked Drummond to bring the boxes from the sick room. They're not just first-aid boxes. They have all the stuff the doctor needs for when our boys get injured. Take whatever you think might be useful, pills and the like, in case the going should get too tough.'

Avedissian said that he would but did not want to dwell too long on the prospects of group suicide.

233

Drummond returned with the medicine boxes and he was sweating with fear. 'God, if Kell ever finds out,' he muttered.

'He won't,' O'Neill reassured him. 'Relax, man.'

Avedissian got to work sifting through the contents of the boxes and was aware of O'Neill getting to work on Drummond again; he was asking probing questions but disguising them effectively as concern.

'So who do you have to worry about with Kell gone? Who's left in the Long House anyway?'

'Just the Feeley brothers and me.'

'Just the four of you? Well, there you are then. Kell will never ever know. Where have all the rest gone anyway?'

'England. All other operations have stopped for this one.'

Avedissian gave Kathleen a pain-killing injection before cleaning her burns and applying antiseptic dressings. The injection took almost immediate effect and a slight overdose made her euphoric. She looked up at Drummond and said with what sounded like a drunken giggle, 'Enjoying the view?'

Drummond became embarrassed. 'Certainly not, Miss O'Neill,' he stammered, 'I'm just sorry that . . . well you know . . .' His voice trailed off.

'I appreciate your doing this, Liam,' said O'Neill.

Drummond became even more embarrassed and looked down at his feet before saying, 'You were always a gentleman, Mr O'Neill. The lads always had respect for you.'

O'Neill hit Drummond hard on the back of the neck and the man fell to the floor. O'Neill chopped him again to make sure.

Avedissian had seen it coming. 'What now?' he asked.

O'Neill searched the unconscious man with his one hand and then repeated the operation before saying, 'There's poetic justice for you. He trusted me so much that he didn't bring his gun with him this time. We've no gun and there's three of them between us and the door.'

234

'Where will they be?' asked Avedissian.

'In the duty room at the end of the passage. We have to pass it to get to the stairs.'

'Couldn't we sneak past?' asked Avedissian.

'Not a chance. The door at the head of the stairs has an electronic lock on it. It's controlled from inside the duty room.'

'What about guns?'

'The armoury is kept locked. The key is in the duty room.'

Avedissian looked at the medical boxes which seemed to be their only resource and asked after some thought, 'Do they drink tea?'

'I suppose so. Why?'

'Where do they make it?'

'In the duty room. They have a stove.'

'Pity,' said Avedissian.

O'Neill suddenly realised what Avedissian had been considering and added, 'But they have to get the water from the room across the way.'

'Then there's a chance,' said Avedissian. 'If I can get this lot . . .' he held up a bottle of pills '. . . into their tea, we can put them out for a week.'

O'Neill filled Avedissian in on the details of the room layout in the passage and of the inside of the room where the men would get water. He wanted to know exactly where the sink was and where the kettle would be, for he would not be able to turn on the light.

'It should be OK,' said O'Neill. 'People don't usually have to turn the light on in that room anyway when they fill the kettle. There's enough light from the corridor.'

Avedissian crushed up the number of pills he thought would be necessary to achieve the desired effect and poured the powder into an empty pill box for the time being. 'I hope to God they all take milk and sugar,' he said as he prepared to move out into the corridor. He checked on Kathleen and saw that she was sleeping comfortably before listening at the door prior to opening it. The corridor outside seemed quiet.

'Good luck,' said O'Neill.

Avedissian thought the corridor was never ending as he tiptoed along it, scarcely daring to breathe. He was convinced that, at any second, someone would come out from the duty room at the end and start shooting. He passed the halfway mark and could now see the room that he was making for. He kept his eyes fixed on it as he steeled himself for the final few metres. He was inside it.

As O'Neill had predicted, there was enough light from the corridor to see things inside the room but he was uncomfortable with the fact that the door was wide open and gave it a little push. It made a noise like a giant redwood about to fall. Avedissian froze in fear but, after a few seconds, he could hear that the muted sound of voices coming from the duty room had not changed. He exhaled slowly and left the door as it was.

The kettle was on the shelf above the sink where O'Neill had said it would be. Avedissian took it down slowly and carefully, avoiding any action that could give rise to noise, and poured the contents of the pill box into it. He swirled the powder around in the little water that lay in the bottom and put the kettle back on the shelf with pained slowness.

Avedissian turned to leave the room but stopped when he heard the level of sound from across the corridor increase suddenly. Someone was coming out and he would be trapped! He stepped quickly back into the shadow behind the room door and prayed. If someone came in and switched on the light he was a dead man.

A short, broad man with a bull neck came into the room, still engaged in conversation with those across the corridor. He did not touch the light switch but took the kettle down from the shelf and filled it under the tap. He was so close to Avedissian that Avedissian thought he must smell his fear but the man appeared to notice nothing amiss. He rattled the lid on to the kettle at the second attempt and left the room.

Avedissian remained motionless for a few moments, still partially paralysed by nightmare thoughts of how close he had come to dying but the fact that he had apparently got away with it filtered through to him and restored his courage. He ventured out into the corridor again and returned to O'Neill and Kathleen.

O'Neill greeted him with an anxious look.

'It's done,' said Avedissian. 'Now we wait.'

'How long?'

Avedissian tried to guess how long it would take for the kettle to boil, how long it would take the man to make and drink the tea, assuming they drank it at all for there was a chance that they would be put off by the taste, and how long it would take for the drugs to act. He said, 'Better give them thirty minutes to be on the safe side.' He suddenly had an awful thought. He looked down at the man on the floor and said, 'Won't they miss him?'

As if in answer to Avedissian's question, the door at the end of the passage opened and a voice called out, 'Liam! Tea's ready!'

Avedissian and O'Neill were turned to stone. They waited for the door to close again but it did not. Someone was waiting for an answer! O'Neill stood up and faced the opposite direction from the source of the shout. He called out, 'Just comin'' and then stopped breathing as he waited for a reaction. The door at the end of the passage closed.

Avidissian examined Kathleen. She was still sleeping peacefully and mercifully free of pain after her ordeal thanks to the analgesics. He lifted one of her eyelids and saw that she was not too deeply sedated for her to be brought round when they had to leave. She groaned and moved her face away in response to him touching her eyes. Avedissian looked at Drummond lying on the floor and said, 'I think I'll give him a shot to make sure he stays out for the next few hours.' He gave the unconscious man an injection.

O'Neill said, 'I think it's time. Shall we risk it?'

Avedissian felt his stomach go into knots again but he nodded and said, 'Let's check it out.'

They left Kathleen in the cell, while they crept along the passage towards the duty room, their hopes increasing with the fact that they could hear no sound at all coming from within. O'Neill found it difficult to put his faith in the power of drugs so it was Avedissian who finally put his hand on the handle of the duty room door and turned it slowly open.

Two men lay slumped over the table, a third lay on the floor where he had fallen off his seat. O'Neill unlocked the door to the head of the stairs but still continued to rummage around. Avedissian asked him what he was doing.

'I'm looking for some clue to what the little bastard is up to,' replied O'Neill. 'He could still start a civil war.'

Avedissian helped O'Neill in the search but when, after five minutes, they had drawn a blank he suggested that they stop.

'Let's try Kell's room,' said O'Neill. He looked down at the unconscious men and said, 'I take it they will be out for some time?'

'A long time,' replied Avedissian.

'Look at this,' said O'Neill, handing Avedissian a piece of paper. It was a photocopy of a map. Ordnance Survey, thought Avedissian, and said so to O'Neill.. He had recognised the style but not the area. There was a circle round a village called Valham. 'Mean anything?' asked O'Neill.

'Nothing, but let's take it.'

O'Neill asked Avedissian to help him put back the medical boxes in the sick room and drag the unconscious Drummond along to join the others. 'I don't want him getting all the blame for this,' he said. Avedissian liked the gesture. This done, they brought Kathleen round and helped her along the passage and up the stairs.

They were out in the Belfast night. The streets were wet but it had stopped raining and the air had never smelled so good to them. For Avedissian, at least, the smell of freedom became a reality.

There was no real decision to be made. Their first objective had to be to get out of the country, for Ireland was no longer a place for any of them. Avedissian suggested that they should make for his flat in London. Any new plans could be made from there. It was agreed.

Avedissian's worry that the O'Neills might have trouble with heightened security on the Ireland-England routes proved to be unfounded. There had been no IRA action for some time and memories are short even with the best of intentions. They made the crossing unhindered.

THIRTEEN

IT WAS NOT UNTIL A LONDON TAXI DRIVER gave them a
second look that Avedissian realised how dirty and dishevelled they must seem. Up until then, their thoughts had
been solely concerned with escape so it was only now, in the
depths of London traffic, that they could relax a little and
consider that they had really done it. They had escaped from
the clutches of Finbarr Kell.

Avedissian looked at Kathleen as they waited at traffic
lights and saw the pain lines round her eyes. She had not
complained at all since leaving Belfast but he knew that the
effects of the pain-killer he had given her must have worn off
some hours ago. He asked her gently if it was bad. She smiled
at him and said that she was all right, he was not to worry.

They drank whisky when they got into Avedissian's flat
while they waited for an immersion heater to provide hot
water. No one said anything about it only being eleven in the
morning. For the moment time was unimportant; they
needed a drink.

Avedissian let the O'Neills bathe first while he scavenged
through the kitchen cupboards and found whatever tinned
food there was to prepare a passable meal, then he dressed
Kathleen's burns before cleaning himself up and settling
down to eat.

'God, I feel better,' said O'Neill and they all agreed. O'Neill
was all right in the clothes that Avedissian had given him but

Kathleen looked like a waif from the storm in a shirt that swamped her and jeans bunched up into pleats at the waist.

Their anxiety had subsided, they had cleaned up and they had eaten. It was time to talk about what they were going to do next. All were agreed that everything had to take second place to finding out what Kell was up to and stopping him if at all possible. At the moment the best they could do would be to warn the authorities that a big IRA operation was under way in England.

'What's the way to do that?' asked Avedissian.

'We could warn them by phone,' said Kathleen.

'Would they believe us? Wouldn't they ask for some kind of identification?'

'More than that, they would want to know what the operation involved and who and what were at risk,' said O'Neill.

'And we couldn't tell them because we don't know,' added Avedissian.

'But if Martin told them who he was they might take the warning seriously,' suggested Kathleen.

'Martin O'Neill is dead as far as the authorities are concerned,' said Avedissian. 'The call would be dismissed as a hoax.'

They considered for a moment before Avedissian said, 'There is one person who would believe that we were telling the truth.'

'Who?'

'Bryant.'

Kathleen looked down at the table and fidgeted nervously. 'I couldn't bear to face that man again,' she said in a whisper.

Avedissian put a hand on her shoulder and said quietly, 'I feel the same. I've got a score to settle with that rat, but we must think rationally. Bryant has the resources to stop Kell.'

'How would you get to Bryant?' asked O'Neill.

'I've had cause to think about that a lot,' replied Avedissian. 'Officially I have no way of reaching him but unofficially I think I can do it.'

'Go on,' said O'Neill.

'When I was taken to see Bryant in London I had to wait in a room that looked out into a lane. It was night-time and there was a neon sign on the building opposite. It said Staplex Bindings. If I can get their address from the phone book I think I can find the building that Bryant uses.'

'That's worth a try,' said O'Neill.

Kathleen, unable to comtemplate the prospect of becoming involved with Bryant again, stayed silent.

Avedissian looked up the phone book and said, 'I've got it.'

'Do you want us to go too?' asked O'Neill.

Avedissian shook his head and said, 'It's best if I go alone. There's no time to lose. You and Kathleen can get to work on that map we took from Kell's room. Find out where that village is and what is special about it.'

'We'll get some clothes too,' said O'Neill.

'Be careful,' said Kathleen as Avedissian prepared to leave. He kissed her and told her there was no need to worry. He would be back soon.

Avedissian took a taxi to the Staplex works. It was a journey of about fifteen minutes but would have been shorter had it not been for heavy traffic. He crossed the road and walked past the building until he came to the entrance to the lane he remembered. He looked at the neon sign above the goods entrance and then at the building opposite. It seemed dark and featureless, just another anonymous building, but there, on the third floor, was a window with a large plant in it. It was the room where he had been asked to wait on the night he had been brought from the training school at Llangern.

Avedissian walked up one side of the lane and came back on the other, casually looking at the doors leading into the

242

building. All were securely locked. But maybe that was all to the good, he thought. His best plan would be to wait for Bryant either to enter or leave the building. That way the element of surprise would remain with him. If he were to go in blind he would be playing a game where he was an amateur among professionals.

Avedissian grew tired of waiting. It had been over three hours and still no one had entered or left. He began to have visions of the building being empty. Perhaps it was only used on odd occasions, not on a regular basis at all. He had almost convinced himself that this was the case when at five-thirty, the front door opened and a woman came out. He recognised her. It was Sarah Milek, the secretary he had first met at Cambridge.

Sarah Milek walked down the lane and turned left, with Avedissian some thirty metres behind. She turned left again into another narrow lane and approached a line of lock-up garages before pausing to search in her handbag for the key to one of the doors. Avedissian waited until she had opened it and was lifting up the door before running up behind her and hustling her inside. He clamped his hand over her mouth to stifle her scream and whispered in her ear. 'Don't panic, Miss Milek. It's an old friend. Remember me?' He took his hand away.

'You!' gasped Sarah Milek.

'Surprised? Could that be because I'm supposed to be dead, I wonder?'

'I'm glad you're not.'

'Of course you are. Where's Bryant?' snapped Avedissian.

'I see,' said Sarah Milek, 'You've come for your revenge.'

'That was my original intention,' agreed Avedissian. 'But circumstances have dictated that I need Bryant's help.'

'Help?' said an astonished Sarah Milek.

'The IRA have been planning a big operation here in England. It's going to happen any day now and Kell's people are already here. It's Kell's way of paying Bryant back for trying to trick him.'

'But there hasn't been time for Kell to mount anything big,' protested Sarah Milek.

'You're wrong,' said Avedissian. 'Kell knew all along that there had been no royal kidnap. He started working on his own scheme right back at the beginning and just kept stringing Bryant along.'

'But he tried to raise money from bank raids.'

'Wrong again. Kell planted Kathleen O'Neill on Bryant and used her to settle an old score with the INLA and convince Bryant that she was genuine at the same time. Her brother hadn't been killed by Kell at all. He's still alive. He's here with me in London. That's how I know about Kell's plans.'

'And Kathleen O'Neill?'

'She's here too.'

'What happened to the boy?' asked Sarah Milek tentatively.

'He's dead. I buried him in a field in Illinois.'

'I'm sorry . . . I know you can't believe that, but I am. It was the most horrible plan.'

'So why didn't you stop it?' demanded Avedissian.

'It was Bryant's doing – him and his bitter hatred of the Irish.'

'Why?'

'He thinks that being so long in the Irish section has destroyed his career. He believes that successive governments have refused to tackle the IRA head-on as he would like. He has always believed that the fight should have been taken to the enemy. Fight fire with fire, that sort of thing, but every scheme he has come up with over the years has been turned down as being either too aggressive or too politically sensitive. He has always taken the rejection of his plans personally; he has become paranoid about the "Public School Mafia" as he calls them. Sometimes I think he hates our side as much as he does the opposition.'

'And his latest scheme?'

'He saw a photograph in a newspaper of a handicapped child whose parents had been killed in a car crash and noticed that the boy bore a superficial resemblance to one of the royal children. It gave him an idea for an operation that he thought would prove to the powers that be that he should be running the section instead of playing number two.'

'Why did nobody stop him?'

'This time Bryant was clever. He sold the idea to Sir Michael as purely a confidence trick to destroy NORAID and undermine IRA morale. There was no mention of ever using a real child, but he maintained that, for the scheme to have a chance of success, everyone would have to act and behave as if the kidnap had really happened, and Sir Michael agreed.'

'Why didn't it stay that way?'

'Bryant was obsessed with the operation. He saw this as his one big chance to show how good he was.'

'So he planned his own version all along?'

Sarah Milek nodded. 'He also diverted funds from within the section to employ some dubious operatives of his own.'

'And the boy?'

'The child was still in temporary accommodation after the crash while the social services decided what to do with him. Bryant came up with transfer forms for a children's home at the other end of the country, on the grounds that some distant relation of the boy had been located and adoption might be a possibility. The local authorities were only too happy to see their problem solved.'

'But surely Sir Michael must have suspected something was going on while Bryant was doing all this?' Avedissian protested.

'He did, but at the wrong moment his past caught up with him.'

'What do you mean?'

'One of Bryant's people came up with something on Sir

Michael himself, a series of indiscretions involving young boys. Bryant virtually took over the operation and the section from then on. Sir Michael became little more than a figurehead. Bryant ran the show.'

'That's why the old man committed suicide,' said Avedissian, remembering the story in the papers.

'He couldn't bear the shame,' said Sarah Milek.

'But Bryant's scheme failed,' said Avedissian.

'It's true that he didn't get the money, but the INLA was wiped out in Belfast and Bryant got the credit for that. He also set up the ambush that killed Kevin O'Donnell. His record says that he will be made head of section in the near future in spite of any opposition from high places.'

'Why doesn't somebody tell the truth about him? You, for instance?' asked Avedissian.

'I only know what Sir Michael told me before he died and even then I suspect that there are bits of the story I don't know. I don't really know much about what he was using the outsiders for.'

'He used them to wire bombs to cars,' said Avedissian quietly.

'What?'

'It doesn't matter. You know enough,' accused Avedissian.

'Knowing something and proving it are two different things.'

'There must be someone you could go to?'

'I'm not that brave, Doctor. Bryant is a powerful man. He's above the law, whatever politicians might say, and, quite frankly, he scares me. You don't cross a man like Bryant and get away with it.'

Avedissian closed his eyes and whispered, 'Now where have I heard that before?'

'Pardon?'

Avedissian ignored the question and said, 'I have to talk to Bryant. Where is he?'

246

'He's at a meeting. He's one of the advisers on security matters for the royal birthday party,' said Sarah Milek. When Avedissian looked blank she added, 'There's to be a specially televised birthday party tomorrow. The *Blue Peter* programme is hosting a party for handicapped young people from all over the country. Members of the Royal Family will attend.'

Avedissian remembered reading about it, but now that he knew that Bryant was involved he saw it in a different light and alarm bells started to ring inside his head. 'Where is it to be held?' he asked.

'That is being kept secret,' said Sarah Milek.

'God, that could be it!' gasped Avedissian.

'Could be what?'

'Kell! He's going to hit the party!'

'But . . .'

'That's what he meant by the "last thing anyone would think of in the circumstances"' A hit on the very child he was supposed to be negotiating for on the other side of the Atlantic!'

'But how? Security is always tight on these occasions.'

'I don't know, but I'm almost sure that must be it. Can Bryant be contacted?'

'Yes if it's urgent.'

'It's urgent.'

'Come back to the office.'

Avedissian waited impatiently while Sarah Milek telephoned Bryant. He heard her say why she was calling but could not hear Bryant's response when she told him who was with her. He took the phone and put it to his ear.

'Well, Doctor, this is a surprise,' said the voice that Avedissian remembered.

'I'll bet,' said Avedissian evenly. 'But the boy and Paul Jarvis won't be coming back to embarrass you. They are both dead.'

'I'm sorry. War can be very unpleasant, Doctor, and that's what it is, a war.'

'And being "a war" excuses everything? How comfortable. Do you think the child understood it was "a war" when his skull was caved in? You make me sick to my stomach.'

'Whingeing sentimentality doesn't do a lot for my constitution either, Doctor. Don't you realise what was at stake? A chance to wipe out NORAID, cut off that running sore for good, and you expect me to listen to your maudlin crap about one orphan boy who would probably have grown up to be another street sweeper in Luton!'

'You bastard!'

'Of course I'm a bastard, Doctor. If it wasn't for bastards like me then fifty-odd million people in this country could not sit comfortably on their arses watching *Dallas* and pretending that they are not the sort of people who could ever do what I do. It's called hypocrisy, Doctor, but, being in the profession you're in, there's no need to tell you that, or are you going to pretend that all you nice, middle-class fellows really are interested in athlete's foot and lorry drivers' piles?'

'You need psychiatric help, Bryant. You're sick.'

'If we're going to start talking about psychiatry, Doctor, then you are really batting on my wicket . . .'

'Don't you care about anything, Bryant?'

'Winning, Doctor. I care about winning.'

'Just like Kell.'

'What do you mean?'

'Kell knew all along that you were trying to set him up. He's been planning to pay you back and I think I know how.'

'Go on.'

'He is going to hit the royal birthday party tomorrow.'

'I suppose he wrote and told you all this,' sneered Bryant.

Avedissian told him how he and Kathleen had come to be captured by Kell after attempting to free her brother.

'Her brother!' exclaimed Bryant. 'You're resurrecting her brother? Really, Doctor, this is too much. I appreciate how badly you would like to play the Lone Ranger and hunt me down but surely you don't expect me to believe all this twaddle?'

'It's true, I swear it. The O'Neills are here with me in London. I suggest we meet and . . .'

'Oh come on, this is Boy Scout stuff. If you will take my advice, Doctor, cash in your chips while you're ahead. Find a nice little job somewhere and try to make the best of things.'

'Until you find me?'

'I no longer have any interest in you, Doctor. You can't hurt me. Who would believe the ramblings of a struck-off doctor sliding towards alcoholism? You wouldn't even make an amusing pub bore with a story like yours.'

Avedissian controlled himself and said as evenly as he could, 'What I have told you is true! Kell is already here in England. If you won't work with me and the O'Neills and you won't call off the party, then at least tighten security. Put more men in the field!'

'Security is already tight, Doctor. There is no possibility of an attack succeeding. The entire estate will be cordoned off. You couldn't get a tank through even if you knew where the place was.'

Avedissian thought he saw how he could convince Bryant to take him seriously. He said, 'Kell already knows where the party is being held.'

Bryant fell silent for a moment before saying quietly, 'I'm all ears.'

'It's to be in Valham,' announced Avedissian.

'Never heard of it,' said Bryant.

'Then nearby.'

'There is no place called Valham, or whatever it was, within a fifty-mile radius of this estate,' said Bryant finally.

Avedissian was utterly deflated. It had to be the party Kell was interested in, or was he letting his own arrogance blind him? Could there be another target? 'I don't know for certain that it's the party Kell is going to hit,' he conceded. 'Only that it's something very big.'

'Take my advice, Doctor,' said Bryant. 'Quit while you're ahead.' The phone went dead.

'He didn't believe you?' asked Sarah Milek, although she already knew the answer.

Avedissian shook his head. 'Arrogant fool,' he muttered. He turned to Sarah Milek and asked, 'What does Valham mean to you?'

'Nothing.'

'I don't want to know any secrets. Just tell me if it seems like a valid target for Kell to be interested in.'

'I wasn't lying,' said Sarah Milek. 'I genuinely have never heard of it. But we can look it up if you like.' She brought down a book of road maps from the bookshelf and looked up the index before flicking through the pages. 'There,' she announced. 'It's a village in Norfolk.'

'Bryant said that it was nowhere near where the royal party is being held . . . Did he just say that to keep me away from there or was he telling the truth?'

Sarah Milek looked at him suspiciously.

'I am not trying to find out how to get at Bryant, I promise you,' said Avedissian.

'Bryant wasn't lying. The party is not even in the same county.'

Avedissian felt a sense of hopelessness and of time running out. He asked Sarah Milek for a phone number so that he could make contact if he came up with anything else.

'You can have mine,' she replied. 'I can't give you Bryant's.'

Avedissian looked at his watch and made a face. 'Too late,' he murmured.

'For what?'

'To rent a car.'

Sarah Milek considered for a moment before holding out her hand and dropping her car keys into Avedissian's palm.

'But you . . .'

'I can get a taxi. Bring it back when you've finished.'

Avedissian was taken aback. He stood there with a puzzled expression on his face while Sarah Milek walked away. She turned and said, 'Call it conscience.'

Avedissian returned to the flat and told Kathleen and her brother of his failure to convince Bryant of an imminent IRA strike.

'At least you warned him,' said Kathleen. 'Surely he'll tighten security anyway?'

'Maybe,' whispered Avedissian, pacing up and down in frustration. 'It's just that I can't get it out of my mind that it's the royal birthday party that Kell's going to hit.'

'Royal birthday party?'

Avedissian told them about the *Blue Peter* party and how it seemed to fit in with what Kell had said.

'I agree,' said O'Neill.

'The trouble is that the party is to be nowhere near Valham, not even in the same county.'

'We found out that Valham is a village in Norfolk,' said Kathleen.

'Me too. Anything else?'

Kathleen shook her head and said, 'No, it seems to be a small village, nothing else.'

'So why would Kell keep a map of a Norfolk village?'

Silence fell on the room.

'Time is running out. I think we should go there,' said Avedissian. 'Sarah Milek loaned me her car.'

'It's better than just sitting around,' said O'Neill.

'And there's always the chance that we might see the reason for Kell's interest as soon as we get there,' added Kathleen.

'When do we leave?'

'First light,' said Avedissian, looking out the window at the rain that had started to fall.

They set off from the flat at five-thirty. The rain of the previous evening had passed and it was a beautifully clear morning with the air so still that the sound of milk bottles being delivered seemed uncommonly loud. They headed north on the M11 and made good time, sitting in the outside lane for most of the way until they reached Cambridge, where they stopped to snatch a quick breakfast. They then veered north-west into Norfolk.

The roads narrowed with the passing of the miles and the hedgerows grew ever more anxious to encroach upon their right of way.

'Are you sure this is the right road?' asked Kathleen, as they were forced to slow to a crawl on what seemed like little more than a farm track.

'It's about a mile and a half along here,' said O'Neill, his finger tracing their route on Kell's map.

'If you say so,' said Kathleen, unconvinced.

Avedissian stopped the car as they came to a rotting wooden sign-board that was almost totally obscured by foliage. 'What does that say?' he asked O'Neill, who was in a better position to see.

'Valham,' replied O'Neill.

The lane opened out to reveal a picture post-card scene, a cluster of cottages that looked as if they had been there since the beginning of time, but there was a small church at the end of the cluster whose crumbling tower proclaimed its Norman origins.

'One shop,' said Kathleen as they crawled past.

'And a pub,' added O'Neill as they came to an inn beneath the trees called the Mouse and Spade.

'Everything you need,' said Avedissian.

'It's beautiful,' said Kathleen.

'So what did Kell see in it?'

'Let's ask questions,' said Avedissian. 'It's too early for the pub. Martin, you try the shop. We'll try the church.'

'What are we looking for?'

'Anything that Kell might see as a target. Play it by ear.'

Avedissian and Kathleen walked towards the church and entered its precincts through a small iron gate. Their feet scrunched on the gravel and they had to duck down to clear the lower branches of a yew tree that possibly pre-dated the building itself. Gravestones competed in a losing battle with weeds and moss. They had been forced to retreat in disarray to the shadow of the church itself.

Avedissian turned the black handle on the church door and pushed it open. They went inside to be met with the smell of dusty hymn books and threadbare hassocks. Dust in the air was highlighted by sunlight coming in through a window high above the altar.

'Good morning,' said a voice from the gloom at the far end.

They waited while a figure, clad in black, emerged from the shadows and turned in to the centre aisle after bowing to the altar. He came towards them. 'I'm the vicar, Simon Welsby. Can I help you or are you just looking?'

'Actually we're lost,' said Avedissian on the spur of the moment. 'We were making for the base but somehow ended up in Valham.'

'The base? What base would that be?' asked Welsby.

'The military establishment,' tried Avedissian.

'My dear chap, there's no military establishment near Valham.'

'Not so much military, more scientific Civil Service really.'

'Oh I see, research and all that?'

'Exactly.'

'In this area you say . . . and I didn't know . . .'

Avedissian and Kathleen wished Welsby good-morning

and returned to the car where they found O'Neill waiting. 'Nothing,' he said.

'Nothing,' they agreed.

'One good thing,' said O'Neill.

Avedissian and Kathleen both turned towards him.

'The pub's open.'

They had to wait outside while the landlord cleared away a number of full crates of lemonade from the doorway. He seemed ill tempered and keen to voice his displeasure. 'I dunno,' he grumbled. 'Some folks has queer ideas.'

'Problems?' asked Avedissian.

The man paused to mop his brow and straighten his back. 'They order six crates for their trip and I humps them all out for them. Then they don't even bother to pick them up! I dunno.'

'Sign of the times,' sympathised Avedissian.

The man finished clearing the passage and said, 'Right then, come away in. What'll it be?'

They took their drinks out to the back garden of the inn and nursed them in a general air of pessimism.

'I don't see what else we can do,' said Kathleen and O'Neill agreed.

'There must be some kind of manor house that goes with a village this old,' said Avedissian, thinking out loud.

'We can ask,' said Kathleen.

The landlord's wife had arrived in the bar to be regaled with complaints from her husband about the uncollected lemonade and the sound drifted out into the garden where silence now reigned. 'Maybe they will come for it later, dear,' soothed the woman.

'Don't be stupid, woman, they've already gone. I phoned the school.'

'Must have forgotten in the excitement, dear.'

'Downright thoughtlessness I call it,' grumbled the man.

'Yes, dear,' said the woman with a conspiratorial shrug to Avedissian and the others as she came out into the garden to collect glasses. 'Men!' she whispered in mock collusion. 'Talk about us women moaning!'

Avedissian took the opportunity to ask the woman about a manor house and she covered her mouth before saying in an exaggerated whisper, 'Just as well you didn't ask Will about that. He might have gone through the roof! Our manor house, Trelford, was turned into a residential school some years ago. It was the school that ordered the lemonade!'

'Oh I see,' said Avedissian, but his heart was not in it. Their last chance of finding something that Kell might be interested in in Valham seemed to have gone. They got up to leave.

As they walked slowly back to the car Avedissian took a detour to look over a stone bridge at the village stream and Kathleen joined him. She saw the troubled look on his face and said, 'You've done all you can. You know you have.'

'There has to be something,' said Avedissian. 'It's just that we can't see it.'

Instead of turning the car, Avedissian drove out the other end of the village, hoping to loop round and re-join the main road. The road on this side of the village seemed even narrower than the one they had come in on and twisted hither and thither as if tracing the bed of some long-forgotten stream. Above them tall trees stretched out to intermingle their branches in a canopy that blocked out the sun.

Half a mile from the village they came to a pair of stone entrance pillars that had been deprived of the gates they once held. A modern-looking board was fixed to one of them, incongruous with its local authority writing. Trelford House School, it said. They glanced up the drive as they passed but could not see anything for the trees.

They drove on but suddenly Avedissian applied the brakes so hard that Kathleen, sitting in the back, was flung violently forward. 'What on earth?' she exclaimed.

'The school! It was the school!' said Avedissian excitedly.

'What about it? It was the one the landlord's wife told us about,' said Kathleen, exchanging puzzled looks with her brother.

'Don't you see? It was the *school* that Kell was interested in!'

'But why would Kell care about a school?' asked Kathleen.

'Because of the kind of school it is! The signboard! It said Trelford House School . . . "for Handicapped Young People".'

Kathleen and O'Neill still looked blank, completely unable to share Avedissian's excitement.

'Trelford must be one of the places to receive an invitation to the royal party! The landlord said that they were going on a trip today but they didn't pick up their lemonade! It's my guess that Kell is running the trip now. Kell doesn't need a tank to get through security. He has an official invitation!'

'My God, he'll be waved straight through!' said Kathleen.

'The question is, how do we stop him?' said Avedissian.

'Kell must have left men at the house. They wouldn't all go,' said O'Neill.

'We'll check it out. Make sure we're not barking up the wrong tree,' said Avedissian. He and O'Neill went back to take a look at the house while Kathleen found somewhere more suitable to park the car.

There was plenty of good ground cover up to about thirty metres from the house itself, where the trees stopped at the edge of a lawn. Avedissian and O'Neill crouched in the bushes where they could see the front of the house. There was no sign of anything being amiss. It seemed still and quiet.

After a few moments they heard a child cry out. It did not sound like a baby, more like a child of ten or eleven with a speech impediment. A deaf child perhaps. A woman moved across in front of one of the windows; she was followed by a man. O'Neill caught his breath and said, 'You were right. He's one of Kell's men.'

Avedissian took little pleasure in being proved right for time was weighing heavily against them. It was already after mid-day and the chances of finding out where the party was being held and getting there on time seemed remote, particularly if, as Bryant had said, it was not even being held in Norfolk. Their one chance of finding out anything seemed to lie within the house but that left them with the problem of how two unarmed men, one with only one arm, could take control of Trelford House. Avedissian suggested they find out more about the IRA presence in the school and O'Neill agreed. It was decided that O'Neill would remain hidden in the bushes and signal to Avedissian when it was clear for him to cross the front of the house.

Avedissian skirted through the shrubbery and emerged to look back for O'Neill's signal. A few seconds later O'Neill stood up to wave him across with a gesture of his hand. Their eyes only met for an instant but it was long enough for Avedissian to realise where he had seen that gesture before. He sprinted into the shadow of the wall but his mind was on other things. It had been O'Neill in the farmyard all those years ago.

Avedissian worked his way along the wall, listening under each window in turn. The front rooms seemed to be unoccupied. He started on the side, but it was not until he had rounded the back corner of the house that he could hear sounds coming from within. He managed to get a look through one of the windows and saw that some fifteen to twenty children were in a large back room being looked after by three women wearing nurses' uniforms. Two men were also present, one sat by the door with a gun in his lap, the other paced up and down.

The nurses were obviously under strain but the children, all badly handicapped, showed little sign of knowing what was going on. Victims of cerebral palsy moved as if controlled by unseen strings, others seemed totally preoccupied by what they were or were not doing. Some stared into space. Some stared at the floor.

Avedissian heard one of the nurses say loudly, as if arguing with a guard, 'I will have to change him. He's soiled himself!'

The nurse won the argument and wheeled out the boy, who lolled in the chair as if his bones had been removed. The sound of running water came from a room further along the wall of the house and Avedissian realised that this might be the chance he had been looking for. If he could speak to that nurse before she returned then maybe she could tell him what he needed to know.

He crept along the back wall till he was underneath the window with the frosted panes; it was slightly open at the foot. Avedissian put his hands on the bars that fronted the window and tried to attract the woman's attention. She seemed to be completely engrossed in what she was doing. She spoke to the boy as she cleaned him up, keeping up a trivial one-sided conversation but there was affection in her voice and that was all that mattered.

'*Pssst*!' Avedissian tried again during a brief lull in the words and this time he was heard. The woman came to kneel down by the gap. 'Have you come to rescue us?' she asked excitedly, with a quick glance over her shoulder at the bathroom door. 'You must stop them! You must stop the minibus!'

'There's not much time,' whispered Avedissian. 'Please just answer my questions.'

The woman calmed down and nodded.

'Where is the royal party being held?'

'Crookham House. It's in Leicestershire.'

'How many children have gone from here?'

'Twelve. They are in the school minibus.'

'How many men?'

'Three, including the horrible little one in the pram.'

'Did they take any of the staff?'

'Two. Miss Sanders and Miss Crispin.'

'Help will be with you soon. I promise. Just keep calm and everything will be all right.'

Avedissian crawled along the base of the wall to the front corner of the house and waited till O'Neill waved him across. They crept back through the bushes together to the gate and ran along the road to join Kathleen. 'A phone! We must get to a phone!' said Avedissian. Kathleen, who was still in the driving seat, drove off along the winding road at breakneck speed. She screeched to a halt outside a call box and Avedissian, searching for coins in his pocket, dashed out to make the call.

He called the number that Sarah Milek had given him and shifted his feet impatiently while he waited for an answer. Impatience became despair as he realised that there was not going to be any answer. Sarah Milek wasn't there! As a last resort he made an anonymous call to the police and raised the alarm about Trelford School, urging caution with a warning that the IRA would be armed. Could the police get a warning to the security people at the royal birthday party?

The police operator who took the call was obviously of the opinion that he had a lunatic on the line and behaved accordingly, at once trying to humour and calm Avedissian and persuade him that he needed some kind of help. 'I'm serious!' insisted Avedissian.

'Of course, sir,' said the patronising voice. 'Perhaps we could start with your name and address . . .'

Avedissian slammed down the phone and rushed out to the car. He looked at his watch and said, 'Three hours! We've got three hours! It's just possible!'

Kathleen made to get out of the driving seat but Avedissian told her to stay where she was. 'You're a better driver,' he said. 'Head east to Leicestershire!'

Avedissian and O'Neill searched through road maps in the car for Crookham but had no success until they found it listed in the National Trust book. They agreed on the best way to get to it when they came off the main road while Kathleen concentrated on the immediate problem of getting free of the winding Norfolk lanes that held them like a net.

Once on the main road they picked up speed but time was still running against them. They passed a mileage indicator sign with depressingly high figures on it. Kathleen pressed her foot harder to the floor but there was no place left for it to go. Avedissian felt the knots tighten in his stomach.

After thirty minutes O'Neill passed the National Trust book over to Avedissian saying, 'You'd better have this. You can give Kathleen directions when the time comes.'

Avedissian took it and said to O'Neill, 'We have met before.'

O'Neill looked at him strangely and waited for an explanation.

'We met in a farmyard once. I was wearing a uniform at the time and there was a child between us.'

O'Neill stared at Avedissian. 'It was you?' he whispered.

Avedissian nodded and both of them relived the moment.

'I owe you my life,' said Avedissian.

'It was worth saving,' said O'Neill.

'What was that?' asked Kathleen above the noise of the engine.

'Some other time,' said Avedissian.

Roadworks outside Peterborough slowed their progress to an agonising crawl for nearly three miles and even when they had cleared them Kathleen was left with a long chain of commercial traffic to leap-frog past before they could make any real headway again. More than once blaring horns and blazing headlights signalled displeasure as Kathleen forced the issue. It was four p.m. when Avedissian said, 'Turn left at the next junction,' and they were on the road for Crookham.

FOURTEEN

THEY WERE BACK INTO COUNTRY LANES and the resultant drop in speed caused an almost unbearable increase in tension in the car. 'The royals must be there by now,' said Kathleen anxiously.

'Just keep going,' said Avedissian.

'Which way?' demanded Kathleen as they came to a road junction.

'Right,' replied Avedissian.

'How much further?'

'Not much. Take the next turning on the left. Crookham should be at the foot of . . .'

The direction became irrelevant as Kathleen turned left and came upon a police vehicle parked broadside in the road. A white-sleeved officer waved them to a standstill while two colleagues, both armed, looked on.

'This road is closed, madam,' said one of the policemen, leaning on the roof of the car to speak to Kathleen through the open driver's window. Although it was Kathleen he was addressing, his eyes took in Avedissian and O'Neill at the same time. 'Where were you making for?'

'Crookham,' said Avedissian. 'We have to contact security! It's a matter of life and death!'

The policeman looked uneasy and signalled to his colleagues to join him. 'I think you'd all better get out of the car,' he said, taking one step back.

Avedissian got out first, saying, 'Contact Mr Bryant, it's urgent!'

'There's not a moment to lose!' pleaded Kathleen.

'You're Irish,' said one of the armed policemen, hearing Kathleen's accent and taking out his revolver. 'Stand away from the car!'

'For God's sake!' exclaimed Avedissian. 'There's going to be a hit on the royals. Get Bryant! Warn him!'

The three policemen looked uneasily at each other. 'Who are you?' one demanded.

'There's no time for all that! Call Bryant on your radio! Tell him that Avedissian says that Kell is already inside!'

Avedissian's persistence paid off. One of the policemen clutched his handset nervously and said, 'Urgent message for Mr Bryant!'

A Land-Rover screamed up the road in low gear and stopped at the barrier. Bryant jumped out of the passenger seat with his radio in his left hand and the jacket of his suit flapping open to reveal a shoulder holster. The policemen stiffened as he ran towards them but he ignored them and came straight up to Avedissian. 'Well, Doctor? What's this about Kell?'

Circumstances prevented Avedissian from lingering on the thought that this was the moment that he had imagined many times over since Harry's death, the moment when he would confront Bryant face to face. He said, 'Kell and two others are already inside. The IRA took over a handicapped children's home in Norfolk and travelled with the official party.'

Bryant paled visibly. He said, 'There are over six hundred and fifty people inside. They are all over the place . . .'

Avedissian said, 'The O'Neills know Kell's men. They can help.'

'Come with me!' ordered Bryant as he turned on his heel and hurried back to the Land-Rover.

The vehicle swept into the grounds of Crookham with Avedissian and the O'Neills aboard as the strains of the National Anthem drifted over the coloured marquees announcing the arrival of the Royal Party. 'What school was it?' demanded Bryant.

'Trelford House . . . in Valham.'

They drew up outside a long caravan and Bryant jumped out to run inside. He returned with a sheaf of papers and got on board again. 'Trelford were listed to park in sector "F"' he said to the driver. 'Take it easy, we don't want to scare them.'

'They were in the school minibus,' said Avedissian over the driver's shoulder as he drove towards sector 'F' at a steady pace.

'Then it may have the school markings on it,' said Bryant.

Bryant held his handset to his mouth and started issuing orders to unseen men, suffixing every instruction with the warning to act naturally.

'I've seen it,' said the driver calmly, keeping his eyes straight ahead.

'Where?' asked Bryant.

'Up to the right with its rear doors towards us. It's white with the school name on the side.'

'Well done,' said Bryant softly. 'Drive past and nobody look directly at it!' Bryant spoke into his radio again.

They drove casually past and Bryant said, 'Pull up behind the trees.' The driver made a right turn and parked so that a clump of trees stood between the Land-Rover and the minibus. 'There were people in the bus,' said Bryant. 'Everyone else is down by the house for the walkabout . . . If Kell is still in the bus it could be a mortar attack . . . All they would have to do is fling open the rear doors and start firing . . . We're going to have to take it out.'

'But the children inside the bus . . . !' said Kathleen.

'We've no alternative,' said Bryant.

'You could get the royals out of here!' said O'Neill.

'It's too late. Kell would start firing as soon as he suspected something was wrong.'

The others conceded the point.

Bryant used his radio to ask if people were in position. Two voices confirmed that they were.

'Murray, can you see anything?' Bryant asked.

A burst of static was followed by a voice saying, 'I can only see one man in the van with the children . . . and it looks like . . . one, maybe two women.'

'The other two may be down on the floor,' said Bryant. 'Jackson! If these van doors should open let them have it!'

'Understood,' said the voice from the handset.

'We've got it covered,' said Bryant quietly to the others in the Land-Rover. He checked the ground between the minibus and the edge of the garden where the children were waiting for the royal walkabout and saw that it was clear. There was a fifty-metre grassy slope leading down from where the vehicles were parked to the lawn of the house. Avedissian did the same but felt distinctly uneasy. 'Something is wrong,' he said.

The O'Neills looked at him and Bryant said, 'What do you mean?'

'This isn't it. This isn't what Kell meant.'

'What are you talking about?' demanded Bryant.

'Kell had something other than a mortar attack in mind, I'm sure of it. He was too cocky, too sure of success, and he was . . . more involved . . .'

'You're not making sense,' said Bryant.

'I think I know what you mean,' said O'Neill. 'All that business with Nelligan, saying that it was going to be like old times again, as if Kell was actually going to be doing something, not just coming along for the ride.'

'What could he possibly do?' asked Bryant.

'I don't know,' confessed Avedissian. 'Ask your man if he can see the other two in the minibus yet.'

Bryant called Murray and got a negative reply.

Avedissian looked down at the crowd on the lawn with growing apprehension. Rows of handicapped children waited with their nurses, attendants and teachers to meet the royal group as it made its way slowly along the line in the sunshine of the late afternoon. A party of blind children carrying Union Jack flags was at the head of the queue.

Avedissian looked down the line to the more severely physically handicapped in their wheelchairs and invalid carriages, some growing restless with the wait and being reassured by their nurses. He suddenly saw the nightmare that was about to come true. 'Kell's not in the minibus!' he hissed. 'He's down there in the line . . . in his pram!'

There was pandemonium for a moment in the Land-Rover as everyone realised that Avedissian had to be right.

'Hold it!' shouted Bryant. There was sudden silence. 'If that's so we've got to get him out of the line. It's our only chance. Any attempt to divert the royals and he will open fire.'

'We've got to find him first!' said Avedissian getting out of the vehicle and looking down at the throngs of people. 'We have to get down there.'

'Wait!' said Bryant. He turned to the driver and said, 'The glasses. Quick!'

The driver handed Bryant a leather case and Bryant said to Avedissian, 'Use these! If Kell is in his pram he must have an attendant. See if you recognise anyone!'

Avedissian handed the glasses straight over to O'Neill who put them to his eyes and started scanning the line-up on the lawn. As the seconds passed anxiety grew to an almost unbearable level.

'C'mon . . . c'mon,' whispered Bryant.

'There!' said O'Neill. 'I can only see his back, but it's Nelligan. He's wearing a white coat and standing behind what could be Kell's pram . . . I can't see for sure, there's someone in the way. He's beside that bunch of older kids in invalid carriages at the far end.'

Bryant snatched back the glasses and pointed them in the direction O'Neill had indicated. 'The big man?' he asked.

'That's him.'

'He's near the very end. If Kell intends waiting until the royals are right beside him we have a few minutes left.'

'He may not,' said Kathleen.

'Knowing Kell, I think he will,' said O'Neill. 'It would appeal to his sense of the dramatic.'

'How do we get him out of there?'

Bryant was sweating visibly. 'We'll have to go in there and pull him out,' he said.

'But the moment you approach him . . . I mean he must have an automatic weapon in his hands under the covers,' said Avedissian.

'If we can take the big man out we can get to Kell from behind. All we have to do is turn him away, destroy his field of fire.'

'I can get to him,' said Kathleen. The others looked at her. 'Get me a nurse's uniform, quick!'

Bryant radioed for a uniform and got a question in reply. 'You stop the first one you see and bring her here!' he snapped. 'And get Miller up here!' While they waited he radioed to the other units and withdrew most of them from covering the minibus to redeploy them in the area behind where Nelligan and Kell were situated. 'Keep down and do nothing!' he added.

Another Land-Rover drew up beside them and a puzzled nurse was abruptly persuaded to part with her uniform. Kathleen hurriedly donned the cape and adjusted the cap. 'How do I look?' she asked.

'You'll do,' replied Avedissian.

'Who is going to deal with Nelligan?'

'Miller is,' said Bryant, indicating the man who had arrived in the other Land-Rover with the nurse. 'Go to it!' He put his radio to his mouth again and asked for someone called Dell. 'The fireworks set up for the staff and television crew party later . . . if you hear anything that sounds like a shot, set them off . . . That's what I said, set them off.'

Bryant told the driver to circle slowly round behind the disabled children at the far end of the lawn and stop about thirty metres behind the line. Kathleen and Miller were almost up to the edge of the crowd. Kathleen saw Miller put away his radio and bring out an evil-looking knife which he immediately slipped up his sleeve out of sight. He saw Kathleen looking at it but did not say anything. 'All you have to do,' he whispered, 'is turn Kell's pram round a little without him suspecting anything. Turn him away from the royals!'

'You deal with Nelligan and I'll turn Kell,' said Kathleen.

Kathleen left Miller and moved to the right through the crowd so that she was some ten metres to the right of where Kell was positioned and slightly behind his field of view. She could not see him at all, for the hood on his pram had been raised to prevent any close scrutiny from those around him. Nelligan had positioned him beside the carriages of two severely handicapped albino teenagers who were being similarly protected, but in their case from the sunlight.

As she saw Miller move up through the crowd behind Nelligan, Kathleen said in a loud voice, as if she had some official role to play, 'Can everyone see? It won't be long now. Perhaps if we move these chairs just a little to the right . . .' She moved the carriage nearest to her and found the child's nurse helping her automatically. The desire to comply with the wishes of apparent officialdom spread up the line and Kathleen saw Miller take his chance. Nelligan keeled over backwards without a sound but people in his vicinity began to fuss about the man who had "fainted".

Kathleen saw immediately that Kell must know something

was wrong and rushed towards his pram. She reached it in time to see the muzzle of an automatic weapon appear from inside it. 'No you don't!' she cried as she flung herself at the pram and pivoted it round on its back wheels. A burst of fire tore harmlessly into the air as Kell pulled the trigger. People screamed and scattered in all directions.

Kathleen, who had fallen to her knees with the effort of turning the pram, fought to regain control of it as another burst of fire from Kell cut down Miller who rushed up to help her. As she realised that Kell was struggling to turn the gun on her she pushed the pram away from her as hard as she could, but it only got as far as Nelligan's prostrate body. The force that she had imparted to it, however, was sufficient to tip it forwards when it hit Nelligan's feet so that Kell's legless torso was thrown out on to the ground. He fell, still holding his weapon, and rolled over to fire at Bryant's men who were approaching across the open ground.

After only one burst Kathleen saw that Kell, determined to achieve the aim of the operation at all costs, was trying to roll over again and open fire at his original targets. She could see the Royal Party being hurriedly escorted away across the wide lawn but they were still within range. She was nearest to Kell but was helpless to stop him.

Among the others, it was Martin O'Neill who realised Kell's intention first and rushed up in the open to throw his body at Kell in an attempt to smother his fire. Kell turned the gun as he heard O'Neill approach and fired as O'Neill launched himself. O'Neill was cut to pieces but his dead body fell over Kell and trapped the gun momentarily. Kathleen, who was still nearest, rushed towards Kell and joined the tangle of bodies in an attempt to wrestle the gun away while Avedissian and Bryant and his men sprinted over the final few metres.

Bryant shouted to his men, 'They are all IRA! Destroy them!'

269

'No!' cried Avedissian in utter horror. 'Wait!' But the bullets tore into the three on the ground and then the shooting stopped.

Avedissian was stunned with grief and anger. He knelt down beside the broken bodies and cradled Kathleen's head in his arms. There was a flicker of life left in her eyes. 'Oh my love,' he whispered, unable to stop tears welling up in his eyes as he put his cheek against hers.

Kathleen tried to speak. 'Thank you,' she said. 'For a moment . . . you almost made me believe . . . it was possible.' Her head fell back and she was dead.

Avedissian was beside himself with rage. He got up and threw himself at Bryant, intent on killing him with his bare hands, nothing else mattered. He got within a few feet of him but Bryant side-stepped smartly and hit him on the side of the head as he charged past. Avedissian fell to the ground, dazed from the blow but the strength of his anger keeping him conscious. He rolled over and looked at Bryant saying, 'Go on, kill me too. That's your style isn't it? No loose ends?'

Bryant was not looking at Avedissian. He was looking at the shambles the party had become, panic-stricken people, running policemen, screaming sirens and, overhead, the ridiculous whine of fireworks that he had hoped might mask a single shot but which now were only adding to the confusion. The royals were safe but it was a mess that his career would never recover from. He looked down at Avedissian and rasped, 'The O'Neills were terrorists, Irish terrorists, the scum of the earth. Go home, Doctor. This isn't your world. It never was.'

Avedissian watched as Bryant walked over to the bodies to take a last look at Kell and the O'Neills. As he pulled Kell's body free of the others and stood over it Avedissian caught a slight movement out of the corner of his eye. Nelligan was not dead! Miller had knifed him from behind, and it had been assumed that he was dead, but his hand was moving and he had his gun in it. Avedissian opened his mouth to cry out a warning but the words froze on his lips.

The bullet ripped into Bryant's chest, and, with a last startled look at the world, he crumpled slowly to lie on top of Kell.

Nelligan's body jerked on the ground as Bryant's men riddled it with bullets and the killing was finally over.

Avedissian was left sitting alone on the ground. When his head cleared he got to his feet and walked over to where Bryant and Kell lay together in death. He looked at them long and hard and then said quietly, 'If any people ever deserved each other . . . you two did.'

Avedissian collected Sarah Milek's car and stopped at a telephone box. He called Directory Enquiries and made his request. The operator gave him the number.

'Children in Need,' said the voice.

'I'd like to make a donation.'

'Thank you, sir. Small donations can be . . .'

'A large one.'

'In that case, sir, perhaps I can send you the relevant information?'

Avedissian said not and asked for the charity's bank account details.

'Might I ask how much, sir, if it's not too impertinent?'

'Twenty-five million dollars,' said Avedissian.